# Praise for *Mister Sandman*

"The family at the center of *Mister Sandman* is uniquely, whimsically dysfunctional. But it is the unexpected birth of Joan Canary, half idiot savant and half changeling, that catalyzes the individual idiosyncrasies and personal secrets of the people around her, melding them into a clan defined by its eccentricity... Joan's possibly brain-damaged brilliance lies at the heart of both the narrative and the symbolism of this delightfully quirky novel, in which the Canary family's life emerges as a weird yet often affecting group composition."

—*The New York Times Book Review*

"One of the strangest—and most heartwarming—paens to family ties you'll ever read. A+."

—*Entertainment Weekly*

"There is an astonishing sensibility in Barbara Gowdy's *Mister Sandman,* which bounds, spritelike, into the farthest corners of lunacy while staying tethered to the author's very real understanding of love."          —*Elle*

"With *Mister Sandman,* Gowdy will surely join the ranks of Lorrie Moore, Kazuo Ishiguro and other great dark-humored literary beguilers. The novel is a true literary original, a perfectly pitched creation in which story, ideas and authorial voice merge so explosively, so felicitously that the reader feels compelled to exclaim 'Yes!' on almost every page."

—*L.A. Weekly*

"Some puritanical streak in many of us insists that art must be medicinal, glumly virtuous and difficult to swallow. Canadian Barbara Gowdy insolently explodes such constipated pretensions. *Mister Sandman* cocks a snoot at conventions, both moral and literary, and is so brilliantly crafted and flat-out fun to read that she makes jubilant sinners of us all."
   —Katherine Dunn, *Washington Post Book World*

"It's truly a monumentally entertaining, brilliantly constructed novel...Barbara Gowdy is poised to be the next big thing."   —*Bloomsbury Review*

"Count this wickedly funny and moving novel by a Canadian writer the year's sleeper. It's unlikely that anything else will come along that will equal its combination of audacious concept, inspired characterization, frank sexuality, ribald humor and poignant message...Gowdy's raucous, tender novel is a find indeed."
   —*Publishers Weekly*

"*Mister Sandman* displays the same quirkiness, the same mordant sense of humor, the same ear for the vernacular, the same innocent-eyed acceptance of the bizarre, that characterizes her two previous novels...Gowdy surprises and delights; she also—which is rare—gives us moments which are at the same time preposterous and strangely moving."
   —Margaret Atwood, *Times Literary Supplement*
   "Books of the Year"

# MISTER SANDMAN

ALSO BY BARBARA GOWDY

*Falling Angels*

*So Seldom We Look on Love*

*Through the Green Valley*

# MISTER SANDMAN

## A NOVEL

## Barbara Gowdy

HARCOURT BRACE & COMPANY

*San Diego   New York   London*

*Mister Sandman* was first published in the United States in 1996
by Steerforth Press.

Library of Congress Cataloging-in-Publication Data
Gowdy, Barbara
Mister sandman: a novel/Barbara Gowdy.—1st Harvest ed.
p.     cm.—(A Harvest book)
ISBN 0-15-600577-8
I. Title.
[PR9199.3.G658M57    1998]
813'.54—dc21    97-28209

Text set in Adobe Garamond
Printed in the United States of America
First Harvest edition 1998

C E F D B

## Author's Acknowledgements

For their guidance and generosity I thank these people:
Susan Cole, Dr. Rick Davis, Clark Deller, Christopher Dewdney,
Irene Dewdney, Brian Fawcett, Robert and Claire Gowdy, Susan Swan
and Tim Wilson. Special thanks to Jan Whitford for her faith and
constancy, and to Patrick Crean for his brilliance and tact.

Grateful acknowledgement is made to the following
for permission to reprint previously published material:

Lyric excerpt of "Jeepers Creepers" by Harry Warren
and Johnny Mercer. © 1938 WARNER BROS. INC.
(Renewed) All Rights Reserved. Used By Permission.

Lyric excerpt of "God Bless The Child" by Billie Holiday and
Arthur Herzog Jr. © 1941 – Edward B. Marks Music Company.
Copyright renewed. Used by permission. All rights reserved.

Lyric excerpts of "Mister Sandman," Lyrics and Music by Pat
Ballard © 1954 (Renewed) EDWIN H. MORRIS & COMPANY, A
Division of MPL Communications, Inc. All Rights Reserved.

Lyric excerpt of "The Trolley Song," Music by RALPH BLANE,
Lyrics by HUGH MARTIN. © 1943, 1944 (Renewed 1971, 1972)
METRO-GOLDWYN-MAYER INC. All Rights Administered by
EMI FEIST CATALOG INC. (Publishing) and WARNER BROS.
PUBLICATIONS INC. (Print). All Rights Reserved. Reprinted
by Permission of Warner Bros. Publications Inc.

Lyric excerpts of "I Cain't Say No" by Richard Rodgers
and Oscar Hammerstein II. Copyright © 1943 by
Williamson Music. Copyright Renewed. International
Copyright Secured. Used by Permission. All Rights Reserved.

I am also grateful to the Canada Council and to the Ontario Arts
Council for financial support during the writing of this book.

*For Christopher Dewdney*

# MISTER SANDMAN

# ONE

JOAN CANARY was the Reincarnation Baby. Big news at the time, at least in the Vancouver papers. This is going back, 1956. Joan was that newborn who supposedly screamed, "Oh, no, not again!" at a pitch so shrill that one of the old women attending the birth clawed out her hearing aid. The other old woman fainted. She was the one who grabbed the umbilical cord and pulled Joan head-first onto the floor.

Joan's mother, Doris Canary, attributed everything to the brain damage. Joan's inability to talk it goes without saying, but also her reclusiveness, her sensitivity to light, her size, her colouring . . . you name it. Joan's real mother, Sonja Canary, attributed everything to Joan's past-life experiences. Sonja was *there* for Joan's famous first cry, and it's true she had thought it was one of the old women screaming, "Flo! Flo! She's insane!" but that didn't make any sense because the woman who could have screamed it had throat cancer. If Joan was either brain-damaged or reincarnated, Sonja preferred reincarnated. She would, being the real mother.

To be fair, though, there was something unearthly about Joan. She was born with those pale green eyes, and the hair on her head, when it finally grew in, was like milkweed tuft. That fine, that white. And look how tiny she was! Nobody in the family was tiny. Nobody in the family was anything like her, her real parents least of all. Sonja was fat, and had dark brown corkscrew hair and brown eyes. The real father was an orange-haired giant, eyes a flat creamy blue like seat-cover plastic. He had remarkably white skin, and Joan did, too, but without the freckles, pimples and hair. Flawless. Joan was flawless. Another way of saying not like any of them. Sonja, of course, went further, she said that Joan was not of this world, and it drove Doris Canary crazy. Baloney! Doris said. Brain-damaged, brain-damaged, brain-damaged! she said. Face it. Ask the neurologists.

Doris even told strangers that Joan was brain-damaged. Her husband, Gordon, never publicly contradicted her but he winced and sighed. "It's the truth," Doris would say then, as if normally she wasn't a brazen liar. As if Gordon had ever agreed with the brain-damaged diagnosis let alone that you could point to anything and call it the truth. "The truth is only a version" was one of his maxims.

(Which Sonja heard as "The truth is only aversion" and, although she had no idea what it meant, automatically quoted whenever the subject of truth was raised.)

# TWO

GORDON AND DORIS were Sonja's parents. They had one other child—Marcy—who had left for kindergarten that June first morning in 1956 when Sonja vomited into her cereal bowl.

"We'll say *I'm* the one who's having it," Doris announced once the cards were on the table, these being that Sonja had missed three menstrual periods, that she had been bringing up in the toilet for weeks, that the young man she'd had intercourse with was someone she'd known only for an hour, that what this young man had told her to call him was Yours, and that "Try the slammer" was the superintendent's suggestion when, a week ago, she'd gone to his apartment hoping to find him.

"We'll say it's mine and Dad's," Doris said. "When you have a baby at our age it's referred to as an afterthought."

By now Sonja was sucking her fingers and sitting on Doris's lap, and Doris was patting Sonja's belly and feeling like the biggest Babushka doll in a nest of dolls within dolls, although she and Sonja were both the same height—five-foot-two—and tomorrow, at the doctor's, they'd find out that they now weighed the same, as well—153 pounds.

(The doctor would be chosen randomly out of the phone book for the sake of secrecy. He would keep mixing Sonja and Doris up,

3

that was how alike the two of them were. Small, flat-featured faces like faces painted on balloons. Dark, curly hair. For the appointment they would hide behind sunglasses, and since only Sonja would remove hers the doctor would assume, wrongly, that her dopey expression was inherited. He'd assume that they were both putting him on—Sonja acting dumber and more innocent than she was, Doris pretending to be overjoyed—and he'd be wrong again. They were putting him on, all right. Sonja was fifteen, not nineteen, and there was no husband overseas. But Sonja *was* innocent. In all of those fifteen years, maybe ten minutes had been devoted to thinking about sex and another minute or so to having it. And, no, Doris wasn't overjoyed, but that was how she always sounded. Thrilled, bursting with news that would knock your socks off.)

Even that morning at the breakfast table, if you didn't know Doris you'd think that having a daughter pregnant out of wedlock was her dream come true. In her breathy little-girl voice she said that as soon as Sonja was out of school, the end of the month, the two of them would go stay with Aunt Mildred in Vancouver until after the baby was born.

"She's starting to lose her marbles," Doris said about Aunt Mildred. "She'll hardly know we're there. We'll tell everyone here she's on her last legs and needs us, her only living relatives, to look after her, and we'll just keep stringing that out." She clapped her hands once. "Play it by ear!"

"Okay," Sonja said dreamily.

Gordon went along, too. Out of being stunned, out of no choice. He stood just inside the kitchen doorway (he'd been about to leave for work, he had his coat and hat on) and kept reaching up and touching the ceiling to reassure himself that he still could, although being a stringbean wasn't something that normally heartened him. At the part when Doris said they would tell people the baby was theirs, "Now hold on" came out of his mouth, and Doris waited, but he was a desperado pretending that the finger in his trench-coat pocket was a gun. Abortion, adoption . . . he couldn't even *say* the words.

This was his daughter.

Their other daughter they would keep in the dark. Doris pointed out that you couldn't expect a six-year-old to hold in a secret as big as this one. Marcy would stay in Toronto with Gordon, and Doris would hire somebody to babysit her after school.

"Can we afford all this?" Gordon asked when Sonja was out of the room. Doris was the one who banked his salary and handled the bills.

"Sweetie, you just leave it to me," she said, her tone even more thrilled and hush-hush than usual so that he allowed himself to envision a secret nest egg, whereas all they had was a huge long shot, something like a five-hundred-to-one chance that she would be crowned queen.

---

Any day now she should hear. It was pure luck she saw the ad. She'd been unwrapping frozen chicken livers from a newspaper and had spotted the words "To All Ladies in Dire Straits."

"Are you wrestling with severe money difficulties?" the ad had gone on. "Caring for ailing loved ones? Recently widowed? Are you doing everything in your power to improve your circumstances but still can't seem to get out from under?" And then it had said that if this was you, you might be eligible to win thousands of dollars worth of fantastic prizes by appearing on ABC-TV's *Queen for a Day* show, which was holding auditions at the Royal York Hotel—that very afternoon, as it happened.

The minute Gordon and the girls were out the door Doris phoned a neighbour to come by at noon and fix Marcy's lunch, then she put on her frowziest house dress and rifled through Marcy's box of dress-up clothes for an old purse, cracked high heels, that fake fur stole and the ratty purple turban, her plan being to carry these in a bag and change into them at a restaurant washroom near the hotel. On the subway she hatched her sob story. She'd never actually watched *Queen for a Day* but she knew about it. Housewife contestants took turns describing their miserable lives, after which the studio audience decided who was the most miserable and that's who won. It was such a tasteless idea that Doris had always figured that the contestants were actresses. Or so she told herself until she arrived at the Royal York and walked down the line-up of mangy women, and either they were world-class impostors, every one of them, or she shouldn't be there.

She joined the line anyway. A long wait on hot pavement during which she thought of the men on the *Titanic* who had dressed up in turbans and fake stoles and too-small pointy high heels, and what she wanted to know was, how many of them had been responsible citizens with another baby on the way? Answer her *that*. In her head the buoyant refrain of the *Titanic* song screamed—*It was sad, so sad, oh, it was sad, so sad . . .*

For virtually any occasion Doris knew a song that went with it, or at least she knew the first verse, and she sang it to herself—involuntarily, ceaselessly—until the occasion changed, at which point another song usually took over. This was just background, like a radio playing or her own footsteps, but today it was as if she had crossed wires with Ethel Merman. On the subway *Clang, clang, clang went the trolley, ding, ding, ding went the bell* had blared the whole way. Now that her feet were really starting to hurt *It was sad, so sad* was blending into an ear-splitting "Your Feets Too Big." *Oh, it was sad, so sad that your feets too big.* And, boy, her feet really *were* killing her. By the time she was finally ushered into the room where they were doing the interviewing, her stagger was no act.

A fast-talking, sweat-soaked man in shirtsleeves paced in front of the chair where she was told to sit. "Do you work, Belle?" the man asked. (Doris had given her name as Belle Ladovsky.)

"Twelve-hour shifts in a beanery," Doris said, putting on the vaguely East European accent she had cultivated years ago to audition for the Yiddish niece in a play. "Nothing but beans do I eat." This to suggest that her round figure was from bloating rather than three square meals a day. "The doctor—"

"How'd your husband die?" the man cut in.

Doris hadn't even mentioned a husband yet. A heart attack, she almost said, since what with his heart murmur that was how she had always pictured Gordon going. She had a better idea. "In Korea," she said. "Killed in action." She thought of the saddest thing she could, which was going on seven years since Gordon had made love to her, and her eyes filled.

"How many kids?"

"Eight."

"Any of them sick, deformed?"

"My twins, they are cripples. When my husband died—"

The man stopped pacing. "You mean with crutches?"

"Oh, yes. Crutches, yes."

"So you're saying that those kids could do with a couple of top-of-the-line wheelchairs."

"Yes, of course," Doris said, immediately catching his drift. "But, oy, who can afford—"

"What'll get you on your feet, Belle?"

"Maybe pots and pans," Doris suggested. As she understood it, the queen always won a stupendously expanded version of the humble thing she asked for, plus, the humbler this thing was, the more fur coats and appliances were heaped on her.

"A few measly pots and pans," the man said.

"Then one day, God villing, I open my own beanery."

---

The telegram arrived June fourth, the Monday after they found out that Sonja was pregnant. It said that Belle Ladovsky was one of three lucky audition winners from the Toronto-Buffalo area and would be flown down to New York City on June twelfth for a June thirteenth taping.

All day Doris worked on a story to tell Gordon, but seeing as the only times in eighteen years she'd been away from home overnight was when she was in the hospital giving birth, everything she came up with made it sound as if she were having an affair. Eventually she decided she'd have to resort to the truth. She waited until evening, until after the girls had gone to bed, and then she put on the outfit—the stole, the turban, the dress and shoes, plus a pair of Gordon's old glasses for extra disguise—and went into the living room where Gordon was sitting on the chesterfield, reading a manuscript. She had the audition ad and the telegram as well as the Dutch Masters cigar box that she kept the overdue bills in. Without a word she handed him the ad and when he'd read it she gave him the telegram.

"I take it you're Belle Ladovsky," he said.

She emptied the box onto the coffee table. "I was hoping to spare you this," she said about the bills.

He studied each one, flattening it first under his jumbo hand, unbending folded corners. Because she was wearing his old glasses she couldn't make out which bill he was looking at, but a few of them, like the ones for Sonja's and Marcy's pink bunny-fur muffs, were extravagances, she knew that. *China man, he had a wife, led him such a miserable life* the lyrics in her head went. Why didn't Gordon say something? "Say something," she said to the hunched-over blur of him, feeling as though she were addressing a man in a dream or through frosted glass. Or through time . . . the unsung clerk. The bow-backed, myopic, genius book editor, unappreciated by everyone except for her and a few alcoholic has-been writers whose stacks of unpublishable manuscripts were her footstools and bedside tables.

He didn't speak. He held a bill closer to the light.

"Nobody vill recoknice me in dis get-up," she said, sitting beside him.

He shook his head, at her or the bill there was no telling.

"I'm promisink hew."

When he was done he neatly piled the bills and returned them to the cigar box. "I had no idea," he said into his hands.

"Heck, it's not that bad," she said. "Eleven months out of twelve, I can manage just fine."

"Now this baby—"

"Okay, we need a miracle, and hallelujah!"

Gordon looked at her. Then he looked her up and down as if he had only just registered what she had on. "Jesus, Doris," he whispered.

"Listen to me." She took his hand. Kissed his mountainous knuckles. "Sweetie," she said, her voice trembling with righteous fervour. "I'm a shoo-in."

She was. She got to be the third contestant, a lucky break because it allowed her to top the agony of the other two. The first contestant was an arthritic cleaning woman with nine kids and a bed-ridden husband. Then there was a wall-eyed pea sheller whose husband had ditched her for a good-time girl. Neither of them knew how to build a story let alone how to play to an audience. But you should have seen Doris. When she sobbed, "I am so ashamed to be beggink," two fatsos in the front row sobbed along with her. Before the applause meter had even confirmed it she knew she'd clinched the crown. Her winnings included two full-length fur coats (one sable, one mink), two wheelchairs, a colour television, a twenty-piece set of pots and pans, an electric range and a year's supply of beans. Back in Toronto her explanation to neighbours was that she had entered a draw and what do you know?

She sold the fur coats back to the dealer who'd sold them to the show. Just the money from them alone paid off their debts with enough left over for fibreglass living-room drapes—pea-green, shot with what Doris told the girls was real silver—*and* (here's why Gordon couldn't muster enough annoyance to even shake his head at that lie) a convertible. Baby blue, brand new, their first new car and not one he'd have dreamed of buying if they hadn't hit the jackpot and she hadn't haggled the price down by trading in the beans and wheelchairs.

On the drizzly morning that she and Sonja left for Vancouver, Gordon picked up the car from the dealer's, and so the first family outing was the drive to the train station. To everybody's disappointment the weather obliged them to leave the top up.

"We wouldn't want to ruin the *regally luxuriant, stylishly elegant upholstery,*" Doris said in her tone of confidential exhilaration. She was reading from the sales brochure.

"You see the road but never feel it," she read, twisting around to the girls in the back seat. "This car has glamour plus." She batted her mascaraed eyelashes.

She wasn't one to get "all dolled up," as she put it, but for the train ride she was wearing fire-engine-red lipstick, moss green eye shadow, mascara and a smudge of rouge on each cheek. To the girls her face looked like a movie star's. To Gordon it looked like a clown's, not that he let on. He loved her a great deal, protectively and sheepishly. "What do you think of my new hat?" she'd asked that morning, and he'd said, "Very smart," although it was ridiculously tiny, like a chimpanzee's hat, and her hair springing out from under it made her head look detonated.

She had sewn on an elastic chin strap to keep the hat from blowing off. As she read from the brochure the strap gave the girls the funny impression that her jaw was hinged, like a marionette's. They laughed at her into their hands. "It's a supreme joy and a thrill and a blessing," Doris read, and the girls giggled into the white cotton gloves they were both wearing.

"And," Doris read, "it's all yours!"

Yours being the baby's father's name, Sonja swallowed hard before laughing. She wasn't quite free of him yet but would be once she was on the train. A few weeks from now she'd get a postcard signed "Yours, Dad" and all she'd swallow over was that he hadn't signed it "Love."

(It wouldn't be signed love because Gordon would be feeling unworthy of using the word. He would still be a wreck from having received, the day before, a consolation card. Sent by a man named Al Yothers. The picture on the front of the card would be a cartoon of a squirrel, and inside it would say, "Hope all your troubles will soon be nuttin'." There would be no message, only "A.Y." encircled in a heart. Marcy would see it—she would come into the kitchen while he was still staring at it—and she would ask if it was from her mother and sister. Because her hopeful, lovelorn face would be slaying him he'd answer yes. He'd say, "It's for you," and then have to account for the A.Y. "All yours," he'd come up with. "A.Y. means all yours," he'd say, and she'd think a minute and say, "Like the convertible!" which would first bewilder and then grieve him, since by that time the car would be scrap metal.)

That day, the day Sonja and Doris left for Vancouver, the car didn't have a scratch and it cruised along as smoothly and quietly as a car sailing off a cliff.

———————

Doris had splurged on a sleeping cabin. There was a sink, toilet and what was supposed to be a double bed but turned out to be more like a good-sized single.

"Let's see how the springs hold up anyways," she said, and with the old Negro porter right there she climbed on and started jumping in her high heels, then bounced onto her back and thought it was a scream when her dress billowed up and the porter saw her garters.

That was the first sign of the new her. Up until then she had been a woman who flushed when the doctor pressed the stethoscope against her breast and who, once she was in a chair, preferred to stay put. Try telling that to the people who were on the train. On that train she couldn't even sit through a meal. Ten times she'd get up to stretch her legs, visit the ladies' room, cuddle somebody's squalling baby, yank the baby out of the mother's arms and stride with it like a mad sentry, up and down, up and down, almost running. At night in bed she was still so keyed up that Sonja had to wrap her arms around her to keep her from thrashing.

Sonja was the opposite—so relaxed on that trip she couldn't detect her own pulse. Every morning she squeezed herself into a lounge chair in the observation car and more or less stayed put, snoozing, eating Animal Crackers and Tootsie Roll Pops from the snack counter, reading her Nancy Drew book, looking out the window. Off and on she pressed her hand over her heart to try to feel her heartbeat while under her new Miss Chubette dress with its Peter Pan collar and daisy-shaped buttons her baby's cells multiplied.

Now that her morning sickness was over and nobody had seemed to notice that her stomach was swelling, she didn't think about the baby too much apart from something precious that she was temporarily in charge of, as when you're the one with the tickets or the money. For the most part she felt nothing but cosy and puffy. She felt like an angel food cake. Her only distress, and it was a very slight one, arose at either of these two thoughts: that Marcy would forget to feed her hamster, Sniffers, and that, because she'd already missed too many lessons to ever get back into Miss Gore's tap class, her dancing days were over. Her ultimate view on both prospects was, Oh well.

Sometimes Doris perched on the seat beside her to see how she was doing, and Sonja curled up with her fingers in her mouth and her head on her mother's lap and let herself be lulled by the rhythm of her mother's breakneck chatter, its pleasing accompaniment to the rhythm of the train. Frankly, she didn't actually hear much of what Doris was going on about.

One morning, though, the third morning, she had her head in Doris's lap and Doris said, "I wonder what the heck's gotten into me?" and Sonja heard that.

"What, Mommy?" Sonja asked.

"Sweetie, you tell me and we'll both know." She knocked both her fists on Sonja's skull, absently and too hard, but as Sonja usually had to see blood before it occurred to her that she hurt, she didn't mind.

"You're still excited about winning the draw," Sonja suggested.

"Well, that's the truth," Doris said.

"The truth is only aversion," Sonja reminded her.

"I feel like I've eaten Mexican jumping beans," Doris said. She laughed, her new high-speed hyena laugh. "Brother, listen to me go."

She was panting.

# THREE

JOAN was born on Friday, November thirtieth, 1956, at around one-thirty p.m. Pacific time in the basement guest room of Dearness Old Folks' Home. The same room that, two years earlier, a seventy-year-old woman named Alice Gunn wrote backwards in the window grime ROT IN HELL then choked herself to death with her rubber restraining belt.

"Callous Alice" the newspapers called her in their features about Joan, because that old tragedy was dredged up and tied in to the reincarnation story. A week after Joan's birth, by which time both Doris and Sonja thought it was safe to leave her on her own for a few minutes, a reporter sneaked into the room and took her picture and then drove to White Rock and showed the snapshot to Alice's ninety-seven-year-old mother, who after Alice's death had changed old folks' homes.

"That's Ali, all right," Alice's mother was quoted as saying. "I'd know those bug eyes anywhere." She said, "Tell her new mother I'm still paying monthly instalments on the headstone, if she'd care to pitch in."

Not just Doris and Sonja but everyone at Dearness took exception to the bug-eyes crack. Everyone at Dearness was bowled over by Joan's beauty, even the old men were. Men who found the soup-spoons too heavy asked to hold her. One man believed that

Joan was the reincarnation of his first wife, Lila, who in a recent seance had talked of returning to earth for "another go-round." When Joan started making that odd clicking sound she sometimes did, he said, "Yep, hear that? Those are her teeth, those are her new uppers," resting his case. "Well, Lila!" he said, propping Joan astride his scrawny knee, "I took the nervous breakdown, expect you heard."

Even Aunt Mildred was under Joan's spell, and she was the one who'd predicted that Joan would be a midget or a dwarf, "something deformed and bunched-up like" because of the tucked-in, round-shouldered way Sonja had carried herself when she was pregnant.

Aunt Mildred had gone downhill a lot further than Doris had realized. On the phone back in June she'd said come on out, failing to mention not only her throat cancer but also that she had lost her house to creditors and was moving into an old folks' home just a week before Doris and Sonja were due to arrive.

"For crying out loud, why didn't you tell us?" Doris said when they finally located her after a morning of taking taxis all over Vancouver.

"Give me the name again?" Aunt Mildred rasped.

"Doris! Gordon's wife!"

Aunt Mildred shook her head. "Doesn't ring a bell, honey."

Doris decided they might as well stay at Dearness anyway, might as well move into the basement guest apartment for the time being since it was dirt cheap and included meals. She booked it for the maximum allowable duration of two weeks, signing in both herself and Sonja under fake last names (and when the reincarnation story hit the headlines was she glad she had!). That same day she found a cottage for them to live in when the two weeks were up, but four days before they were supposed to go there she fell in love with a nurse named Harmony La Londe. Unhinged by this voodoo rapture and by the thought of Harmony being out of her sight for more than a few hours, she staged a little drama in Dearness's office. She pretended to telephone Gordon, then over the dial tone pretended to be hearing that he had been fired from his job and there would be no money for her and Sonja's return train fare, not for many months. She hung up slowly. She sat there blinking, one hand over her mouth. She allowed the woman who owned Dearness to pry the news out of her and she said, with dignity, "I'm very grateful," when the woman said, "You and your daughter stay right here for as long as you need to."

———————

"You are a liar," Harmony La Londe said upon hearing this story. She sounded nothing but charmed. She found Doris exotic, if you can believe it. When all she knew about Doris was that Doris was a housewife from Toronto who had tried to swing on the hot-water pipes, she said, "Are you exotic or what?" This from a lesbian Negro career woman who wore see-through negligées and had painted her apartment to match her parrot.

On the ceiling of the basement corridor the water pipes were runged like monkey bars, and early one morning when Doris was on her way to the lounge for coffee she saw that a ladder had been left propped against the wall next to the stairwell. Out of pure high energy and without thinking, she climbed the ladder and reached for the nearest pipe. Harmony heard the yelp. "Are you all right?" she called from her door.

"I had a little accident!" Doris said, scuttling down the ladder.

Harmony hurried toward her. She was wearing a red chiffon negligée, she looked on fire. Doris extended her hand and there were two pink slashes—one across her fingers, one across her palm. "Better get that under cold water," Harmony said.

As Dearness's head nurse, Harmony lived rent free in what had once been a second guest apartment. Doris followed her down the hall. "Ow, ow," she said, graduating to "Wow" when she walked through Harmony's door. The layout was the same as Doris and Sonja's apartment but the walls were painted a brilliant lime green, and instead of venetian blinds there were drapes, orange with a black dust-web pattern. In the centre of the room, in a glittery cage that hung like a chandelier from the ceiling, a parrot squawked and flapped around.

"That's Giselle," Harmony said. "She's the jealous type."

The bathroom was sunny yellow. Harmony turned on the tap and took hold of Doris's wrist to direct her hand under the water. As if Doris were a child. No, as if she were an old lady, Doris realized. But Harmony was the older one here. In her short, slicked-back hair (Doris presumed she'd had it straightened) were single white strands like cracks. Not a line on her face, but ancient eyes and furrowed bony hands that made Doris's plump white hands look like they belonged to a lady of leisure.

"That better?" Harmony asked.

"I'll say. Listen, I hope I didn't wake you."

"Oh, no, no, it's my day off. I was just lounging around." She turned off the tap, then dabbed Doris's hand with the corner of an orange towel. "What were you doing, anyway?"

Doris told her.

Harmony laughed. "You crazy?"

"Sometimes I wonder."

"You really wanted to swing on the pipes?" She had stepped out into the hall and opened the closet there. Doris saw shelves crammed with bottles and vials, medicines, bandages.

"Good thing I didn't, eh?" Doris said. "I'd have brought down the whole plumbing system."

Harmony took a tube of salve from the back of one of the shelves. "Mrs.—"

"Oh, call me Doris."

"Doris." She turned and planted a fist on her hip. "Are you exotic, or what?"

"*Me?*"

Doris wasn't aware that she had been avoiding glancing at the negligée until she glanced at it. She only wanted to give it an exaggerated once-over, as if to say, You're the exotic one around here! But the light coming from the living room had made the chiffon transparent, and so what Doris found herself looking at was her first naked woman. The high, conical breasts, the darkness of the nipples, the darkness at the crotch and the long thighs pouring down. She stared, all right. For how long? ("Long enough," Harmony said later.) Say, fifteen seconds. Dead seconds, so evacuated of everything except for Harmony's body that staring seemed natural to Doris, a serenely clinical act, a polite one even, until the bird started squawking, "Giselle! Giselle!"

"Yes, you," Harmony said then. Quietly. She stepped back into the bathroom and took hold of Doris's wrist again to apply the salve.

"God, God, God," Doris thought. She felt faint from embarrassment. Her vision blurred. Now what? Don't tell her she was going to cry!

"There you go," Harmony said.

Doris whispered, "Thanks." Okay, it was over.

No, it wasn't. Harmony still held her wrist. Doris looked at both their hands, hers the most helpless thing she had ever seen. She watched Harmony lift it like food to her mouth.

"A kiss to make it better," Harmony said before her lips touched down.

---

Five months later, ten days late, Sonja's water broke. It was Friday, early afternoon, and the Jolly Kitchenaires—the little band of wheelchair-bound ladies who met after lunch in the dining room to bang cutlery on cookware and belt out show tunes—were working on "I'm Just a Girl Who Can't Say No." You could hear them all the way down in the basement, that's how loud they were. Happily, languidly, Sonja was pencilling loops in a notebook, eating licorice Allsorts and trying to balance her grammar book on her head while, sitting next to her at the card table, her starry-eyed little tutor, Miss Florence Butson, cooed encouragement. (It turns out that a retired teacher of penmanship and deportment isn't the same thing as a retired teacher of English after all, but at a nursing home you take what you can get in the way of tutors was how Sonja and Doris were looking at it.)

Doris wasn't in the apartment that afternoon. She was hardly ever there, being too full of pep to just sit, she said, and when she did fly in, by then Sonja was usually asleep. But Sonja was often awakened by her mother's hands on her belly. First thing in the morning Doris would go for Sonja's belly again, feeling for the feet and hands, listening to the heartbeat through Sonja's navel. In her sleep she sometimes moaned, "Baby . . . baby," and Sonja pressed her mother's hand against herself and said, "Right here, Mommy. Feel, Mommy."

Nobody had prepared Sonja for her water breaking, so when she felt the sudden pressure she thought she was dying to go to the bathroom. She came to her feet, forgetting about the book, which slid off her head and onto the floor, right under the downpour.

"Oh, my," said Miss Butson and scraped back her chair.

Sonja waddled in the direction of the bathroom. Halfway there a knifing pain bowed her backwards and she fell hard on her rear end, bringing a table and lamp crashing down with her.

"When a person tries to kiss a girl!" shrilled the Jolly Kitchenaires.

Another pain. Another. Unaccustomed as she was to pain,

Sonja wasn't a good screamer and could manage only a few broken whinnies.

"I'm going for a nurse," Miss Butson said, scurrying for the door as it opened and "I can't be prissy and quaint!" blared in together with Aunt Mildred.

"What's all the racket?" Aunt Mildred rasped.

"She just fell right over!" Miss Butson said at a hysterical pitch.

"I want my mommy," Sonja whimpered.

"Is she having it?" Aunt Mildred got down on her knees, joints cracking like popcorn. "Let's take a look-see," she said, throwing up Sonja's soaking dress and peering in. "Huh," she said.

"What?" cried Miss Butson.

"Get up," Aunt Mildred ordered Sonja.

Another pain. During its long trajectory Aunt Mildred moved behind her and hooked her under the arms. "Well, don't just stand there like a nitwit," she rasped at Miss Butson.

Miss Butson clutched Sonja's hands and tugged, her sweet, milky eyes ogling Sonja with an expression of terror-stricken reassurance. Sonja was no help. Between pains she felt numb from the neck down. She felt like a tiny, melting snowman's head. "Whut you goin' to do when a feller gits flirty?" shrieked the Kitchenaires. Finally Aunt Mildred growled at Miss Butson to get out of the way, then mustering astonishing strength managed to heave Sonja onto the high four-poster bed.

"Now then," she wheezed.

"Is it the baby?" Miss Butson asked, tremulous.

With one quavering hand Aunt Mildred fumbled at her cardigan pocket while regarding Sonja under half-closed, leathery eyelids. She pawed out a cigarette and a book of matches. When she had the cigarette lit she took a deep drag, lips puckering like a draw-string purse. "I'll tell you what you do with left-over mashed potatoes," she said to Miss Butson.

Miss Butson made a whimpering sound.

"What you do is—" She frowned at Miss Butson. "What is it again?"

The next pain produced a dozen little pains that flew like sparks. "Better get her drawers off," Aunt Mildred said. Sonja felt hands scrambling on her belly, and then her underpants being jerked down her legs. The caressing coils of vein and the crib-like little bones, the cosy pink-and-white chamber she had envisioned her baby living in she now envisioned being scraped away by the slow, sinking rotation of a cement-block thing. "Make way," her aunt said, and Sonja felt her mouth opening wider and wider as if obeying or as if pantomiming her other end, but the cry skidded in her throat.

"It's out."

"Oh, my."

"What do you know about that, it just jumped right out."

"Oh, my."

"You got a hold of it there, Flo?"

"Yes, yes I think so . . ."

"Let me see," Sonja murmured.

"It's a girl."

"You've got yourself a girl, honey."

"Let me see," Sonja said.

"She's not breathing!"

"You've got to smack her."

"Please," Sonja said.

"Go on, Flo, really whack her one."

"I can't . . ."

"Give her here."

"Mind your cigarette."

A loud slap, a faint bleat . . .

Then . . .

"FLO! FLO! SHE'S INSANE!"

Or was it, "OH! NO! NOT AGAIN!"

Whichever, that famous, disputed scream was loud. Even the Jolly Kitchenaires heard what they agreed among themselves sounded like bad news in the hot-water pipes, likely a rupture.

---

Write off that ear-splitting cry as something mechanical or as a hysterical, multiple hallucination and you still have the mystery of why a head-first fall onto the floor didn't kill her let alone cave in or crack her skull. The only visible injury was a bruise to the left of her soft spot, a mauve quarter-sized circle from which radiated a wavy starburst of hair-thin veins so that you had to wonder (or at least Sonja did) if the bruise wasn't transmitting urgent bulletins from the afterlife.

There was the mystery of Doris calling her Joan, being inspired to call her this the first time she held her in her arms although Anne was the name that she and Gordon and Sonja had agreed on for a girl. Not until almost three years later, when Gordon looked up from his crossword puzzle and said, "*Sonja* is an anagram of *Joan's*," did anybody realize that Doris had unwittingly branded her with her real maternity.

Her beauty was a kind of mystery, not just because it was genetically inexplicable but because it was so seductive. People always say, What a beautiful baby! but here was a baby who inspired adoration even in the blind. At Dearness the blind faltered their hands over her face and limbs and like everyone else compared her to the disadvantage of all other babies, including their own. The picture of her that the photographer took to show Callous Alice's mother also appeared in three Vancouver newspapers and generated hundreds of claims that she was the reincarnation of this or that beloved relative, pleas and orders to hand her over.

The newspapers were notified by Aunt Mildred, another curiosity when you consider that her hip broke when she fainted and she had to climb two flights of stairs to get to a phone. Fortunately, by the time the first two reporters showed up, Doris had everything more or less under control. No pictures, she said, no disturbing the mother or the baby, but as she couldn't put a lid on Aunt Mildred, let alone the other residents, all of whom were declaring they'd heard something mighty eerie, she left it to them to answer the reporters' questions. Nothing to worry about there. Thanks to her, everyone in the home was under the impression that Sonja's last name was Gorman, that she was nineteen, and that she was the bride of a doctor who had been sent to the British Honduras as part of a U.N. relief effort.

Until the to-do died down, Sonja and the baby should stay put in the guest apartment, Doris decided. She brought them their meals and otherwise took over, and it didn't occur to Sonja to feel anything aside from off the hook. The ache she sometimes felt watching her mother give Joan her bottle she thought was her womb shrinking. "There it goes again," she'd think and feel a reverential affection for the complicated workings of her body. When Joan's whimpers made her breasts leak she went into the bathroom to squeeze the milk into the sink. Formula was better for babies, her mother said, which was just as well in Sonja's view. She couldn't imagine her breasts being sucked by an innocent baby, especially a baby who was supposed to be her sister. Who, for that matter, might still be Callous Alice, although most of the old people who had been willing to entertain that notion had changed their minds. With a few exceptions they now called Joan Joan.

Everybody bore gifts. Lots of knitwear and blankets, a red and orange hand-quilted blanket from the Negro nurse, which Sonja thought was a bit loud for a baby but which Doris went into raptures over. Some of the residents brought money. One old couple, old pals of Alice's, showed up with a Black Velvet Chocolates box containing twenty-five silver dollars. This couple was one of the few exceptions. "Cold, hard cash, Ali!" the man said with a wink at Joan, and then he started pestering her with questions about the hereafter. "Blink once for yes," he said.

"It's her huge eyes," Doris said one night after the visitors had gone. *Jeepers, creepers, where'd you get those peepers?* she sang, venting the song in her mind. She cleared her throat (and Joan made a similar sound, imitating Doris, you'd swear) and said, "The way they seem to see right through you."

"Maybe they do see right through you," Sonja said. Leaning over her mother's arm, she lightly touched a finger to Joan's bruise, a thing she did from time to time in case she picked up a message. "Ali?" she called softly.

"Cut it out!" Doris said, and then cooed, "Sorry" because Joan had flinched. Turning back to Sonja she whispered, "I've had it up to here with that mumbo jumbo."

And she meant it, even though she herself couldn't shake the feeling that there was something going on with this kid. A few crossed wires from the fall. She'd had two babies, she knew the score. A newborn shouldn't be able to focus on you the way Joan did, right across a room, it wasn't supposed to follow you with its eyes like that. Then there was her extreme sensitivity to light and noise, and all those unbaby-like sounds she came out with. The throat-clearing, the droning, the clicking, hissing.

Do you want to know the truth? For a while there, Doris was also looking at Joan and asking, "Ali?" Not out loud, but she was asking it. Later she'd look back and think no wonder. For one thing she didn't know then that Joan was brain-damaged, added to which she herself was hardly in her right mind around the time that Joan was born. Doris was wild . . . an out-of-control, madly-in-love nymphomaniac but carrying on as if she wasn't, like a murderer you find out was a clown at children's parties. She was either keyed up or so absent-minded that she felt she went into trances. Take the night she was jiggling Joan to bring on a burp, and Sonja drew her attention to how red Joan's face was turning.

"She looks embarrassed," Sonja chuckled. And only then did Doris realize not only that she was *holding* Joan but that she was shaking the poor kid like a ketchup bottle.

This was when Joan was five weeks old.

This was when Doris and Sonja had the same dream.

It happened on the train ride home. What with all the money from the Dearness crowd Doris had splurged on a cabin again, one with a good-sized double bed this time. It was the second afternoon, and Doris had put Joan in her basket and then she and Sonja decided to have a nap along with her. After a few minutes, because Joan was wide awake, cawing and clicking, they moved her into the bed, and that calmed her down.

They all slept—even Joan, who hardly slept at all, even Doris, who never slept soundly any more. When Doris opened her eyes about an hour later, Sonja was also blinking awake. At the end of the bed, over the sink, was a big mirror, and for a few minutes in the grey light the two of them lay there looking at each other . . . their pie-plate faces (identical except that Sonja's was fatter these days), their corkscrew hair smoking out, and the train rocking them in time. And a little farther down, in the space where they had each lifted an arm to make room, Joan's round, bald head like a planet.

Doris, for once, was okay, despite having had a nightmare about Harmony. She smiled, and as if an invisible connection went taut, Sonja's mouth straightened into a smile, too.

"I had the nuttiest dream," Sonja whispered, addressing Doris in the mirror.

"Join the club, Sweetie."

"You know that Negro nurse?"

Doris waited.

"Melody," Sonja said. "You know . . ."

"Harmony!" Doris said too vivaciously, too loud. "Harmony!"

"What?"

25

Doris started pulling a thread from the sleeve of her cardigan. "Her name," she said, trying to keep a grip on her voice, "is Harmony."

"Oh, that's right, Harmony. Well, anyways, I dreamt she was in that play you were in when you were an actress. Julius . . . no, *Romeo and Juliet*. She was an old lady and she said, 'I'm falling apart,' and then she really did. Her arm fell off, and then her foot and her other arm. Then her head."

In the mirror Doris witnessed herself blanching.

"And then . . . And then she changed into a big fish, one of those . . . oh, what is it . . . ?"

"A dolphin!" Doris burst out.

"What?"

"She changed into a dolphin!" Doris could hear herself—the crazy, tickled-pink gush of her voice.

"How did you know that?" Sonja asked, turning to look at Doris in the flesh.

Doris held her breath.

"Mommy, how'd you know she changed into a dolphin?"

Doris was unravelling her entire sleeve. "A guess," she got out in an exhalation.

"Well, jeepers, good guess." She resumed looking at Doris in the mirror. "Anyways, she was a dolphin but with legs, black legs, and then . . . then I woke up."

At which point Joan woke up and turned her head to stare at Doris while making *tsk-tsk* noises, just like scolding, and Doris thought, "It's *her*," by which she meant that Joan being between them was how the dream had passed from her to Sonja, or from Sonja to her. Joan had conducted it! And then the even more harrowing possibility struck her that Joan had made the dream up! A dream about Harmony! "She *knows*," Doris thought, completely spooked, while Sonja, oblivious, touched Joan's bruise and sang, "Bunny, little bunny," but Joan was fixed on Doris, her eyes like ponds.

# FOUR

A YEAR before all this, one Thursday afternoon in early November while Gordon is eating a ham sandwich at his desk, an orange-haired giant swaggers into his office. At first sight Gordon is in love, so the young man is ringed in fireworks, but anyone would stop chewing. The office is suddenly doll-housed, and the young man is in it like a dreamer, blinking around, scratching his throat. His throat is alpine. His forearms are clubs fleeced with orange. Orange froths out of the v of his white T-shirt and is greased back in rivulets on his head.

"Knock knock," the young man says, knocking on Gordon's bookshelf.

Gordon swallows his food.

"Secretary said go right in," the young man drawls.

A few hours earlier a guy with a drawl phoned wanting financial backing to write a first-hand account of the stevedore life—"The real *On the Waterfront*." Gordon told this guy to drop in around noon. "Yes, hello," he says now, coming to his feet. "Gordon Canary." He reaches across the desk to shake hands. It doesn't often happen that he has to look up to look into another man's eyes.

"Al Yothers," the young man says, smacking his palm into Gordon's. "You done with this?" He lets go of Gordon's hand and picks up the half-empty cup of coffee on the desk.

Gordon gestures. "Uh—"

Al strolls over to the window and takes a sip.

"It'll be stone cold," Gordon says.

Al kicks the radiator. "Air blocking the flow."

"I beg your pardon?"

"Air pockets." He turns the latch on the window and shoves, the muscles of his arm leaping into relief.

"It's painted shut," Gordon says. With a sound of splintering it opens. Al tosses out the coffee.

"Hey—"

Al glances at him. Now he's trying to loosen the screw at the end of the radiator. "No can do," he says. He sets the cup on the window ledge and withdraws a screwdriver from his back pocket.

Gordon finally gets it. He drops into his chair. "I asked for someone to see about it two weeks ago."

"You know how they say 'two weeks' in England?" Al says. A few turns of the bolt, and air hisses out. "Fortnight," he answers before Gordon can grasp the question.

Gordon waits, but apparently that's all Al has to say on the subject.

Al squats, retrieving the cup. His thighs are like sandbags but his buttocks are as small as a boy's. A ripple of spine where his T-shirt rides up. "It's real backed up," he says.

*Gordon is squatting next to him, saying something. Saying "How does the air get in there anyway?" or something, meanwhile sliding his hand around Al's waist. No, he's standing, they're both standing. Gordon is behind him. He reaches around and unbuckles Al's belt, unzips his fly. Al grips both sides of the window frame. Two strokes and he's hard and turning. His eyes are closed, mouth open. The door is closed. Locked. Before going over to him Gordon has shut and locked the door and told Margo to hold his calls. No, he has sent her out for another coffee and sandwich, and to the bank . . .*

"When was the last time you had this drained?" Al asks, glancing at him.

A split-second too late Gordon looks up. Al's eyes narrow. What amazes Gordon isn't just how far he has let his imagination go, it's the sense of nostalgia that's egging him on, as if in some life, and it isn't this one, he has actually danced this dance. By the time Al turns back to the radiator Gordon's legs are trembling so badly the change in his pocket jingles. "Last winter," he says.

Al doesn't speak for a minute. Then he says, "Tell you what, Mr. Canary." A jet of black water shoots into the cup, and he quickly tightens the bolt. "How about I keep this just loose enough so's you can drain it yourself from time to time?" He straightens. Slips the screwdriver into his back pocket.

"All right," Gordon says too eagerly. "Good idea."

Al strolls over and sets the coffee cup back on the desk. There is a dime in Gordon's paper-clip saucer, and he picks it up. "This here's your screwdriver," he says, flicking it off the end of his thumb.

Gordon fails to catch it. Laughs. "Right," he says, covering it with his hand where it has landed on a manuscript. "Good idea. Well, yes, certainly, I'll do it myself next time."

"It's a deal," Al says.

His smirk goes straight to Gordon's heart.

———————

Gordon sits like a pillar of salt. A good five minutes go by and then he places both hands flat on his desk and looks around his office. Everything before his eyes he is homesick for. His phone rings and he waits for Margo to pick it up at her end but it rings and rings and with each ring it's as if his chances of saving himself diminish. He reaches for his coffee. He has the cup tipped at his mouth before he realizes that that black stuff isn't dregs. In the same second it hits him that it isn't too late! This affair in the wreckage of which he is staggering, it hasn't happened yet!

He stands, goes over to the window and pulls it shut. Cracks his knuckles, paces. Sits back down at his desk and dials home.

"Hello?" Marcy says in her high, expectant child's voice.

"It's Daddy, honey. Is Mommy there?"

"Oh, hi, Daddy. Mommy's outside hanging up the laundry. I'll get her."

"No, no, that's okay. Just tell her I phoned, nothing important." He checks his watch. Twelve-thirty. "Are you eating your lunch?"

"I just finished." She breathes noisily. "You know what?"

"What?" He presses the receiver against his ear. He wants to hear her blood circulating.

"I forgot to say grace"—she's whispering—"and my sandwich went mouldy."

"Honey, it would have been mouldy before, and you just didn't notice." What the hell were they teaching her at Sunday school?

"No, it *wasn't* mouldy before!" she cries.

"Okay, all right. Did Mommy make you another sandwich?"

"I ate the mouldy one," she says piously.

That evening at the supper table he feels like someone who hears that the plane he decided not to board has exploded in midair. Doris and the girls seem like apparitions, Doris's round face infinitely alive and kindly, a guardian moon. In bed he clings to her capsized body, and as if Al Yothers were nothing more than the catalyst to return him at last to this sanctified threshold, he gets an erection.

"Doris," he moans.

But she's asleep.

And there goes his erection.

Not his high hopes, though. Not his feeling that everything is going to be fine, that this is only the beginning, etc. An erection, even a short-lived one, that's something in this bed.

The next day at the office, whenever he is in the corridors, he keeps an eye out for Al Yothers. To avoid him, he thinks. There is a proofreader named Tom Hooks, a surly kid with insolent little hips and fluttering blue eyes, whom he has taken mighty pains not to look at. Today, however, standing behind him at the Gestetner machine, he stares at the boy to reassure himself that his desire isn't fatally pinned to one man but is spread out, restored to its old, harmless sprawl. Back in his office he sits at his desk and pictures Al Yothers over at the radiator, and feels, well, no more aroused than he is already. He wonders if he has ever been even half this aroused with Doris. He doubts it, although he remembers the first few years of their marriage as a time of perfect happiness. Maybe the way it works is, if you're that happy once it vaccinates you against the possibility of being that happy again. He sits there rubbing his thighs, and the part of him that is feeling how long and bony they are, experiencing them as if with the hands of another man and thinking, worriedly, that they're like a pair of goddamn banisters, that part seems like the last of it. The little brush fire that will burn itself out.

It's just after four o'clock when the stevedore phones and says, "Hey," and Gordon's guts drain. He thinks it's Al. "Al," he says, and sees bombs blooming.

"No Frank," the stevedore says. "Frank Amis. Say, about yesterday . . ."

Yesterday he got held up. A shipment of pork bellies. He suggests a meeting tonight, five-thirty at the Lakeview Tavern, adding that this thing is big, real big.

Gordon says, "Drop by the office tomorrow."

"I might not be alive tomorrow," Frank says, which Gordon doesn't fall for, but his head is in his hand and his heart is still banging, and so it happens that Frank is talking his kind of language. "All right, five-thirty," he says. He then phones Doris to tell her he'll be late.

At five-twenty, as he is putting on his coat, Frank calls back and shouts over what sounds like a foghorn that he'll have to take a rain check. Gordon phones Doris to say he'll be on time after all, gets a busy signal, waits five minutes, tries again. Still busy. He gives up and leaves the office.

A few minutes later he is standing at a red light across from the parking lot. The lot adjoins the cemetery where, filling the last available space on the Canary family headstone, his name, date of birth and a dash are etched. This was his mother's doing, a deathbed effort at immortalizing her denial that he married Doris and created more Canarys. "You've got to hand it to her," Doris laughed at his mother's burial, while he reeled at the dash. He never visits the grave or even walks through the cemetery's praised gardens, although tonight the place beguiles him. The sky above it is mauve and soft, frayed by naked tree branches, the moon like a place where the sky has thinned out, or like a moon long gone, a fossil moon. He toys with the idea of a stroll. He looks at his watch, then glances behind him for some reason, and there, hunched under the awning of a tavern, is a giant.

Al Yothers.

It's him, all right. The orange hair. He has on a black leather jacket. He looks furtive and menacing, until he catches sight of Gordon, and then his face opens like a child's.

"Hey!" he calls.

Gordon pretends not to hear. He turns back around.

"Hey! Mr. Canary!"

Gordon takes a deep breath and turns again. The boy is trotting over to him. "Oh, hello," Gordon says.

"Al Yothers." He holds out his hand.

Gordon shakes it. "Yes, I remember."

"I wanted to ask if your rad was giving out any heat."

Between the thumb and forefinger of his left hand he holds a stogie. Gordon stares at it and says, "Yes, I'm quite comfortable now, thank you."

"Glad to hear it." Al takes a last puff and flicks the cigar to the sidewalk, crushing it under the heel of his black boot. "I got a few complaints this morning about the friggin' things still being ice cold."

"Mine's doing fine."

Al nods. He smiles and looks down, not shyly but as if Gordon wouldn't get the joke.

"Well, goodnight," Gordon says because he knows that Al is going to ask if he wants to have a drink in that tavern behind them. Because his life up until now calls for some show of resistance, however counterfeit.

———————

The tavern turns out to be a new Chinese restaurant that hasn't changed the old sign, but they go in anyway, Al saying he hasn't eaten "Chink chow" in years. When they are seated he removes his leather jacket and hangs it on the back of his chair. Today he's wearing a blue janitor's shirt with "Al" stitched on the pocket, which holds another cigar. He yawns and stretches. He seems breathtakingly young and exotic to Gordon, his big white hands like shells. "Hoo Wah Family Restaurant," he drawls, reading the aluminum-foil letters hanging from a string behind the bar. He looks at Gordon. "You a family man?"

"Yes, I am," Gordon says quietly.

"The family man is the cornerstone of civilization. Am I right, Charlie?" This addressed to the waiter, who has brought their menus.

"Family man," the waiter says energetically. "Very good."

"Famry man," Al mimics before the waiter is out of earshot. He withdraws the other cigar, lights it. Exhales out his nostrils. His nostrils are huge, gorilla-sized. He looks up at the ceiling, and Gordon gazes at the pillar of his neck as he knows he is being invited to. Gordon is someone counting the seconds between lightning and thunder. It's out of his hands, it's imminent. A recurring dream that he should know to manoeuvre his way through except that in this dream he's a sucker. This is the dream where he opens the door to midair and strides right out.

"What is it?" he says. Al is looking at him now, squinting.

"Shoot," Al says, "you're the spittin' image of that fella on TV, who am I thinking of?"

Gordon takes off his hat and sets it on the chair beside him. "You're from the South," he says, changing the subject.

"Greenville, South Carolina. Population 58,161 as of 1953." He nods to Gordon's left. "Your coat fell."

It has slipped off the chair. When Gordon picks it up he feels something sticky on the lapel. It was his father's coat, high-quality camel-hair, an heirloom, and normally Gordon would be anxious to clean it right away but he just hangs it on a hook in the wall behind him, then sits down with the feeling of having crossed a point of no return. Another one. He wonders if what an affair amounts to is a series of points of no return. "Shoot," the boy is saying, "that skinny fella with the curly hair," still trying to figure out who Gordon looks like, and as Gordon can only imagine being mortified by the comparison he says, "Are your folks still in Greenville?"

"They were killed in a car accident when I was two months and two days old."

"Jesus. I'm sorry."

"Nuns raised me. I was Al for Alan but the sisters christened me Albert after Albert the Great, 1193 to 1280 A.D." He picks up his menu and blinks hard, and Gordon fears he has opened a wound, but this isn't grief, this is memorization. A few moments later Al looks up and starts reciting: "Moo goo guy pan—sliced chicken with mushrooms and mixed Chinese vegetables. Tai dop voy—chicken, shrimps, barbecued pork with mixed Chinese vegetables.

Soo guy—buttered breast of chicken with almonds and sauce. Ma po dow fu—bean curd with minced pork and hot sauce."

Gordon laughs, amazed.

Al signals the waiter. Word for word, in the same inert voice and gazing above the menu at a spot on the wall, he repeats the recital, adding three more dishes while the waiter and Gordon pretend that there's nothing unusual about ordering this way. "A big amount of food" is the waiter's only reaction, which it is. Gordon thanks God that Doris gave him ten dollars this morning. It goes without saying that the bill will be on him, not just because he makes more money but because (this also goes without saying) he will be the one to fall in love.

That he already *is* in love he doesn't yet know. He sits there like a man who still takes an interest in everyday life. When the soup arrives he makes a show of savouring the aroma, and the steam fogs his glasses. The noodles are as fine as corn tassel. He winds them around his spoon. Al dices his up with a knife and fork. Al holds the floor, the theme being "Chinks," their eating habits (slurping, shovelling it in), the food they themselves eat (Labrador retrievers and stray cats), their feelings (none). Anyone else and Gordon wouldn't still be sitting there, but it's as though he has to let the boy dig this hole because if they're headed anywhere together, it's down there.

All the same, he is glad they are by themselves in a corner and relieved when Al, after a pause, moves on to encyclopedias. Does Gordon own a set? He owns several . . . no, not the *Encyclopaedia Britannica,* although they have two sets at his office. Has Gordon read it?

"I refer to it now and again," Gordon says. "Of course."

"I've read it right through twice," Al says. "All twenty-four volumes, start to finish. I'm on my third go-round, up to the D's."

"You're kidding."

"Everything you need to know is there. All the facts there are

and ever were. That's all I'm interested in. The facts. The truth."
He drains his glass of rice wine.

"Well," Gordon says, "the truth is only a version—"

Al bangs down his glass. "Test me on a D fact. Something before Delilah."

Gordon laughs.

"Go ahead," Al says, frowning.

Gordon opens his hands. "Daphne."

"From Greek mythology," Al fires back. "The nymph that turned into a lily pad."

Gordon is curiously relieved. "Laurel tree, actually," he says. "She turned into a laurel tree."

Al blinks. "You sure about that?"

"Yes. Yes, quite sure."

Al's face goes slack. "Daphne, laurel tree," he says. "Daphne, laurel tree."

"You got the gist right," Gordon says.

Al shoves aside his soup bowl and folds his mammoth arms and says, "Gimme some C's. I've got the C's down cold."

Gordon doesn't want to do this. A quiz is not what he's here for. "I seem to be drawing a blank," he says.

"Go on," Al says impatiently.

So Gordon says, "Lewis Carroll." Al gets that right. Gordon says King Charles. And concerto. The rest of the food arrives, and he says Cervantes, cubism, Castries, curlew—facts and things, words that would be in an encyclopedia, although it doesn't seem to matter, Al takes a stab at anything and isn't frustrated when he is wrong, even when he is idiotically wrong. Glassy-eyed he listens to the right definition and then repeats it twice. Every time he is idiotically wrong Gordon's tender feelings dilate a little.

They carry on like this—at Al's insistence sticking with the C's—until the check arrives, by which time Gordon is down to words like chop suey and China. "Check," he says, reaching for it.

36

"A resident of Czechoslovakia," Al says.

If he's joking, Gordon can't tell.

Al picks up one of the fortune cookies from the tray and cracks it open. "The person should take it easy," he reads. He comes to his feet. "Shoot, I was hoping to take it hard."

Gordon is standing to get his wallet out of his coat pocket. When Al says that, Gordon freezes, and then so does Al. They stand there looking at each other like a pair of gunslingers.

"I know a place we can go to," Al says. "Just up the street." He strokes his own head. Gingerly pats it as you would an unfriendly cat.

# FIVE

ONE NIGHT when Sonja and Doris are in Vancouver, Marcy dreams that Sonja is being stabbed in the stomach by a man whose head is on fire. She wakes up crying. She gets out of bed and goes into the living room to tell her father that he'd better phone Vancouver right away. The living room is dark but she knows that her father is in there because his "Mister Sandman" record is playing.

Yes, he's there. On the floor. "Lie beside me," he interrupts the telling of the dream. He paws at the tears on her face, and she smells the familiar pencil odour of his fingers. She tugs at his hand until he is on his feet. He sways. He clutches her shoulder so hard her knees buckle. Thinking that his leg must still be sore from the car accident, she takes his hand and leads him down the hall to the kitchen, where the phone is. Three times he gives the operator the wrong number, although Marcy is piping it at him. Through the threadbare cotton of her pyjamas, which have a red-and-yellow watering-can pattern, she pinches her thin arms.

Finally her father hands her the receiver, but she has to speak to two other women before Sonja's crackly, faraway voice comes on the line. Marcy is not especially relieved that Sonja doesn't know what she's talking about. Marcy says, "I'm *warning* you." She says,

"No, I think he's a fireman . . . or something . . . ," her voice un-ravelling as in her mind the dream unravels.

"Say goodbye now," her father slurs.

Marcy has two recurring dreams. One about a talking baby and one about a little girl playing the piano in a room where Marcy and a man wrestle on a bed. There's a dog in this dream as well, a poodle biting its leash. The man says, "Ah, come on, it's like balling in front of the dog." In the dream Marcy understands what the man means by "balling."

Her dreams wake her up. If she doesn't fall right back to sleep she's apt to start fretting over all the pages in her school textbooks the teacher hasn't even got to yet. She'll touch the dolls that are aligned like bridesmaids on each side of her. Lightly, so as not to wake them, she'll feel their brittle dresses and the rigid brush of their eyelashes. Eventually she'll climb out of bed and go to her desk and pore over her exercise books in the bar of streetlight where her curtains don't meet. It's not out of the question that she'll sit there for hours, erasing and rewriting entire pages.

She has straight, coarse hair the colour of cardboard. She wor-ries that it is actually fur, as she has seen hair so coarse and that colour only on dogs. She is prone to styes that puff and redden her eyelids and that (as she will eventually discover) give the new neighbours across the street the impression that she lives in a vio-lent household. She is ruining her eyes, and like her father will wear glasses. Not for another four and a half years, though. In the meantime she prays for twenty-twenty vision, human hair and the death of the tub of lard. She prays on her knees in her closet where she believes that sparks of static electricity indicate the presence of Jesus.

Jesus is present during her babysitter's bubble baths as well, the sound of static electricity and the bubbles bursting being identi-cal. Being the sound of Jesus. Worshipfully, Marcy washes her babysitter's back, which because it is covered in moles is a starry sky. The soap circles Marcy makes are clouds. Sometimes, to scare herself, she prints AL WAS HERE in the soap, believing that this means BEWARE. The babysitter moans with pleasure. Jeanie is her name, Jeanie with the cornflake-coloured hair. When she is lying on the floor in front of the TV Marcy straddles her back and brushes her hair. To Marcy, Jeanie's dandruff is confetti.

Jeanie has told Marcy that the scar under her eye is from when her mother hit her with the buckle end of a belt. Jeanie cries not because of her mother but because her boyfriend dumped her for a tub of lard who shaves her arms. Marcy strokes Jeanie's slender, unshaved arm and dips her finger into Jell-O powder for Jeanie to lick off. She feeds her Cheez Whiz on Windmill cookies. "There you go," she says soothingly, coaxing a cookie into Jeanie's mouth. "Is that good? Mmm, good."

Before Jeanie was her babysitter Marcy heard that you could give her a jar of worms and she'd eat them by the handful. Did Jeanie really? "That's classified information," is all that Marcy can get out of her. Jeanie admits to having been a worm *picker,* however. Picking and selling worms to fishermen for a quarter a can. She has a secret method. First you mix three tablespoons of Keen's hot mustard in a glass of water. You fill a second glass with plain water. Then you crawl around your lawn knocking the tops off of the tiny clumps of earth that are actually worm mounds. When you have uncovered twenty or so holes you pour a bit of the mustard mixture down each one.

"Now wait," Jeanie tells Marcy the day she demonstrates the method. "And don't move, they feel our vibrations."

Marcy hugs her knees. Maybe her Thursday underpants are showing. She has "Day of the Week" underwear—Monday, Tuesday, Wednesday and so on stitched across the back of seven pairs. To wear a pair that didn't match the day would be unthinkable to her, crazy, like eating breakfast in the middle of the night. She hugs her knees to keep perfectly still. She is prepared to stay like that for a long time but within seconds worms start shooting up all around her. It's a fountain of worms. Long, plump, segmented, writhing and craving up out of the grass. Marcy jumps to her feet.

"Big fat juicy ones, long slim slimy ones," Jeanie sings, plucking up the worms and dropping them into the glass of plain water.

Marcy is terrified. "Do they love us?" she cries, knowing it's a stupid, babyish question, humiliating herself and yet asking it again. "Do the worms love us?"

Jeanie snorts. "Are you out of your mind? We've just burned them. They hate our guts."

A little later, because her devotion is undiminished but also to distract Jeanie from mixing more Keen's hot mustard and water, Marcy brings Sonja's precious tap-dance shoes into the kitchen and urges Jeanie to try them on. "They're broken," Jeanie says when she can't get them to click. Marcy returns the shoes to the box that says "Private Property" and comes back into the kitchen with her piggy bank whose contents add up to five dollars and thirty-seven cents, her life savings. "It's all for you," she announces. "I present it unto you."

"Don't tell your father, okay?" Jeanie says, shaking out the coins.

With the money, Jeanie buys tomato-red nail polish and a Ouija board that zooms out the answers but is a bad speller.

This is July, when Marcy is still the person she has been all her life. She is crazy about Jeanie, but not yet swooning over her. This is before everything. Before Marcy is pregnant, although pregnancy is on her mind because her mother is pregnant. Sometime before Christmas her mother and Sonja will return from Vancouver with what Marcy imagines will be more or less an alive doll. Her dream! She understands that babies come from a seed given to the mother by the father, and so while her mother is away and it is her father who makes breakfast and supper, nothing goes into her mouth that she hasn't first picked through for a seed that doesn't match the others. A suspicious-looking seed. She is aware of the ignominy of unwed mothers, there being a home for unwed mothers at the end of the street where if you climb the brick wall you sometimes catch a glimpse of them in their white maternity dresses, drifting around the back lawn like dandelion seeds.

---

It is not until the beginning of November that Marcy has her first talking-baby dream. When she wakes up, her ears still ringing, she can't remember what the baby said. But was it loud!

The next afternoon while she is soaping Jeanie's back she is suddenly inspired to let her hand slide under Jeanie's arm and touch her bosom. She knows a hymn, "The Mothers of Salem," in which Jesus says, "For I will receive them and hold them to my bosom," and calling this hymn to mind as her hand circles closer and closer to Jeanie's left breast provides not just absolution, not just permission, but encouragement. Jeanie pretends she doesn't notice anything, whereas Marcy feels strips of velvety light coiling up and down her legs.

A few nights later she dreams that she is pregnant. In the morning she awakens to a pot belly and the inflation of the black, unknowable world. She climbs out of bed and uses her hand mirror to try to see in through her navel. She swallowed a seed, she thinks. Somehow she swallowed a darned seed! She presses her stomach with her fingers and feels a stem-like thing. An arm! In common with Sonja she has the idea that babies in the womb are like baby birds, their heads drooped back and their mouths wide open waiting for food to drop in. With a sense that it ought to be a snap, she resolves to let the baby wait until it starves to death.

For two days she eats nothing. Her father tries to bribe her with promises of money and Creamsicles but Marcy shakes her head. She says she's the one who eats all the food that Jeanie wolfs down. "I'm stuffed," she says. "Look," she says, brazenly drawing her father's attention to her pot belly.

On the third day she eats a slice of summer sausage and two crusts of bread. She squares this with herself by chewing until the food is a paste so that there is hardly anything left for the baby. Just as her mother craved liver and onions when she was pregnant, Marcy craved the slice of summer sausage. "I have cravings," she thinks, a bit disturbed by such irrefutable evidence of her condition.

Nobody knows, not even Jeanie. Marcy is too ashamed. When she wakes up in the middle of the night her big anxiety is what if the baby doesn't die? "Please let it die," she prays. In her fervour she pulls her hair out in clumps. She makes deals with God. To be good. To be silent. She Scotch-tapes her lips together so that she can't talk. She knows that she is too young to marry, and yet as an alternative to being an unwed mother she finds herself reflecting upon Dug, the boy Jeanie's Ouija board said was going to be her husband. Except that Marcy doesn't know any Dugs, not yet.

The dream that invariably wakes her up these nights is the talking-baby one. It's not her baby, and it's not her mother's, either. If only when she woke up she could remember what the baby said, then she might know who it belonged to. She's not certain but she thinks it's a girl. On the way to and from school she searches for it in the bulrushes along the river. She is frightened of quicksand and won't step where the earth is wet.

Meanwhile, throughout November and despite her baby worries, she is obsessed with giving Jeanie baths. After school, as soon as Jeanie arrives and lets them into the house, Marcy chirps, "How would you like a nice, relaxing soak in the tub?" In bed at night she has found that if she presses her palm between her legs she can bring on "the feeling," just by thinking about washing Jeanie's breasts. Not without guilt though. The suspicion that she is doing something wrong has entered the picture and loiters during the day in the creases of clothes and between the slats of the venetian blinds in her classroom, and yet "the feeling" itself, when it washes over her, is white and glorious, like heaven. Her ensuing prayers tend to cancel each other out. "Thank you, Jesus," she says, heartfelt. "Thank you, dear Lord." And just as heartfelt, "Please forgive me, Jesus."

---

The night before her mother's baby is born, Marcy's baby dies. A sharp cramp wakes her from a dream about it dying. She goes into the bathroom and sits on the toilet because in her dream that was how it happened. She was on the toilet and the baby dropped out of her down there, still alive, a puny blue baby that could do the dog-paddle. Eventually it sunk but not before holding up one tiny finger, then two fingers, then—last chance—three fingers. When Marcy was sure that it had drowned she fished it out of the bowl and put it in a Pez dispenser for burial.

Her father is still up, listening to his "Mister Sandman" record. "Please turn on your magic beam," Marcy softly sings along to quell an unnameable fear. "Bring me a, bring me a, bring me a—" she sings where the record always sticks. She sits on the toilet for half an hour, in the dark. Finally she gets off and switches on the light to assure herself of her flat stomach. There is blue lint in her navel. Knowing it is only lint, she nevertheless picks it out and saves it to bury.

That following day, just when it doesn't matter any more, she meets a Dug. He reminds her of her dream poodle, his tight, curly blond hair and brown, snappy eyes. *She* doesn't make fun of his baggy Bermuda shorts. When the teacher says, "This is Doug Green all the way from London, England," if he had been a poodle, Marcy would have held her flat palm under his nose and said, "Good boy." She would like to bite his chubby legs.

At recess, intending flattery and consolation, she tells him he has ruby-red lips. He is alone beside the Elmer the Safety Elephant flagpole. He says, "Don't talk rubbish," and proceeds to do a series of hectic, crab-like cartwheels. The kind of cartwheels they do in England, she supposes. She tells him she has a crown at her house (the *Queen for a Day* crown, although Marcy has been led to believe it's her mother's lost prom-queen crown, only recently discovered in the attic). She brags that her father once mailed the Queen of England six books and that the Queen phoned him to say thank you. (This is a dream, not a memory, induced by her belief that the words "Send her victorious" are actually "Send her six storybooks".)

The boy says, "Watch this," and stands on his head. His shorts riding up produce in her the sentiment that her field of prospective husbands is narrowing.

On the way home from school he runs up behind her and says, "You better watch out or I'll kiss you," then keeps running. She stands still as white flowers open in her head. Boys gallop by her, all of them wearing Davy Crockett coonskin hats, the first such hats she has seen not on TV, herds of boys with tails on their heads. She has to go to the bathroom. She crouches behind a cedar hedge, and while she is peeing remembers the Pez container in her pencil case. Next to where she has peed she digs a hole with a sharp stone and buries her baby, finishing up with the singing of "What Can Little Hands Do to Please the King of Heaven?"

By the time she arrives home Jeanie is already there, watching *Secret Storm*. Jeanie declines a bath, so Marcy brushes her hair instead. Almost in a trance Marcy runs the brush and her hand over Jeanie's hair until Jeanie grunts and rolls onto her back. Marcy falls off her but climbs on again, astride her stomach. They look at each other, Marcy revelling in Jeanie's eyes. She has heard her father refer to Jeanie's eyes as beady, and she believes this to mean like jewels, sparkling.

"You know what?" Marcy says. Her throat aches. Her chest aches with a kind of bursting.

"What?" Jeanie says.

Marcy is suddenly inspired. "You better watch out!"

"Or what?" Jeanie asks in a sarcastic voice.

"Or I'll kiss you!" Marcy cries to her own enthralled disbelief.

Jeanie tries to heave her off, but Marcy drops forward and clings with her wiry arms and legs. "Jeanie!" she cries, earnest now, her entire body chiming with joyful noise. "I love you *so* much!"

# SIX

TO THE FOUR OF THEM baby Joan was what the new car was until Gordon smashed it into a tree. They often stood together in a group and just looked at her. They ran their hands over her body and strove to find words worthy enough and took her for spins around the block to show her off. At the very thought of her they laughed. They had their picture taken with her.

To the four of them baby Joan was what the sales brochure had *said* the new car was. Glamour plus. A supreme thrill, and a joy, and a blessing.

Now that they were back home Doris's apprehension about her was gone. Now that they were away from those senile Dearness crackpots was how she saw it. (*Just like the nuts that fall, I'm a little cracked, that's all!* were her theme lyrics for the whole bunch of them.) Strangely, she felt redeemed when she was holding Joan, as if Joan were the miraculous flowering of her own illicit sex.

Sonja felt redeemed all of the time. Those days of shame back when she'd first learned she was pregnant out of wedlock were no longer even a memory, let alone an unpleasant one, and any time Yours crossed her mind, after she had shuddered at the recollection of his nostrils, she thought almost fondly, "What a character." Without him there would be no Joan, there wasn't any getting around that. And the way he had pounced on her and got it over and done with in no time, that struck her as pretty smart now, like a doctor slipping the needle into your arm when your mouth is open for the thermometer. She never did see his penis, so it wasn't as if she had nightmares about it, although she'd had two weird dreams about green hammers—going into Ted's Cigar Store and all they were selling was green hammers, and a dream about her father having green hammers for arms.

There'd been a hammer with a chipped green handle lying in a nail box on Yours's windowsill. When she felt something pushing between her legs, it happened so suddenly and the thing was so solid she thought he was trying to stick the hammer handle up her. With his hand over her mouth she couldn't cry out. The blood on the fingers of his other hand, which he showed to her while she was still pinned down, was from splinters, she thought. What's more she thought it was *his* blood. *She* wasn't hurt. She hardly felt a thing. "Serves you right," she said as soon as his hand left her mouth. She was embarrassed to have been touched down there, she was scared to death because he was obviously a mental case after all, but even when he zipped himself back up she didn't catch on. She had to see the unbloodied hammer still lying in the nail box before another possibility struck her.

"Did we go all the way?" she asked.

He patted down her skirt and brushed a coil of hair out of her eyes. "We sure did," he said, smiling as if remembering a wonderful, romantic time.

"We *did?*"

His eyes emptied. "You give a fella the come hither, what do you expect?"

It was like missing the last bus. It was like losing her wallet. And she knew, she *knew* that she was pregnant. Yes, there it was—already!—another, faster heartbeat behind her own. Yours got up and left the room and she just sat there, listening to her two hearts. When he came back he had a facecloth. For her, she thought, but he used it to wipe the blood on the chesterfield. He asked if she could name the four blood groups.

They had met for the first and last time less than an hour before, at the Swan Restaurant next door to where her father worked. She had gone downtown for a polio shot and to bring her father a manuscript he'd left at home, since his office was in the same building as the doctor's. "Gin Alley" the manuscript was called. On the bus she opened it to read the recipes but it was a story about a man named Ratface.

"Potboiler means *trash*," her father said when she asked why he was always going on about how his company published nothing except cookbooks. "Private-eye novels, shoot-'em-up hoodlum novels." He spoke nicely but he looked at her as if he couldn't believe how stupid she was, and suddenly she craved apple pie à la mode. And then she remembered that she was next door to where they had the best apple pie she had ever tasted! Her father smiled and said, "Oh, I get it, you were pulling my leg." With his finger he wiped away the saliva at the corner of her mouth.

It was a Thursday morning. Phys. ed., math, chemistry—all her worst subjects were on Thursday morning. So she was in no hurry. She ordered two pieces of pie and a glass of chocolate milk, using up her whole allowance. She was just digging in when a huge man with nostrils the size of quarters sat beside her at the counter and extended a pack of Lucky Strikes. "No, thank you," she said, "I don't smoke," and he said in a Southern accent, "I'm with you a hundred percent, stunts your growth."

She glanced at him. He winked. She looked down but couldn't help smiling. Stunts your growth, she thought. That was a good one.

He pocketed the cigarettes and withdrew a cigar, turning to the woman on his other side for a light. Then he turned back to Sonja and stared at her. After a few minutes he said, "You know who you

look like? Elizabeth Taylor. I'll bet folks tell you that all the time.
I'll bet folks stop you on the street for your autograph."

She laughed. "Every day and twice on Sundays." She knew that
she looked nothing like Elizabeth Taylor.

"Shoot," he said. "Elizabeth Taylor." He sat there staring until
she wondered if he thought she *was* Elizabeth Taylor. She wondered if he was a mental case. She gave him another quick glance.

"You're of Greek origin, aren't you?" he said.

She shook her head.

"If you were, folks would say you were Aphrodite. Know who
she was?"

"No." Looking straight at her pie.

"Goddess of love, beauty and fertility. Daughter of Zeus."

At this point the waitress came over, but he waved her away,
saying he didn't need food, he was feasting his eyes. Sonja ate
steadily and tried to ignore him and his cigar smoke. She tried to
remember what fertility meant. She knew it was rude. Another
few minutes passed and then he tapped a finger on the cover of
her geography notebook and drawled. "Soncha." He traced the
letters with a ridged, yellow fingernail. "Soncha, now there's a
classy name. Pleased to make your acquaintance, Soncha."

"Sonja," she couldn't help correcting.

"Sonja." He nodded. "Sonja. As in I wanya, Sonja?"

She let out an embarrassed laugh. "No," she murmured.

"You know what you can call me?"

She started eating faster, shovelling in the last forkfuls.

"Take a guess."

She sighed, flustered.

"Go ahead, guess."

"Red?" she tried with her mouth full. He had red hair.

"Try again."

She swallowed. Scanned him sidelong. "Stretch?"

"Yours," he said. "You can call me yours." He set his cigar in the ashtray and wrested her hand from her glass. She had an idea that he was going to perform a magic trick, the one where a coin suddenly appears in your palm. "I bet this is as soft as beeswax," he said. He balled up her hands between his. "Mmm, darlin'," he said.

She wondered what to do. She didn't want to be rude. She didn't want to upset him and make him snap. His hands were the size of baseball gloves, quite pale. By comparison her hand was a little clump of brown bread dough he was working. When he began to pull on her fingers, she tried to tug away, and he gave her a heavy-lidded, broken-down look.

"I'm not allowed to date yet," she said. It was true, although up until now it had been beside the point. She tugged at her hand again but he folded it in both of his and brought his cupped hands to his lips.

"Well, then, how about we just be close friends," he said.

To get rid of him she agreed to walk with him as far as the corner. He said, "It's a deal," slapping the counter with both hands and coming to his feet. He was even taller than she'd thought, his black boots long and pointed, like a court jester's. But with cleats. Out on the sidewalk, for every scraping chink from him, her penny loafers produced three feeble little slaps, and trying to change her pace didn't make any difference, he automatically adjusted. He said that she was so graceful, she must be a ballerina.

"A tap-dancer," she admitted.

"Hey, show me a few steps," he said, but she said it didn't work without tap shoes. They walked on. He kept looking at her, she could feel it. She looked straight ahead, clutching her books to her chest, scurrying alongside what felt like the sway of steel girders.

When they reached the corner he badgered her to walk with him just three more blocks, and seeing as she wasn't really going out of her way, she gave in. "Oh, all right" was her half of the conversation until they arrived at his place. It turned out to be in a new apartment building. He said she'd see a grown man cry like a baby if she didn't take a ride in his elevator.

"Oh, all right," she said and followed him through the ritzy lobby. Partly out of curiosity because she'd never been in a high-rise. Partly out of sheer surrender.

The elevator was mirrored, even the ceiling, which he came up to. He punched the highest button, nine, then clamped her shoulders and turned her in a circle. He said, "No matter which way you look, darlin', there we are."

It was true. Her so short and chubby and him so tall she thought for a minute they must be fun-house mirrors, except that he'd been that tall outside.

"You and me," he said.

He turned her again.

"Going on to infinity," he said.

# SEVEN

"SHE's not *like* any of us," Sonja would marvel at least once a day as the weeks and months passed and Joan's face articulated into gorgeousness, especially around the eyes, whose expression was so intent and focused that combined with her astonishing ability to mimic sounds and to hum the first two bars of "In the Mood" on key it seemed obvious that the family had a genius on its hands.

When she was about eighteen months old, however, Doris began to wonder. Here Joan was doing amazing impressions of creaking hinges, screeching tires, radio static, and yet she hadn't uttered a comprehensible word yet, not even "Mama" or "Dada," and when you spoke to her she just went on staring at you in her detached way until (if you were pressing for a response) she cooed or chirped or mooed or gobbled or made some other animal sound. For two months now, she'd been walking and feeding herself. But throw a ball at her, and her hands didn't so much as twitch to catch it. Or try to get her to wave or clap, or to give you a kiss or hug. Or to laugh. Or to even smile! Good luck getting her to go outside without covering her eyes with her hands. The worst was that she couldn't bear the sight of anyone except the immediate family. Somebody rang the doorbell, and first she reproduced the sound and then she sank to the floor, and not even putting Glenn Miller on the record player could persuade her to get up.

By the time she was two and a half she still had not said a single word to any of them, and she spent much of the day either down in the windowless laundry room or in her and Marcy's closet. Mostly in the closet, which was not as cramped as you might think because it had once been a dressing room. She had unearthed her old potty from under a stack of blankets and she was using it again, presumably to cut down on outings. Back in a corner she listened at barely audible volume to the big-band station on the transistor radio that Doris won on *Queen for a Day*. How did she know that the aerial had to be poked into the room for good reception? The other mystery was what was she doing with Sonja's old high-school textbooks and Gordon's *Webster's Dictionary* and *Pears Cyclopaedia*? There they were, in two stacks. Never opened as far as anybody had witnessed. She had also brought in the Eaton's and Simpson's catalogues and a box of old *Life* magazines, and these she studied with the excessive intensity that she studied herself in reflective surfaces—mirrors, windows, the toaster, spoons . . .

You could coax her up from the laundry room but not out of the closet. Once she was in the closet you might as well be appealing to a cat, her green eyes shining and vigilant. Stroke her hair, squeeze her feet in their white newborn shoes, the pleasure was all yours. She would emerge when she was good and ready. When you were gone. You wouldn't hear her walk down the hall, you'd hear her pipsqueak hum, or you'd turn off a light and a second later hear that dry click again, *behind* you this time.

Dr. Ackerman, their family doctor, an elegant, burly man with black eyebrows like fur stoles, declared her "As healthy as . . . " He opened his hands balletically.

"A horse?" Doris said.

He smiled. He asked Doris if she had considered Einstein. "A genius," he said in his soothing bass, "who didn't speak a word until he was . . . " Another opening of the hands.

"Did he act like that?" Doris said, indicating Joan. In a chair in the farthest corner of his office Joan sat with her eyes squeezed shut and her palms pressed over her ears. A little ghost (only when she was out of the closet did Doris appreciate how white her skin and hair were), her lips moving quickly as if in desperate prayer, but Doris knew that what she was doing was faintly echoing a repeated sound—the clock, maybe.

"Joan is high-strung," Dr. Ackerman said, his lovelorn gaze floating over to her. "That's all."

"High-strung?" Doris said after a minute.

"There's nothing physically the matter with her eyes. There's nothing physically the matter with her ears. So, that leaves us with?" His smile wafted back to Doris.

Doris waited. "Nerves?" she said finally, sceptically.

A single, savoured nod.

"Well, how do you explain this closet business if it's nerves? I'm telling you, she just sits there hour after hour. I've never heard of a kid sitting still for that long."

"And you stand for it?" He was still smiling but as if despite a tragedy.

"How do you mean?"

"I mean it seems to me she has the whole family worried as . . . "

"Can be," Doris admitted.

"Have you thought of trying . . . " He clapped. Up by his ear, like a Spanish dancer.

"What?"

Another three claps. A suggestive lift of the eyebrows.

"Applauding?"

"Warming her fanny." His tone so kindly that it took Doris another minute.

"Spanking her?" she said.

He might as well have asked if she had tried slamming her across the head with a two-by-four. As far as Doris was concerned he might as well have said string her up.

What she and Gordon did instead was make the closet more hospitable. If she must hide, they preferred her to be upstairs where it was warm and dry and from where she didn't materialize clutching centipedes. Gordon removed all the boxes and blankets and clothes and installed a piece of thick-pile rose carpet. On the inside of the closet door he taped a miniature reproduction from *Life* magazine: Monet's "Garden at Argenteuil," and right next to it, on the wall, he hung a three-foot-high mirror (which from then on she always sat facing so that at least she now faced the door as well). He hooked up a shaded twenty-five-watt light designed to illuminate a small circle while keeping the rest of the closet in relative darkness, but before doing that he bought her a pair of pink-framed sunglasses (why hadn't he thought of sunglasses sooner? he wondered guiltily) and once she had them on, that was it, she wouldn't remove them to undress, to go to bed, wash her face, those sunglasses were glued to her. The wax earplugs that he bought a few days later were not such a hit. Them she used to patch a hole in the closet wall where some plaster had fallen away.

She seemed happy enough, but Doris could hardly stand the sight of her stowed in there with only reading material and a radio like some blind midget scholar hiding from the Nazis, so she collected her dolls and stuffed animals from the shelf where they were gathering dust, loaded them into the wicker laundry basket and put that in, frankly surprised it wasn't pushed back out the same day and then realizing that why it wasn't was because, with the boxes gone, it served as a partial barricade when the closet door was opened.

Which it only was for getting or hanging up clothes or when any of them were paying a visit. To Joan's credit she suffered the door to remain open during visits from the family.

And there were a lot of these, a regular pilgrimage throughout the day—Doris always racing in, Sonja dropping by whenever she felt like taking a break from pin-clipping, Marcy joining her before and after school, and Gordon going straight there as soon as he arrived home from work. The half hour before supper that he used to spend reading the newspaper Gordon now spent stretched out on the floor.

The truth was, the best part of the day those bleak days in his life was lying with his head in his daughter's closet. Shoes and tie off, listening to the turned-down radio, so unwound he often found himself talking to her as if she were the family dog. "I'm just not a corporate man," he might say. Or even, "Between you and me I'm not cut out for married life." Once, to his horror, he realized that he had asked her if she'd ever contemplated suicide. He was a private person, tormented by almost everything he felt. But here he was spilling his guts to a toddler. It was eerie, inconceivable. Sometimes the words he'd just said would boomerang back to him and he'd come to as if out of a coma. Aghast, but refreshed as well, he had to admit—and usually assuring himself he'd only *imagined* he'd spoken out loud—he'd sit up and take a peek at her sitting back there so straight with her legs out and a magazine opened on her lap.

He couldn't see the expression in her eyes, not with the sunglasses on, but her lips were almost always parted, and this, combined with her utter stillness, gave her a highly expectant look. He would reach in and pat her barrette-laden head. What fine hair! Like spider webs, her ears poking through the strands. He might click his tongue or whistle through his teeth to hear her imitation. To be wowed by her.

---

Gordon wasn't alone in confessing to Joan or using her as a sounding board. They all did it, although maybe not so involuntarily.

Without a pang, Doris tried out lies on her. When the mail arrived and the sound of it coming through the slot sent Joan fleeing into the closet (if she wasn't there already), Doris would chase after her and sit in the closet doorway to open the letters, never failing to get a charge out of Joan's perfect echo of the envelopes ripping. If there were any overdue notices or final invoices Doris would announce them and ask how they were going to weasel out of paying. Joan would look at her, seemingly rapt. Then Doris would say something like, "I know! I'll tell them I moved the bank account and they mustn't have transferred the money yet!" If she snapped her fingers, Joan immediately snapped hers.

When a letter arrived from Harmony, Doris would read parts of that, too. Harmony had a one-tracked, colourful mind. "My woman," Harmony wrote, "I pine for your breasts like fattened geese. In reveries I taste your mango honey." These were not the parts Doris read. "The mist falls like arpeggios" was what she skipped to, that kind of thing. Harmony's envelopes were lilac-scented and had her initials embossed on the flap. "Feel," Doris would say, extending the envelope into the closet, and Joan would touch the HLL with the tips of all ten fingers like a person reading braille. Then Doris would hold the envelope under Joan's nose and say, "Smell," and Joan's nostrils would flare and contract daintily. Sometimes she gobbled, a sign of pleasure.

For her part Sonja read to Joan from the *TV Guide* in a vain attempt to entice her into the living room or just because Sonja had the *TV Guide* handy. Lying on Joan's bed, she recited the childrens' show listings and, in case something rang a bell, the synopses from old movies and "Yesterday's Newsreel."

" 'Yesterday's Newsreel' looks at 1936 and the death of King George. King George! Do you remember him, Bunny?"

From inside the closet, Joan clicked her tongue.

"You do?"

Joan mooed.

"You don't?"

Sonja watched TV all day. After failing grade eleven she had left school and was now working at home for the Schropps Pin Company. Her job was counting bobby-pins and clipping them on cards, twenty-four to a card, and she did this at the fold-out writing table in front of the TV while eating Planters peanuts and licorice Allsorts, her fat hands skittering from the box of pins to the box of cards to the food to her mouth.

After Joan was born, Sonja never lost the weight. Now she was up to 210 pounds, but the bigger she got the happier and lighter she felt, as if she were being inflated to the point where a little breeze would lift her out of her chair and bounce her around the room. Maybe it wasn't the extra pounds that were making her so happy, though. She had another theory, a hare-brained one, she knew, that Schropps had coated the bobby-pins with something like a laughing gas to keep the clippers in good spirits, because she could wake up on the wrong side of the bed but the minute she started working she'd be calm, completely relaxed all over except for her hands. Her hands, when she worked, felt mechanically operated, the way her feet had felt when she was a tap-dancer. Month after month for filling up the most cards she won the five-foot-high cardboard bobby-pin that said "I'm Tops at Schropps." Plus she was hauling in a weekly paycheque of twenty-five dollars. At Doris's insistence twenty of that went straight into the bank, into a "dowry account," even though Sonja couldn't see herself marrying.

"I'm a born career girl," she confessed to Joan from a deep vein of content.

Marcy's confessions were the most intimate, in these years anyway, and the raciest—"We touched his tongue with our tongue." "We had 'the feeling' today." She had picked up Doris's habit of using the the plural pronoun, with the difference that when *she* said "Time for our bath, Joanie" she climbed into the bath, too. Joan was her. The her that was tiny, magical, celestial . . . not entirely real. If Joan whimpered, Marcy's eyes welled up. To her parents, Marcy pointed out that she could do the talking when she overheard them fretting over Joan's speechlessness. She brushed Joan's wispy hair with Gordon's shaving brush, and her own scalp tingled. She adorned Joan's head with ribbons and barrettes and felt all dressed up.

When Joan was younger and in a high chair, Marcy had fed her. Marcy still insisted on cutting Joan's meat (while Joan covered her ears at the scraping noise). Usually Joan then cut the meat into even smaller portions, and she could do it without a sound. At three and a half she had the table etiquette of a finicky duchess. She ate one pea at a time. She chewed silently and forever and with her mouth closed. She swallowed as if her throat was sore, touching her neck with the tips of her fingers. Doris never bothered to put out napkins, but Joan always had a tissue handy to dab the corners of her mouth. Where had she learned such manners? Not from any of them, although to make her life easier they had all become fastidious, quiet eaters. There were no raw carrots or celery to munch on, for instance, and they kept their voices down. If Marcy wanted to say something directly to Joan, to be extra quiet she often only thought it.

In bed at night Marcy's communication with Joan was entirely telepathic. Doris used to shout "Go to sleep!" if Marcy talked, so now, as soon as Doris was out of the room, Marcy left her own bed and climbed into Joan's and "thought" to her. Her challenge was to keep thinking conversation until Joan fell asleep, but she never managed it. The last thing she saw every night before drifting off was the first thing she saw every morning—Joan looking at her (the green plastic lenses of Joan's sunglasses weren't so dark that you couldn't make out her eyes). Joan lying there, staring. And parroting some soothing noise, like a drip or the refrigerator motor.

# EIGHT

IN THE AUTUMN of 1960 Doris took Joan to another doctor, who recommended a third doctor. This third doctor fastened Joan to an electroencephalogram while she sat limply with her eyes shut, apparently asleep except that she imitated the electric shaver cropping patches of her hair. A small desk fan wafted some of the hair in Doris's direction, and as if it were dandelion tuft Doris caught it, balled it up and released it with a wish— "Please don't let her be brain-damaged."

But Doris already knew she was. The diagnosis when it came—after more tests, after x-rays and separate physical examinations by two other neurologists—was only confirmation, in Doris's eyes as pointless as the bathroom scales spelling out that you're broad in the beam. The nature of the damage was scar tissue, almost certainly from the fall at birth. The scar tissue was fickle. It enhanced certain abilities but interfered with others, mainly the ability to vocalize words. So although Joan could reproduce certain sounds and could understand what was said to her, she couldn't talk and likely never would.

"She could if we wanted to!" Marcy protested when Doris broke the news to her.

"We don't know that, Sweetie." In the back of her mind, the song "Happy Talk" babbled.

"She *could!*" She appealed to Joan, who had suddenly appeared in the doorway. "Couldn't we?"

Joan stepped over to Marcy—that cautious, lightfooted way she had of walking in the house, arms trailing, fingers moving like cilia. She stood on tiptoe (she was only half Marcy's height) and sniffed, a thing she sometimes did when you asked her a question, and Doris mentally added "smelling people's faces" to her "Signs of Brain Damage" list.

"Couldn't we?" Marcy repeated.

Joan stepped back and made clucking noises that Marcy took for "Sure."

"She said yes!"

"You know Zorro's servant?" Doris said. "What's his name, Leonardo?"

"Bernardo," Marcy said sullenly.

"Bernardo. Well, you know how Bernardo can't talk but he can hear better than anybody? That's like Joanie. Joanie can't talk but she can make sounds better than anybody."

"We could talk if we wanted to," Marcy said, clasping Joan's hand.

"Listen to me," Doris said. "Parts of Joanie's brain just don't work," she said, her voice reaching the jubilant-sounding pitch it did when she wanted to make no bones about a thing and engendering in Joan a quiver of delight that, through their joined hands, Marcy detected and mistook.

"Mommy, you're upsetting us!" she said. "You're hurting our feelings!"

One of the doctors advised Gordon and Doris that when it came time for Joan to go to school she be sent to the Mother Goose Home for Mentally Retarded Children, a spanking-new factory-like building with portal-sized windows and a few hole-faced Mother Goose characters on the lawn (Humpty Dumpty, Tweedledum and Tweedledee), the kind of statues you stick your own face through and someone takes your picture.

"She's hardly a drooling idiot," Doris said.

"Don't let 'Mentally Retarded' throw you," the doctor said. "They kept the old name for some reason but they're taking in all kinds of kids now. Mongoloids, deaf-mutes, your straight delinquent cases."

"When the time comes, I'll teach her at home," Doris said.

"Are you qualified?"

"Before I got married, I was a teacher."

A Sunday-school teacher when she was twelve, she meant. Not that either she or Gordon cared about the lie. "Do you think you'd be able to manage it?" Gordon said on the drive home. "That's all I'm questioning."

"Oh, for crying out loud!" Doris said. "Look at all the dimwit teachers there are! The only thing they have that I don't are the textbooks."

A few months later, when the three diagnoses were in, she went to Marcy's school after four o'clock, just marched in the unlocked gymnasium door and down to the grade-one classroom and stole two Dick-and-Jane readers, a spelling book and an arithmetic book.

Now that she had the idea of doing the teaching she was raring to get started. As much for her own sake as for Joan's. Scouring magazines for contests and scrawling out hundreds of reasonable facsimiles gave her a kick, but it wasn't enough any more. She knew the signs—not being able to sit still for a second and then, when she did, falling into daydreams about the sexpot cashier at Ted's Cigar Store. Night-time dreams about making love with strange women in public places, such as in front of the meat counter at Dominion.

She had been hoping that she was done with women. Her explanation to herself had been that indulging in women was a stage she'd gone through with a lot of help from voodoo. Lately, though, she'd been wondering if it wasn't Harmony who had set her off, but Joan—the shock of Joan's arrival, the shock of becoming a grandmother.

Oh, who knows? "You haven't touched me in over ten years" was what she intended to throw at Gordon if he ever found out, and you bet it was a good excuse but it wasn't the reason. Her yearning for Gordon and her yearning for women ran on two separate tracks. That much she had always felt, and occasionally she felt the delicacy and the imperiousness of the division, a bit like the reminder when you choke on food that you breathe from one place and swallow from another. The only other thing she was sure of was that loving women was dangerous. Don't think she didn't fight it. Since Harmony there'd been only Robin the Avon Lady, and that was only the one time but enough of a close call to scare her off for good. So she had thought.

Blunt-spoken Robin, who left her with the thrilling, crazy impression that while "normal" women were in their kitchens dreaming up the winning answer to "Why I Love Tenderleaf Tea," there were bands of feverish Valkyrie lesbians out hunting sex. She knew Robin for all of an hour, but for years afterwards she was convinced that Harmony had been exceptional, that most lesbians scorned romance and long love affairs, and you'd never know they were lesbians to look at them. Except for how they looked at *you*. And if you didn't blink when they looked at you like that, you were in the money.

They had red, spiky nails, these lesbians. They showed up at your front door and sang "Ding dong!" On your chesterfield they sat with their left thigh touching your right thigh while they massaged lotion into your hands and your calloused elbows. Into your bare feet. "How does that feel?" they asked. You said, "Like a million bucks." You let them test all their products on you, offering your wrist to be slashed with lipstick. The shade you liked best they applied to your lips. They held your chin and brought their own face so close to yours that you inhaled each other's breath.

They kissed you. You kissed them back because the coast was clear—your husband at work, your oldest girl at a pin-clippers seminar, your middle one at school, and your littlest one in the closet from where, ordinarily with a stranger in the house, you couldn't have budged her. So why *did* she budge? Not needing to use the toilet, she had the potty for that. Maybe it was the tantalizing sound of so many zippers—first the zipper on Robin's suit jacket, then the one on her skirt, and then the broken zipper on her full-length girdle.

The tip-off was a zipping noise so faint that Doris didn't register it for a few seconds. And then she knew, and she looked around and gasped. Joan gasped. Robin gasped. Joan gasped.

"Mommy's just comforting the lady, Joanie, it's okay. Go back to your room." In her mind the song "People Will Say We're in Love" started up. "Go on, honey," she said and was ignored. Meanwhile, she and Robin were both pulling their clothes on, Robin whispering, "Oh my God, my God," and Doris's heart racing, and yet even in those first fluorescent seconds Doris knew that she and Robin were the only horrified ones in the room. "Honey, go back to the closet, I'll come see you in a minute," she said.

Joan took a step closer. Her lips moved, she was doing inaudible imitations. Of what?

Out on the front porch Robin said, "I don't think she really saw anything, do you?"

"She's only three," Doris said. Without conviction she said, "She wouldn't know what she saw." A year later and she would have said that Joan was brain-damaged, and Robin might have been even more relieved, in a guilty way. For Doris it wouldn't have made any difference except that she derived a cheerless relief from being able to deliver the official diagnosis. Brain-damaged. It meant there was no mystery. You fell on your head and your brain scarred. It had nothing to do with disobedience or the supernatural and it wasn't a punishment, not unless any tragic accident was a punishment, and Doris wasn't buying that.

# NINE

T HE SAME DAY that she stole the books, Doris phoned
Gordon at his office and asked him to bring home some
pencils, erasers and paper. The next morning she rode the
bus and subway downtown to a school-supply store and wrote a
cheque from a defunct account for a pointer, coloured construction paper, a pitch pipe, chalk, a blackboard, a blackboard eraser
and a bundle of pale green writing paper, green because Gordon
said that it cast no glare. There was already a desk in Marcy and
Joan's bedroom and she intended to push it in front of the opened
closet door and put the chair right inside. For the teacher's desk
she'd slide the mirror off the vanity and use that.

Back home she hung the blackboard where Marcy's paint-by-
numbers Harlequin clown normally hung. She wrote out the al-
phabet on squares of the coloured paper and taped the squares
around the room just below the ceiling, the idea being to create an
atmosphere as classroom-like as possible, considering. She then let
out the seams on her navy pleated skirt and washed and ironed her
two white blouses. While she worked she whistled "Whistle
While You Work," and not once all day did she think about the
cashier at Ted's Cigar Store.

At exactly nine o'clock the next morning she and Joan stood
facing each other at their desks, Joan dressed in the coral silk

blouse and lime green velvet skirt that she shared with Marcy's two-foot-high Miss Sophisticate doll, her hair festooned with twice as many barrettes and ribbons as usual, thanks to Marcy. And Doris wearing the pleated skirt, one of the white blouses and brown high heels that her swollen feet knuckled out like shoes on fists.

"Okey-dokey," she said, "here we go." She blew the pitch pipe any old place (it didn't matter what came out, she couldn't carry a tune). She waited for Joan to imitate the note, then she sang "O Canada" and "God Save the Queen," hardly above a whisper because her singing usually sent Joan under the bed. As it was, Joan covered her ears. Ignoring this, and how Joan wasn't singing along, she conducted with one hand. She didn't believe in God but the Lord's Prayer was part of a school morning routine, so she raced through it without bothering to ask Joan to close her eyes. This was a child who once you had her attention didn't blink, let alone close her eyes.

She did sit at Marcy's desk, however, perched on two pillows, and she continued to do so every day without protest. Provided that the bedroom curtains were drawn and there was only the one desk light on, provided that the phone didn't ring and nobody came to the door, she stayed put for a good two hours at a time, a lot longer than Doris herself was able to. Doris paced and fidgeted. Whenever she had a minute she pored through magazines for coupons and contest-entry forms. Joan, meanwhile, although alert (unnervingly alert, breathing fast as a bird), sat straight and still. It is no exaggeration to say that she didn't move a muscle unless she was writing or there was some sudden sound from outside the room, and then she gave a little start and trained one rose-petal ear in that direction.

She learned fast. By the end of the first month you could say any number or letter to her and she wrote it. Three months down the road she was adding and subtracting double-digit numbers in her head. Doris would ask, for instance, "What are eleven and thirteen?" and Joan would continue looking at her as if this question, gripping as it might be, was rhetorical, but a few seconds later she would push her sunglasses up her nose, pick up the pencil, write a tidy "24," set the pencil down and then suffer Doris to praise her as she suffered all the family's attentions—patiently and without reciprocation, although she liked to echo the smack of a kiss, not against skin but into the air.

The next step—reading and writing words—seemed foregone. Anyone who could produce a "d" followed by an "o" followed by a "g" should be able to write "dog," if you told her that this is what those three letters in that order amounted to.

You'd think so. But every time Doris asked her to spell "dog," or if she wrote "dog" on the blackboard and asked what it spelled, Joan played dumb. Eventually Doris began to wonder if there was a scar over the part of her brain that allowed her to comprehend the joining of letters, and so she phoned one of the neurologists. "Maybe," he said. He couldn't be more specific than that because the scars were hard to pinpoint. "Think of them as uncharted islands in a fathomless ocean," he advised. He said, "Keep trying!"

Advice that Marcy took passionately. On all fours in the closet Marcy wiggled her bum, softly barking, and said, "Write what animal we are!" She found pictures of dogs in magazines and asked in an excited, encouraging voice, "Joanie, what's this?" She knelt on the floor, and with her nose an inch away from the paper (this was a few months before anyone noticed that she needed glasses), wrote "dog," saying, "Down, around, now a circle . . . ," trying to get Joan to copy her. Joan watched all this, leaning over the magazine in her lap to see the word. Sometimes she even picked up her pencil and held it poised. Sometimes she sniffed the word.

Sonja was the one who thought to bribe her. She used licorice Allsorts, Joan's favourite candy. One afternoon when Joan appeared in the kitchen to refill her water glass, Sonja fetched a piece of paper and a pencil, shut the curtains to make the room more hospitable, enticed Joan to sit at the table, then poured the candy into a bowl and said, "Spell dog and you can help yourself." Joan waited, hands folded on the paper. A few minutes passed and Sonja ate a candy herself. Then another. And another. Joan didn't write dog but she watched Sonja like one, watched her hand go from the bowl to her mouth, watched her chew until Sonja couldn't stand it any longer and said, "Oh, forget it, dig in," and Joan did. She ate, even candy, in little bites, fastidiously.

This tickled Sonja. "You dickens," Sonja laughed with her mouth full, patting Joan's angora hair, and that was the extent of her contribution to Joan's literacy. Like Marcy, she found the brain-damage theory off base, her hunch being that in previous lives Joan had suffered from words. As a gossip, maybe. As a tattle-tale.

Gordon entertained a similar thought. Not that Joan had been reincarnated but that she was deliberately forswearing words out of an instinctive sense that it took only one to flatten you. On his bad days he wondered if her muteness wasn't highly evolved. He wondered why people didn't hit the dirt whenever other people talked. He wondered what possessed people to read! On his bad days he found nothing as discouraging as the sight of reflection that has been dislodged from the preserving climate of the mind and then arranged—all dried out and shrunken—on paper.

On his good days he wasn't prepared to say that Joan could talk if she chose to but he suspected that she could read because when he read to her he sometimes caught her head moving back and forth, very slightly, as though she was following the words with her eyes. He said to Doris, "She'll come around," and he didn't doubt it.

No matter what his mood, if he was home he read to Joan every night before she went to bed. The books were ones he picked up from the library twice a week. Fairy tales mostly, stories about snowy-skinned princesses and girls no bigger than your thumb. Down in the laundry room, the only place she didn't seem to mind leaving the closet for, the two of them sat on the lumpy, spring-sprouting sofa while on the clothesline overhead his laundered white shirts swayed like his own ghosts.

After everyone had gone to bed he devoted himself to the books he had "borrowed" (temporarily stolen) from another library, the university's medical library or his old stomping grounds you might say because when he was eighteen he spent the month of August in a corner cubicle reading about his "affliction," as it was referred to in books with titles like *Curing the Male Homosexual* and *Demonology and Homosexuality.*

Back then, these books were catalogued under "Mental Disorders" and "Sexual Deviance" and were not on the open shelves. So he had always waited until the librarian was alone before handing her a request slip . . . printed in perfect block letters (the last thing he'd wanted was her reading it aloud for clarification!). As the librarian frowned at the slip he would mention that he was a student of psychiatric neuroses, or that he was writing a paper, doing research for Professor So-and-so. He suspected that the librarian would have preferred to have conducted these exchanges in silence, but every time, he couldn't help himself, he blurted out some story. The librarian never met his eye. She brought him the books. He took them to a remote corner cubicle where, behind a bulwark of other, innocently titled books, he read them. They were dry, scholastic, densely footnoted, but also shocking, operatic. Bland passages would explode in such graphically clinical descriptions that he would be driven to the washroom to masturbate.

Which was not at all why he was there that August. He was there for information. And for a kind of punishing reassurance that it was true. He *was* sick. He was ungrown, unmanly. The authors tended to agree that the remedy was to discuss the problem with your priest or pastor (unthinkable!), failing which you might try self-healing—lowering the timbre of your voice, playing football. The premise of *Curing the Male Homosexual* was that you should enter into a serious study of "real" men. (As if, Gordon thought, that wasn't why he was in trouble in the first place.) In this book there were diagrams showing you how to walk and sit in a masculine manner, how to cross your legs, for instance, by lifting your left leg and resting the ankle on your right knee. If you must masturbate, like a real man you should imagine beautiful naked women just as you were ejaculating. If your mind drifted to naked men, the trick was to picture them covered in suppurating sores.

Gordon gave it his best shot. There in his cubicle he practiced leg-crossing, he practiced sitting as if a yardstick were prising apart his thighs. In the library washroom he summoned breasts as he was climaxing, cysts and scabs as he fought his arousal. It was the strangest time. Oddly featureless, even tranquil in stretches. There *was* frustration, off and on, toward the doctors who had written the books. Who *were* these men? Were *they* homosexuals? If they were, why hadn't any of them figured out that the best you could do was the only decent thing you could do: keep your affliction under wraps, live with it.

Almost thirty years later, whenever Gordon walked through the doors of the library, he was struck by how remarkable it was that he'd had the answer to his homosexuality way ahead of any real grasp of what it was. He was a virgin at eighteen, staggeringly innocent about everything, not just the choreography of sex. And yet even before he read those books he'd had a feeling that they weren't going to change anything. Hide it, live with it, he was already weathered by what he would end up doing. It seemed to him now that when it came to all the big decisions he acted and *then* he was driven to act so that his whole life had been lived in the light of consequence rather than of expectation. That sad old light, and here it was incarnate: the yellow flush of a library at sunset, dust motes fat as stars.

He avoided glancing at the table where he used to sit (the tables were the same ones, the same gold wood), striding straight to the books about the brain. Striding as opposed to skulking. The brain as opposed to the mind. No different from when he was eighteen, however, he was looking without much hope but resolutely for an answer as empirical as the circulation of blood.

And was finding that brain damage was where medicine became vague and overblown, wacky even, as if the mind couldn't contemplate its own peril with anything like objectivity. Of an aneurism one neurologist wrote, "Envision a red balloon bursting in a bucket full of noodles." Another spoke of bulges "like ripe berries lodged in the serpentine crevices of a walnut." The damaged brain as a berserk telephone exchange run by demented operators was a popular image.

His own images—the dreams he had when the book slipped from his fingers and he nodded off—tended toward snake clusters and the braided limbs of gas-chamber corpses.

When he came to, past midnight, the living room would clang around him like a place whose dreary familiarity comes from long hours of keeping vigil. He'd turn off the lights, go down the hall to his and Doris's bedroom and jiggle her shoulder to wake her in case she wanted to watch from the window. Then he'd tiptoe to Marcy and Joan's bedroom and stand right at the door.

Never a sound from the other side, but a moment later the door would open and Joan would come out. How she always knew he was there, he had no idea. He'd pick her up, and if it was a cool or rainy night he'd go to the hall closet for shoes and jackets before taking her outside.

This started one night when he'd been about to check on her and Marcy but had paused, because no matter how quiet he was he seemed to wake Joan up. Either that or she was never asleep. He'd had his hand on the knob and had felt it turn from the inside. Don't think that that didn't startle him. When the door opened and it was only Joan in her nightgown (and sunglasses), he lifted her up and pressed her against his hammering heart. Without thinking, he carried her down the hall and out into the front yard.

It was warm and hazy that night. Mid-July. A buttery glow from the sky down, a soft, sulphuric light, and what sounded like a thousand crickets. The air quivered with them. There were also a lot of moths, the small white ones, fluttering like ash under the streetlights. Joan saw them right away. He felt her body tense and then her head began to move in rapid jerks and he realized, astonished, that she was following individual flight paths.

"Moths," he said.

Instantly she slumped in his arms, her normal outdoor behaviour. He was sorry he'd spoken. He stood her on the grass, expecting that she would just run back inside.

She did run. She ran to the door, but stopped. Then—arms trailing and fingers wiggling—she ran across the yard to the shadow of the hedge and crouched down.

He waited, not sure what to do. In the wet grass her footprints were like silver coins she'd thrown to find her way back. She was stark white—her hair, her nightgown. The crickets were like live wire, and after a minute she joined them.

When she fell silent he pretended he couldn't see her. He had a feeling that this was what she wanted. He said, "I wonder where Joanie is."

She made a shivery noise he had never heard from her before. Was that a laugh? Could she actually be laughing? Then she bolted across the lawn to the shadow of the wisteria and crouched.

"Joanie?" he said, and she made that sound again. She darted by him, jumping over the crevice that was his long shadow and crouching in the shadow of the house.

He waited a moment. Aside from the crickets there was a sprinkler going next door. "Where is she?" he said, and she shot back over to the hedge.

A blizzard passed behind his eyes. Why hadn't any of them thought of this before? To take her outside to play *at night,* for Christ's sake? He felt like a scientist who has neglected to do the most obvious thing—turn on the bunsen burner, add water. He wanted to wake up Doris so she could witness it, but he didn't want to break the spell. He couldn't even bring himself to take a step. He just stood there calling, him and the whippoorwill and the crickets, while Joan laughed and zigzagged from shadow to shadow until the entire lawn was spangled with her footprints.

# TEN

T AKING Joan anywhere during the day was like transporting a narcoleptic whose dreams are about the real and present moment, as if she were watching the same television program but on another channel. You'd swear she was in a deep sleep because her breathing slowed and because of how she drooped and grew warm and still, and yet there wasn't a horn or a revving she didn't instantly, almost inaudibly, mimic.

The neurologists agreed that, appearances to the contrary, she was really wide awake. That pretending to be asleep was typical agoraphobic behaviour.

"Neurologists are the brain's stooges" was Gordon's response. By then he'd had it up to here with their categorical abstractions. Not even Marcy had ever caught Joan with her eyes shut in her own bed, not since Joan was a baby anyway, so it seemed logical to him that when Joan finally did shut her eyes (and, sure, it took fear and shyness to get her started, he wasn't arguing with that) she was bound to drop off.

If this was the case, though, it would mean she had no escape from the world, not even in dreams. It would be like trying to leave a room, only to find yourself in an identical room, then trying to leave that room, but the next one was also identical, and so on. A claustrophobic's nightmare. Which, Gordon reasoned, should make it an agoraphobic's nirvana. But maybe not. When she was asleep he studied her face for a sign of pain or ecstasy (as he had once, during sex and with as little elucidation, studied Al Yothers's face).

At their destination Joan preferred to be carried from the car. But if you stood her on her feet she would walk, hands over her ears, eyes shut or blinking rapidly. Inside, she'd head for a chair in the darkest corner, sit and close her eyes again, and if she was faking it, she was good. One day before anyone noticed what they were up to, a group of boys slapped their hands in front of her face and pinched her leg, and until she covered her ears with her hands and started smacking her lips to imitate the slapping, they weren't prepared to believe she was real.

Doris's mother, Grandma Gayler, said that Joan reminded her of the guards at Buckingham Palace. "I used to think those lads were wax," she said, giving Joan a loving, anguished look.

A look meant for England, not Joan. That was how Grandma Gayler always looked when she spoke of England.

Grandma Gayler was born in Toronto and had never travelled farther than Niagara Falls, three hours away by car. She didn't own a television set, she never went to the movies and she read nothing but the Bible. So why she had these wistful memories of England, nobody could figure out. If you asked her, "How do you know the Humber River smells like the Thames?" she'd scratch her knuckles and look cornered. Consequently, nobody had the heart to pin her down about her supposed reminiscences.

She lived in the finished basement of the century-old lakeside house Doris had grown up in. After Grandpa Gayler died she'd moved downstairs and rented out the upper floor. She preferred the basement, she insisted, the coolness in summer, the "good" damp. It was so damp that she had to cover the upholstery with plastic or it would rot, but the carpet she left uncovered because it was a cheap old thing, she said, and as a result mushrooms grew under it. Several times a year mushrooms pushed their way right through the fibre, and these she plucked and ate fried on toast—something the English did, according to her. The walls were mildewed, the wooden arms and legs of the furniture furry with mould. Mould was the antimacassars. Frogs were her "flat mates." After rainstorms, which flooded the apartment and turned her shoes and wastepaper baskets into boats, bullfrogs showed up and preyed on the centipedes. When Grandma Gayler descended on the frogs to show how they wouldn't harm you they made gangly leaps to escape her, but she caught them with a ferocious lightning snatch. "Bad boy," she scolded them, and they wailed like babies.

Every time Doris visited, the first thing she did was dash around squashing the centipedes and harvesting the mushrooms. She scraped the mildew and mould but not from the arms of the maroon wing-backed chair because it was the one Joan liked, and when she sat in it she stroked the arms with both hands, over and over.

Joan was about three when she started acting more at home at Grandma Gayler's, keeping her eyes open in that dark corner though still refusing to leave the chair. Apart from the fuzz on the chair arms she was preoccupied with her reflection in the mirrored picture frame on the table beside her, and with the movie usherette who lived upstairs and who in soft-soled shoes walked briskly and ceaselessly up and down the corridor as if she had to practice her job. Looking up at the ceiling, creaking when a floorboard did, Joan's eyes tracked the usherette like radar.

Until her preoccupation became the piano.

Unbelievably, there was a piano in that saturated basement. Twenty years earlier, when it had been upstairs and when her fingers had been straight, Grandma Gayler had played hymns on it after supper.

"You should sell it," Doris was always telling her now, "before it gets so rusty and out of tune it can't be fixed."

"Well, I don't know," Grandma Gayler would say in an anxious—and these days English-accented—voice.

One afternoon, though (it was a Sunday in February, 1963; Joan would have been six), Grandma Gayler lifted her chin and said, "It so happens I still play it now and again."

"You do?" Doris said suspiciously. Moss sealed the crease where the lid opened.

Grandma Gayler strode across the room, wide arthritic hips gyrating with resolve. She pulled out the bench, sat and lifted the lid, causing the moss to bisect and hang from each end in cords. For a moment she suspended her spiggoty fingers above the keys, then she started banging out a surprisingly in-tune "Tell Me the Stories of Jesus."

Her mouth worked like mad. As if, Marcy thought, she wanted to sing but had forgotten the words, so Marcy supplied them, sliding onto the bench beside her. So then Doris, on the plastic-covered sofa, started singing as well, in her little-girl, off-key voice, and after a few bars Sonja, who'd been lying with her head on Doris's lap—mainly to oblige her mother to stay put—sat up and joined in, also off key.

In the third verse Gordon picked up the lyrics. He had been a choirboy once, a descant. He had a beautiful Bing Crosby bass now, and Doris looked at him and wondered why it was that the best things about the people you loved, the very things you loved them for, could take you off-guard like this. Gordon didn't enjoy these visits to her mother's. For starters, the humidity fogged his glasses. But here he was, singing, "Tell how the sparrow that twitters on yonder tree . . ."

He made it through all six verses, him and Grandma Gayler. And Marcy softly garbling along and pretending to know the words by piping up at the cadences. Doris kept glancing over at Joan, amazed that she wasn't covering her ears. When the singing ended, Doris's eyes were awash. "Well," she said. "Aren't we something?"

Grandma Gayler closed the lid. "So there," she said and pulled herself to her feet and waddled toward the kitchen.

"Oh, Mother," Doris said apologetically. She jumped up to help her with the tea, but Gordon tugged her skirt. He nodded across the room.

It was Joan. She was walking over to the piano, echoing the squishing sounds her feet made in the drenched carpet. "Hey," Sonja said, seeing her, and Doris nudged her to be quiet. Marcy, though, spun around and cried, "Joanie!" then looked at the others through her misted glasses with their blue, pointy frames.

Doris touched a finger to her lips. Joan was climbing onto the bench now. She was so small that she still climbed onto chairs frontwards, like a toddler. When she was seated she opened the piano lid.

"Do you want to hear me play 'Chopsticks?'" Marcy whispered.

Joan mooed—No—and pushed her sunglasses up her nose. She held both hands above the keys and clawed them. Marcy giggled at this parody of Grandma Gayler, then glanced guiltily at her mother. Before she had turned back round Joan was picking out "Tell Me the Stories of Jesus."

"Holy Geez," Gordon murmured after the first half dozen bars.

"Who's that?" Grandma Gayler called.

None of them answered. It was as if a bird had flown in and landed on someone's finger. Grandma Gayler appeared at the kitchen door as Joan clawed her hands above the keys again and started over. This time she added chords.

"Well bless her heart, who taught her that?"

"Shh, Mother," Doris said.

"Shh," Joan echoed but went on playing, jabbing bass notes with her left hand and swinging the rhythm.

Marcy leaned sideways to give her room. Was this a miracle? Marcy was a bit scared.

So was Doris. That old eeriness she hadn't felt since the train ride back from the West Coast. Joan's toy hands were now dancing on the keyboard, all her fingers getting in on the act. Her shoulders were nursing the rhythm like an old lounge lizard's. They were! And now—this was too much—she was playing "In the Mood."

Gordon came to his feet and took a few steps toward her. Doris glanced at him. The ceiling was low and he had to stoop, his head thrust forward. His face had a bright, famished look. Doris got an impression of a papier mâché head wearing glasses, a head composed of hundreds of layers of faces wearing glasses, and the head with the famished look was the innermost and most private one and had punched its way, indecently, through all the others.

"Gracious me," Grandma Gayler said. She patted her heart and looked around the room, catching Sonja's eye. "How long has she been taking lessons?"

Sonja slowly shook her head. There was a dead composer she was trying to remember. That really famous small one with the white hair.

Doris, too, was now thinking about Mozart reincarnated, but telling herself to get a hold of herself. *Did you ever see a cow with a green eyebrow* were the lyrics in the back of her mind. "I don't believe it!" she said. Unintentionally and at that weirdly jubilant pitch of hers. And everything, everyone stopped, even the usherette.

Even Joan, who twisted around and looked with her usual attentiveness.

"Keep going, Sweetie," Doris said, trying to sound normal.

Joan then did two more unprecedented things. First she pushed her sunglasses up onto her head. And then she smiled. With her bare eyes, looking straight at Doris, she smiled.

"Sweetie?" Doris whispered.

Joan chirped and turned back to the piano, back to playing "In the Mood."

# ELEVEN

I N THE SPRING of 1927 when Gordon was twelve, he and
his friend Tony went down to the creek one warm Saturday
and collected snakes coming sluggishly out of hibernation.
Garter snakes, milk snakes, green snakes, rat snakes, lots of little
deKays the colour of golden-brown sugar. A good thirty snakes all
told. Is that possible? Snakes in every spill of sun, on rocks and in
the mouths of their pits. Most of them solitary but some in
groups of four or more, a haphazard tossing and mortally still like
an aftermath.

They threw them into Tony's wagon. There were so many they
didn't bother about the ones that poured like tributaries over the
sides of the wagon as Tony pulled and Gordon pushed it home.

And is it possible that Tony's mother let them unload the
snakes on her front porch? This is how Gordon remembers it. He
and Tony sitting on the porch rail, herding the snakes with sticks
and dropping bait worms on them, but the snakes wouldn't eat, so
the worms dried and the next day their fish-hook shapes were all
over the porch as if to illustrate the manner of death they'd been
braced for.

By then the snakes were gone. Gordon and Tony had kept
them only a few hours before hauling them back to the creek and
tipping them out of the wagon. In every direction and stunningly

fast they burst into the undergrowth. Quicksilver vanishing down the cracks of a floor.

The next time the two of them went snake collecting all they found were a garter snake and a deKay. They decided to keep them in a cardboard box at Tony's, and here again, considering that the snakes would have been too traumatized to eat and would have died pretty quickly, Gordon questions what he remembers, which is days and days of going around bare-chested with a snake wrapped around his neck, him and Tony pretending to be Tarzan.

At that age Gordon's chest was as hairless as the palm of his hand. It was tubular and soft and a source of horror to him because his nipples were growing. Every night, to fend off breasts, he slept prone on a plywood board, inserting it under his chest before lying down. His snake, the garter, was long enough and docile enough that when he wore it around his neck its ends covered his tender, pink nipples, and he didn't feel so self-conscious around Tony, who had nipples like pennies, and a compressed chest, heroically muscled.

Tony's snake didn't really go around his neck. It was only about eight inches long and he had to grasp its head and tail to keep it on. Gordon had offered him the garter, but the garter always seemed to nose toward Tony's groin, and Tony was afraid of it biting him. A snake bite there, he said, even from a non-venomous snake, and you could be paralyzed for life.

Gordon had read two books about snakes and there was nothing about groin bites. He didn't challenge Tony, though, because he believed that Tony knew more than he did about sex and sex organs. Way more. Tony had whiskers and underarm hair and from his navel to the waist of his trousers a stripe of black hair that affected Gordon as if it were an award. As if it were evidence, like a singe or a shadow, that there had been a lot of erections in that vicinity, all of them more adult (bigger, more exciting, more legitimate) than Gordon's.

Not that Gordon could have said for sure that Tony got erections. He and Tony were modest. They were careful not to look at each other urinating. They were pious, Tony especially so, being Catholic. He was always crossing himself in a speedy, nervous fashion that Gordon's mother had initially taken for a palsy. On the shelf above Tony's bed was a pocked, orange-skinned Jesus statuette with crossed eyes that gazed straight down at the mattress. What did Jesus see? Nights drenched in solitary sex, Gordon imagined. Manly sex. Sex that was all right with Jesus. But he couldn't imagine anything that Tony actually did because he couldn't imagine what Tony thought about.

In his own bed that summer he thought about Tony and the garter snake. A quick little scene, all he needed. It went like this: The snake slipped into Tony's trousers. Tony yelled at Gordon to get it out. Gordon fished around a bit and got it out.

This was before Gordon had heard of queers and when he was reconciled to marrying Beryl, a conspiratorial, hairy-armed girl who claimed him at tea dances. And yet he knew that his fantasy was trouble and not all right with Jesus. Some things you know.

Eventually he forgot about it. Or buried it alive, because when he recalled it again, thirty years and a hundred lurid fantasies later, it was like the exhumation of a baby he'd fathered or killed, guilt thundering through him like jungle drums. But that was just for a few seconds ahead of the memory itself, which immediately struck him as pathetic. And so obviously symbolic he wondered whether he was remembering a dream. Snakes like coils of rope. A long, long dream.

---

Al Yothers is describing an attack of crabs he caught in the army when Gordon remembers his first sexual fantasy. Although the memory makes him feel fragile about his young self, that foetal specimen who against all expectations outgrew the jar, he tells Al the fantasy to get him to laugh.

Al laughs, all right. He has a cruel, goofy laugh, but Gordon courts it because when Al laughs at him is the only time Al seems to let loose.

This snake fantasy Al finds so funny he chokes, and Gordon has to thump him on the back. "What a jerk!" Al manages to get out between guffaws. "What a *friggin' jerk!*"

(He said the same thing in response to another masturbation story of Gordon's. The one when Gordon was fourteen and got into ecstasies of soaping himself in the bathtub, and if the bathroom was occupied, taking a cup of water into his bedroom, locking himself in and doing it there, using a bar of his mother's Jergens for its thick lather. He told Al how one day he had just lathered himself up in his bedroom when his father knocked on the door and he realized too late that he had forgotten to lock it. He scrambled into his closet before his father came in, but of course his father found him huddled on the closet floor, naked and soaped all over, limbs, torso, face, looking— he knew, he stood in front of his dresser mirror afterwards—like the deranged victim of a hideous skin condition. And all his father said was, "You're liable to catch cold, son.")

He and Al Yothers are in Al's bed when Gordon tells him the snake fantasy. It's the first time they've been in Al's apartment because before that Gordon thought that a flophouse would be safer, provided they entered it five minutes apart. But on two different occasions a shifty-eyed character wearing a Sternway Jewellers sandwich board stared at him going inside, and he began to get uneasy. And, anyway, those dismal rooms with their stained, brown-flowered wallpaper peeling in fronds and their banging radiators sounding like outrage, and no matter what room they were in some wreck next door coughing his guts out—Gordon found them suicidally depressing, more so when the sheets were clean, any sign of decorum in places like that seeming grotesque to him, like lipstick on a corpse.

So this evening they go to Al's bachelor apartment, and it turns out to be even more depressing. It's new and expensive and what's depressing about that is that when Gordon asks Al how he affords the rent, Al says, "Sugar daddies."

A wrecking ball slams into Gordon's guts. He figured he wasn't the only one. He had no proof, though, and he never imagined Al would just hand it to him. He walks across the room to the two pictures, one of Einstein, one of the Marlboro Man, side by side. Each has been cut out from a magazine, or torn out and carefully trimmed, and nailed—*nailed!* big bloody three-inch spikes!—to the wall. What a dumb cluck, Gordon thinks miserably. He reads the caption under the Marlboro Man: *A lot of man, a lot of cigarette.* The pictures are above the room's only real piece of furniture, a chesterfield upholstered in a prickly tin-coloured fabric. "Maybe you should ask one of your sugar daddies to spring for a chair," Gordon says.

"Maybe I should ask *you* to." Al is crouched in front of the record player. "This—" he says above the zipper sound of the needle bouncing off a record, "is"— he adjusts the needle—"for you."

On comes "Mister Sandman." Gordon doesn't get it. "Bring me a dream," the lyrics go . . . "Make his complexion like peaches and cream." Is *he* the dream, or are the sugar daddies? Or is this a joke?

Al straightens, yawns. Brushes by Gordon, sits on the chesterfield and spreads his tree-trunk arms across the back. "Well?" he says.

In that surly face Gordon sees heaven. He hardens. He's still nauseated, and now he's hard. Fear, guilt, misery, humiliation, where these blossom is where he and Al never fail to meet. "Take your pants off," he says.

"You take them off," says Al, tapping his right hand to the music.

The chesterfield is a pull-out bed. The mattress feels like it's stuffed with baseballs, and the grey sheets are brittle. From semen? Sugar-daddy semen? Gordon envisions huge guts and short pricks, or why would they have to pay for it? But he makes love this time as if he's performing for an applause meter, and forget winning two fur coats, he'd settle for a moan. When it's over and as usual he's the only one sweating and out of breath he asks, "Do you take your other men in your mouth?" He has to ask.

Al lights a cigar. "Does your wife take you in her mouth?"

"Yes, as a matter of fact she does." Or used to. Probably still would, it occurs to him.

Al folds one arm behind his head. In the gloom his orange body hair holds its colour like a horizon. He looks at Gordon and says, "You know what I like about you?"

"No." Hopelessly.

"Guess."

Gordon sighs. "I'm your drill master." Every time they meet, at some point, he has to quiz Al on encyclopedia entries up to D. The encyclopedias are neatly stacked beside the chesterfield, the top one lying open across the others, and before they pulled the chesterfield out, when the light was on, Gordon thought he was hallucinating because there at the top of the page was his own name—"Gordon"—and right next to that, on the top of the previous page—"Gonorrhoea."

"Yep," Al concedes. He exhales in little puffs. "But I'm thinking about something else."

"What?"

"Go on, guess."

Gordon fingers his bony midriff. "I can't imagine," he says. He envisions his rib cage on a sand dune, picked clean.

"I like how you wear your glasses the whole time," Al says.

Gordon thinks about that. Snorts.

"I mean it," Al says, sounding so innocent and sincere that love instantly crams Gordon's chest. He cups the boy's groin, his cool testicles. He moves down his body and sucks one testicle into his mouth.

"Not now," Al says, pushing at Gordon's head.

A whole harvest is still in Gordon's heart. He raises himself up on one elbow. "I lied about that other guy," he confesses. "You're the first guy I've ever . . . I've ever known . . . like this."

Al reaches for the whiskey bottle. "Shoot, you think I haven't figured that one out?"

Gordon eases himself back down on the bed. Was he that inept, that desperate? Is he still? Al gets up and goes down the hall, and Gordon is left in the familiar, sweltering chrysalis of his mortification. He can hardly breathe. He reaches over to extinguish Al's cigar as the toilet flushes, and in the flushing are the orgasmic moans and cries of every one of Al's lovers, the seven or eight hundred Al estimates he's had—"not including hand jobs." Just as the voices lapse away, Al turns the shower on and here they come again. Olive-skinned Mario, Gentle George, all the Bills, Pete the poet, the bull-cocked Roger, and warbling above the rest Tyrone the Irish sergeant major who sang "Mother Machree" while performing anal sex. According to Al the whole U.S. army was queer and horny. "You ought to have signed up," he said, and then, impatiently, "Yeah, sure," when Gordon reminded him that he did sign up, here in Canada, but was declared unfit because he was discovered to have a heart murmur. "You win the hundred-yard dash one day," Al said, "and the next day there's a war and, well what do you know about that? You've got a bum ticker."

"I never won a hundred-yard dash," Gordon said.

By now it's January. The affair has been going on for two months, two nights a week. Incredibly, Doris seems to have no idea. Who'd have thought she'd turn out to be so gullible? Except that when Gordon thinks about it, the lies are hers, not his. Through some twisted coincidence what he is doing and what she wants to believe he is doing dictate that he arrive home drunk and stinking of cigar smoke.

She wants to believe that he's making an effort at last to climb the industry ladder. She thinks he's a genius who is rotting in oblivion because he's too unsociable, too reserved, and now that he's out late she has decided that, as a result of a pep talk she gave him on his fortieth birthday back in October, he is spending his time at the roof bar of the Park Plaza Hotel where all the important writers, editors and journalists go after work to knock back drinks and talk shop. He reels into the bedroom at midnight, and just by agreeing with her he has his alibi. What a set-up. She's so tickled that she gives him extra pocket money for his next night out.

"You don't want to get a reputation as a cheapskate," she says in her thrilled voice, taking out of her change purse a ten-dollar bill that has been folded—for safekeeping?—opening the bill as he imagines his daughters going barefoot, pressing it into his palm and saying things like, "Go on, Sweetie, let your hair down" and "Do what you have to do," so that he sometimes finds himself gazing into her busy little eyes and wondering if he has underestimated her. If she knows, and either she's a saint or the guy in the sandwich board has said, "Humour the sucker until I get a few more pictures."

Part of him wants her to know. Craves her permission, or just to come clean. "Act normal," he has to keep warning himself. Meaning, "Act how you used to act before you screwed Al Yothers and for the first time in your life felt normal." Although the feeling of normalcy lasts only *while* he is screwing Al. Those fifteen or so minutes.

The rest of the time he feels unhinged.

Even when he's happy. Because he knows that his happiness is not only temporary, it's groundless. Does Al love *him*? That's a laugh. And yet like a man loved madly he examines his naked body in the bathroom mirror, and the words "lean" and "sinewy" no longer have an implausible ring. He masturbates in the shower, and his erection should be bronzed. He plays his new "Mister Sandman" forty-five and belts out the line "And lots of wavy hair like Liberace!" During his lunch hour one day, at a thrift shop, he splurges on a giant plum-coloured silk scarf and removes his tie and puts the scarf on in the presence of the beaming old queen who owns the place (suddenly he is seeing queers by the herd), and as the queen slaps his hands away and fussily arranges the scarf himself, working it like origami until it is a tiered and bulging cravat, he is as moved as if he were being decorated for valour on the field of battle.

He wears the scarf less than a block before tearing it off, almost hanging himself to get free of it. His mood can turn on a dime. All it takes is for an oncoming pedestrian to give him a wide berth and he's a pervert. He stuffs the scarf in his pocket and looks up and down the street for a coffee shop or restaurant where there might be a washroom.

In this mood, washrooms are where he lives. He masturbates non-stop, but his erection repels him. It should be shot. He studies his lips in mirrors for syphilis sores, he presses under his ears for swollen glands. "I'm as clean as a whistle," Al is always saying. And, "Ever heard of penicillin?" But in this mood Gordon believes himself to be a venereal sewer. He weeps for his daughters, because he's already dead—or ruined and behind bars—so that makes them orphans. "Marcy is losing weight," he tells Doris. "She's withering away!" he protests, staggered by Doris's unconcern. At the supper table he looks at Sonja's good-natured, vacant face and later says to Doris, "I love her, but I'm telling you I don't detect an active mind there." Then he goes and sits on the toilet, masturbating and weeping for his ruined life, his stupid child.

There's a kind of grisly peace in feeling so low, so depraved, at least when it comes to him and Al. Delete any decency and with it goes the real danger—the romantic dream of the two of them being together always. What you have left is two nights a week, cut and dried, wherein two gigantic queers "do what they have to do" and then go their own ways.

Except that that's nothing like how it is, not when they're actually having sex. They are a pair of gods then. They precipitate lightning and sirens. Beds collapse under them. "Do you know who I am?" Al whispers. "Yours," he whispers. "Daddy, I'm Yours," and Gordon thinks "I was made for this," wondering how, when they're *not* having sex, he can forget the immense relief. Screwing Al is the breakthrough cure. It's worship. Al is as quiet as a church. He, Gordon, is the wild one. "If Doris could only see me now," he can't help thinking.

---

Here is how the affair ends. With Al banging the whiskey bottle on the armrest of the pull-out bed and saying, "Time's up."

Gordon bolts awake. "What—" he says, terrified.

Al is standing beside the bed. He's wearing a white shirt.

"What's going on?" Gordon says.

"You gotta skedaddle."

"What time is it?" Where are his glasses? He swims his hands over the sheets.

"Five to ten." This muttered into his wrist as he applies a cuff-link.

"Is that all?" Gordon finds his glasses and puts them on, then reaches for his boxer shorts on the floor and pulls them up before coming to his feet. He has an erection, and when Al isn't interested in sex he finds Gordon's erections irritating. "What's going on?" he asks again.

"I want you to beat it," Al says, walking away. "That's all."

"Are you expecting company?"

No answer.

"I see," Gordon says.

Silence.

"None of my damn business," Gordon says. Hearing his gut-
tered voice, he has a feeling he has said this before in an apartment
where there was a hammer on the windowsill.

Across the room Al mauls through one of the cardboard boxes
he keeps his clothes in. Gordon buttons his shirt and watches him
as he used to watch any beautiful man. It's a gluttonous, suspense-
ful feeling. It's like something stacked too high. Like something
that should topple but won't.

"Shoot," Al mutters. He throws several odd socks out of the
box. Is he looking for red ones? He has told Gordon that if you go
into a queer bar where nobody knows you, wearing red socks is a
sign that you're not from the vice squad.

No, he's looking for a navy-and-green argyle. He finds one and
holds on to it as he continues his search.

"Does he pay you less if your socks don't match?" Gordon asks.
This is not as sarcastic as it sounds. For the first time he is truly
curious about the sugar daddies.

Al finds the other sock and hops on one foot as he pulls it up.
"You don't know everything, Pops."

Pops? Where did that come from? Things are sliding downhill
fast. Why tonight, though, their best night so far? They did it
three times. In the shower, on the chair with Al straddling his lap,
then half kneeling, half standing on the chesterfield, Gordon's
forehead butting the throat of the Marlboro Man. And when
Gordon was lying on the bed and drifting off he felt Al combing a
hand through his hair.

"I always wanted my hair to be black," Al said, one of his rare
confidences. A few minutes later he added—or did Gordon
dream this?—"I used to shoe-polish it, but you could tell."

Al goes into the kitchen and returns wearing grey flannel trousers and with a belt in each hand. Gordon has never seen him dressed so formally. From belt to belt Al scowls, back and forth while Gordon, overcome now by an almost pleasant lassitude, watches him. Believing himself to be nothing but mildly interested, he asks, "Are we going to see each other again?"

Right past his face, missing him by an inch, one of the belts flies and lands on the bed.

"Jesus," Gordon murmurs.

Al starts threading the other belt through the loops of his trousers. "You cuss too much," he says.

Gordon stands there, radiating some kind of hot wave. Maybe it's relief. After a moment he asks, "What if we meet in the hall at work?" Funnily enough, it hasn't happened yet.

"Me, I'm blowing this turkey-trot town."

Gordon puts on his hat and coat. He walks to the door. No, this is not relief.

"Hey, hold on a minute."

Gordon stops. What he wouldn't give right now. Who he wouldn't sacrifice.

But Al is only handing him a pen. Gordon's fountain pen. "I had to write a message," he says.

He looks sly, up to something. Gordon's heart starts working. "For Christ's sake, Al—" Hearing the profanity, he breaks off, gives a weak laugh.

Al's eyes flicker out.

And Gordon . . . Gordon gets hard again. He can't believe it. He accepts the pen and pockets it in his trousers, letting his fingers brush the tip of his erection. He can't believe it.

"You know who you are?" Al says in a tone of having only just realized.

Gordon waits.

So does Al.

"The pornographer of lost causes," Gordon answers at last, more to himself.

"A taker," Al says.

Gordon blinks, uncomprehending. It's over this time. Dead. He knows it, but his hard prick is like fingernails still growing in the morgue, so he rips apart "taker" for a speck of hope.

"Folks are either givers or takers," Al elaborates. "You go around acting like you're a giver but you're a taker." He shrugs. "Anyhow—" He folds his Paul Bunyan arms over his chest.

"I love you," Gordon says. Even to himself it sounds false and grotesquely inappropriate, a stupid surprise like a squirt in the face from a carnation. Al grimaces. Gordon turns. He reaches for the doorknob, tears warping his vision. "Goodbye," he says.

"Adios," Al says. "Watch your back."

# TWELVE

THIS was six years ago. When Marcy was in grade one, it must have been, because she knew how to read but Joan hadn't been born yet.

It was morning. Marcy pushed open the bathroom door, and her father was in there, shaving. He was in his pyjama bottoms, and on his bare back there were letters.

"Al was here," Marcy said slowly, reading.

Her father went still, holding the razor at his throat. "What did you say?"

She pointed. "On your back. It says, 'Al was here.'"

He jerked around to see in the mirror.

"Who's Al, Daddy?"

"Jesus," he murmured. That scared her. He whipped on his glasses, then grabbed her mother's hand mirror and positioned it to see himself from behind. "Jesus." He looked at her, wide-eyed.

"*I* didn't do it!" Before she could back away he gripped her by the shoulders. He had never hit her, but she thought he was going to. He brought his face right up to hers. His white foam beard, his sour breath. "I didn't!" she cried, trying to squirm free. He was hurting her.

"Shh." With his foot he shut the door. He let go of her and began stroking her head, hard. "Honey, it's okay, it's okay."

"I was just reading what it said," she whimpered.

"I know. Honey, I know you were. Shh. Be quiet."

He told her that it was a joke. Somebody must have done it last night, he said. Written right through his shirt when he was standing at the bar. Some joker. "Al?" she suggested meekly. Yes, that was right. Al. Ruining his good white shirt, which was why he swore. He said that he shouldn't have sworn.

Then he said, "We'd better not tell Mom. You know her, she'll have a fit. I'll just throw the shirt out and buy a new one, and that way we won't upset anybody. Okay? We'll keep it a secret, okay?"

"Okay."

"Promise?"

She promised, although she knew that she hadn't heard the whole story, or even the true one. It didn't make sense. Why would her mother have a fit over a measly shirt? Why would her father? And how could you write on someone's back without the person feeling it?

When she was undressing for bed that night she saw in the mirror that both of her shoulders were bruised, front and back. After the initial awe, after she had studied and fingered the bruises and would have been disappointed if they had turned out to be dirt, she quickly pulled on her pyjama top before her mother came in. Later, under the covers, she fixed her eyes on the line of light beneath the door. What if the man, Al, opened it? She would scream. She kept touching her shoulders, pressing a little for the pain.

Still later—it would have been the next day or the day after that—she went looking for the shirt. She couldn't find it, not in any of the garbage pails, not in the laundry basket, not balled-up somewhere in her father's workshop. Finally she took one of his soiled shirts out of the laundry basket and wrote AL WAS HERE on it herself, using his good fountain pen. She then shoved the shirt into a bag of rags. Because she had crumpled the shirt up before the ink was dry, the "L" had stamped out an "I" and the message actually read ALI WAS HERE. She didn't know this, though.

She is thirteen years old now. She has a nice boyfriend named Al. But "Al was here" is what she writes—her secret code—where otherwise she might draw a skull and crossbones. "Al was here" also means "bruise." Any time Marcy and her friend Pammy spot a bruise on someone they say, "Al was here," Marcy having informed Pammy that gangsters used to say this after they had been roughed up.

"Who's Al?" Pammy asked through her fingers.

"Al Capone," Marcy said. "Of course." She has become an expert liar. She has become a girl after her mother's own heart.

Pammy is the opposite. She cannot tell a lie. Or recognize one. Or get over one. She is a person who believes everything and who is shocked by everything. One hand covering her mouth is her listening. She drives other girls crazy. "You're so *naive,*" they say. But Marcy is in the last, flaming years of her pious period, and she has a feeling that Pammy is a lamb of God. So meek and mild. It was Pammy who pointed out that her own head is peanut-shaped— "See, I have a wide, wide forehead, then I go in here at my eyes, then out again here, and then I have this big chin"—to account for why she doesn't have a boyfriend. "I'm not exactly a femme fatale," she said, shocked at the idea.

To Marcy, all girls are either femme fatales or frumps. To Pammy, they're either femme fatales or not femme fatales. Pammy can't say frump. She can't say anything the least bit mean or even critical, the most obnoxious behaviour alarming her only a fraction more than normal behaviour does. Still, Marcy is careful not to alarm Pammy too much, not to alarm her away. She pretends that she has only one boyfriend and she says, primly, "We *kiss,*" when Pammy petrifies herself by asking if Marcy and her boyfriend neck. It is for another girl to clue Pammy in about hickeys. The two times that Pammy has seen them on Marcy she has said—Marcy is not kidding—"Al was here." Pretty funny, if Pammy only knew.

Actually, not that funny because it isn't Al who gives Marcy hickeys, it's Gary Short, the *Telegram* paperboy. "Punk," her mother says, fishing the newspaper out of the rose bush, but she never complains to *him*, far from it, she overtips—fifty cents, a dollar once—and even flirts, calling after him not to do anything she wouldn't do. It's obvious to Marcy that like everyone else her mother is afraid of getting on his bad side.

Gary Short is a criminal. When he was only eight years old he stole the stethoscope from his father's doctor bag and tried to crack the Dominion store safe. He just strode through the meat department and up the stairs to the office, and nobody saw him, not even Miss Slitz, the old woman who was working there that day. When the alarm sounded (the hitch in Gary's plan: an alarm set to go off after ten unsuccessful spins of the combination), Miss Slitz fainted, and the meat manager ran in to find Gary listening to her chest with the stethoscope. "She's dead," Gary announced. Lucky for him, she wasn't.

Two years later he set fire to his own bed and burned down half his house. But did he? Marcy wonders if the culprit wasn't his retarded brother, Cedric. Why isn't Cedric at the Mother Goose Home? Marcy would like to know. Cedric scares her, his big lolling head and lumpy body, his Jack Benny imitation. "Woo-ell," Cedric says, crossing his arms and slapping his own face.

What nobody would believe is how kind Gary is to Cedric. "Not now, okay, Ceddie?" Gary says. "Later, okay?"

"Woo-ell," Cedric says, stumbling backwards out of the garage.

"Go watch TV and I'll be in soon," Gary says. Then he slides a crowbar through the handles of the garage doors and sits back up on the barrel. And Marcy, who hasn't appreciated the interruption, resumes her stripping, undoing the neck buttons of her powder blue surgical-collared Ben Casey blouse, working her arms out of the sleeves. So as not to knock her glasses off she tugs the blouse down over her hips and steps out of it, carefully because her boots are mucky.

Her teeth chatter. Her breath smokes. Light from the setting sun slices through the slats between the wall boards and fashions gold bracelets all down her arm when she lifts it to drape her blouse on top of her navy-and-green kilt. From the other handle of the lawnmower, which has been hoisted up on a rack, hang her navy cardigan, her red wool jacket and her red-yellow-and-purple angora tam with the grapefruit-sized orange pompom. The tam was made by Sonja. Sonja knits gloves too, but she didn't knit the white angora ones that Marcy is wearing, still wearing as she wiggles her half-slip down her legs. When it is off she holds it out like a silk sash and drops it over her kilt.

She is getting better at these stripteases. Not so hurried and clumsy, more like a lady in a magic act. She wishes she had a bra, though. Nobody in her class (nobody except for the fat, grandmotherly-looking Karen Kennelworth) wears a bra, and usually Marcy doesn't want one, but as she manoeuvres her arms out of her undershirt she imagines reaching behind herself to undo hooks, how that would make her arms wings. How she could dangle a bra from her baby finger and then toss it at him.

No, she would never do that! She can't even look at him. She looks straight ahead, at that piece of wood laddered in light. There or at herself, her white gloves, her clothes peeling off. She is the beautiful, elegant lady. He is the man. With her first boyfriend, Dug, she used to play a game they called "Romantic," where the haughty lady slinked by the man who whistled and said, "Hows about a kiss, baby" and "Hey, good-looking," and the woman said, "Flattery will get you nowhere" and "Fresh!" and slapped at his groping hands but eventually let him kiss her. Sometimes Marcy was the lady, sometimes Dug was. This switching was his idea, and led to fights. "*You* be the man," he'd say. "No," she'd say, "*you* be the man."

She should have pulled down his pants, she thinks now. That would have shown him who was the man. She isn't serious. Her own underpants she has never pulled down for anyone. She has never had to, she has never been made to. The first time Gary suggested she take her clothes off she naturally assumed he meant all of them, and her only qualm was what if her underpants were dirty? It didn't occur to her, either to refuse or that he wouldn't be interested in seeing her bum.

He isn't interested this time, either. As soon as she steps out of her undershirt he jumps down from the barrel and comes over, and she holds out her goose-bumped arms and is perfectly still to be outlined by knives. Neither of them say anything. He touches her left breast first. Her left breast is bigger than her right one, which is not saying much. Both are always sore. Always. Just him dabbing with the palm of his hand hurts. He dabs for a while then pushes her nipple with one finger, in and out, lightly, testing, as if he expects to hear a buzz. Then he starts squeezing and rubbing, not hard but it's torture.

After a minute or so he stops squeezing and begins to rub the nipple back and forth between his thumb and forefinger, the way you turn a knob. Or a combination lock. Why does he do this? She'd give anything to be a mind reader. He is screwing a nail into her it feels like, but she doesn't blame him, he knows not what he does. Darling, she thinks. He moves on to her right breast, and she allows her aching held-out arms to drift down and around his back. Shivering into his jacket, she inhales his steel-bar and Arrowroot-cookie smell. Oh, my dreamboat, she thinks, soft and amazed.

It is no secret to her that she is not a femme fatale. She is a four-eyes. She is a stork. Her feet are already bigger than her mother's. In her basement, in a cupboard under the bar, there is an electric cocktail shaker that is a black-haired lady with huge bare breasts and a round rump skimpily covered in a hula skirt and with tiny, tiny hands glued to a glass. Now *that* is Marcy's idea of a femme fatale. When she notices a boy staring at her own button breasts she is always surprised. What does he see worth gawking at? At the same time she doesn't dismiss the possibility that boys can see more somehow, just as dogs can hear sounds humans can't.

Gary is the only boy who has ever seen her *bare* breasts. Who has ever touched them under her undershirt or squeezed them (he has resumed squeezing). By now her right breast is almost numb, and she is thinking of saying something when he stops and takes a long, satisfied-sounding breath.

"I'm cold," she says.

He hikes up his blue jeans. "I can fix that." The next thing she knows his arms are around her, and his mouth is clamped on her neck. She lets herself go limp to feel him holding her up. For his age—thirteen—he might be small, but he's no weakling. "He is fearfully and wonderfully made," she has told Joan. "His lips are like a Negro's, but a lighter colour, like a hot-dog bun."

Does she ever wish he'd kiss her on the mouth. He never has.

The hickey ends with a loud smack. "Okay, you're branded," he says.

Shy now, she folds her arms over her bare chest, and rubs her upper arms with her gloved hands. "Can't I give you a hickey?" she asks. She has asked once before.

"Well—" He tightens his lips. Sighs. Finally gives his head a shake. Years from now she will be reminded of him by car mechanics and men working in hardware stores. "It's getting late," he says, looking past her at the garage doors, and she knows that he is worried about Cedric in the house waiting for him.

His house is in a well-to-do neighbourhood twenty minutes away from her quadrant of identical, garageless bungalows. When she is halfway home the streetlights come on, producing splashes of light that she walks more slowly through in case they contain heavenly light. The cleansing light of heaven is everywhere, she believes, but in disguise. "Verily, verily," she has been chanting off and on the entire way. "Verily, verily, verily," her nervous, irresolute prelude to certain prayers.

It's not as if she is a fornicator or an adulteress. It is not as if she has been selfish or mean. She has yielded to temptation, and she has been a temptress. "But I have loved much," she protests, thinking of the woman who washed Jesus' feet with her tears and hair and was forgiven. Being forgiven isn't even the point, though. The point is, if she has loved much, why does she need to be forgiven in the first place?

It's an old argument, and she knows who will win. She jumps into it anyway, straight to her biggest weapon—the Song of Solomon. "Thy two breasts are like two young roes that are twins," she thinks, and as always feels shockingly rude and deeply, deeply excited. "My beloved put in his hand by the hole of the door, and my bowels were moved for him!"

She could keep it up, she could remind Jesus of almost every verse after all these months of reading the Song of Solomon aloud to Joan. As the only person in her family who goes to church Marcy has taken Joan's religious education upon herself, and the Song of Solomon is Joan's favourite book, Marcy has decided, containing as it does the passage about a little sister. A little sister who "hath no breasts." Reading this part, Marcy is liable to laugh, which is why she usually leaves it out and goes straight from "We have a little sister" to "What shall we do for our sister in the day when she shall be spoken for?"

The answer is: "If she be a wall, we will build upon her a palace of silver." Here Marcy slows down. "And," she reads, "if she be a door, we will enclose her with boards of cedar." Joan always sucks in her breath at these last words.

A wind has come up. Marcy walks faster. "Just get it over

with," she orders herself and she manages to think "Dear Jesus" but then goes blank. A roar is shuddering through her, a multitude in her bones. She starts to run. "I charge you, O daughters of Jerusalem!" she says out loud. She leaps over a hedge. "Thy breasts are clusters of grapes!" She begins to laugh, she can't help it. "O that thou wert as my brother, that sucked the breasts of my mother!" she says and has to stop, she is laughing so hard. "I'm not joking," she says, addressing Jesus now. Despite her laughter, she is deadly serious. These are the words of God. More than that, they are weapons.

———————

The music is coming from *her* house. Piano music. Somebody must be blaring the radio, Marcy figures, that's how good it sounds. Then she remembers that today is the day the piano was supposed to arrive from Grandma Gayler's and she dashes inside, kicks off her boots and races up the stairs to the living room.

"Please turn on your magic beam," her mother sings along. "Mister Sandman, bring me a dream . . . ," looking over her shoulder and miming "Shh" when Marcy charges in, as if Marcy was the one singing.

To make space for the piano the chesterfield has been pushed in front of the bookshelves. There is that smell, that earthy, wormy smell of Grandma Gayler's basement, and what's this green on the carpet? Marcy bends to touch it. Moss. A trail from her to her mother and Sonja, who stand behind the piano bench with an arm around each other's waists.

Her mother and Sonja are exactly the same height and have exactly the same dark springy hair, but Sonja is twice as wide from the back and she's not moving, unlike her mother, who is bobbing and pitching. As Marcy crosses the room she hallucinates that Sonja is the husk that her mother is thrashing out of. For just a second, her mother is Sonja emerging from hibernation, she is the not-so-fat dancer whom Marcy can remember, with a pang of longing, from a time before Joan was born.

Marcy stands beside her mother. Joan's miniature femme-fatale fingers hop over the keys, picking out a jazzy version of "Mister Sandman," while her right foot pumps as if it reaches the pedal. Even Marcy's parents, who say they don't know if God exists, agree that Joan's piano playing is a miracle. "Forgive me, Lord," Marcy manages to think at last. Her eyes burn. "Play 'What a Friend We Have in Jesus,'" she says, and without a missed beat Joan does.

That night Marcy runs her fingers through Joan's hair in an act of worship over its silkiness. Her own hair, which is coarse, is as a pack of dogs, she would say. Joan's hair is as a flock of angels. While Marcy combs with her fingers she talks about the striptease and being felt up. Joan hums and looks at herself in the mirror, a *Life* magazine opened in her lap.

Every night Marcy sits next to Joan in the closet and reads aloud from the Bible. Then she removes the barrettes and ribbons from Joan's hair and reviews the day with her, taking for granted that the questions and concerns popping into her head are Joan's wordless, humming half of the conversation. "We don't know," she says now, answering the silent question Which one do we love the best? (Marcy still refers to either of them in the plural when they are by themselves.) "We don't *know*," she repeats anxiously when the question is rephrased as Who is our one and only? She then hears, What if Ziggy sees it? and touches her hickey and says, "He won't." What if he did, though, what would he do? Marcy bites the side of her thumbnail. "We'd be in for it," she murmurs, "that's for sure."

Ziggy is her handsome boyfriend, blond and tall and another strong, silent type, another outcast, in his case because he thinks everybody hates him for being a Nazi's son. People claim to have seen a swastika tattoo on his father's arm, but Ziggy told her that on Remembrance Day his father burned it off using paint stripper. "I'll never forget his screams in the night," he said.

Screams? Considering that his father's voice sounds like a record played on slow speed, Marcy detected a lie. "Everybody thinks it's kind of neat about your father's swastika," she said.

"Maybe *you* think its neat," he muttered. "Everyone else hates me."

"Nobody hates you."

He stabbed a finger at his eyes. "It's in their eyes!" he shouted. "The eyes don't fib!"

They don't? Marcy tried to make her eyes pools of love. Never does she love him more than when he blows his stack.

She fell in love with him the usual way for her. One second not loving him and the next second identifying him as an innocent target. Doomed, fingered. One second it was just Ziggy the German boy up ahead of her and the next second it was a boy in some dire peril . . . of anything, there was no telling what. A car accident one day, a girl like her.

It was a Friday, and she was by herself, having given up waiting for Pammy, who, when you walked with her, kept stopping to gasp over whatever you were talking about. Now, on this stretch of the road, there was only Marcy and Ziggy. She mentally scrambled for a good excuse, got one, ran up and delivered it: "My mother was wondering if your mother wanted to join her bridge club."

Her mother doesn't belong to a bridge club. On the other hand his mother doesn't speak English, which Marcy happened to know.

He stopped and frowned at her. "I don't think so," he answered uncertainly, and it occurred to her that he had no idea what a bridge club was.

"Oh, well, that's okay, my mother was just wondering." She

continued to walk alongside him, chatting about school, home-work, their teacher—Miss Torg. "Did you know she shaves her arms?" she asked.

"No." He sounded worried.

"At about three o'clock they get five-o'clock shadow. Haven't you noticed?"

He shook his head.

"Well, it's pretty disgusting."

It was a dirty lie but she had his attention. She told him that her old babysitter shaved her arms *and* ate worms. This was only half a lie. "I used to give her baths," she said. "I washed her bare breasts!" She giggled, startled at herself.

He stopped again. Had she gone too far? In her mind a Nazi shot a silly woman. "I was only six," she said quickly.

He nodded over his shoulder. "Here is my snazzy house."

They were in front of a little red-brick bungalow, the last house before the railway crossing. It was a real dump. The lawn all weeds and piles of dog dirt, a picket fence gaped like an old comb, the front door and eaves feathered with peeling green paint.

He lived *here?*

"The picture of order and efficiency," he said.

She glanced at him. There was a red perfect circle, a bull's-eye, on each of his cheeks. With a jerk of his head he loosened his scarf and extracted a key that hung from a black shoelace around his neck. Oh, so his mother worked, Marcy thought. She began to twist her thumb. If only she could twist her thumb right *off!* Console him with a catastrophe way worse than his house. "It's ex-actly like my Grandma Gayler's place," she lied. "Gee," she said, clasping her homework books to her chest, "I just adore picket fences!"

She beamed at his awful house, keeping it up because she could feel him studying her. A Nazi's son, a German boy. There was no imagining herself in his eyes. Was she too skinny? Too forward?

Was he homesick for plump, yellow-haired girls in braids and white blouses with short puffy sleeves?

"When we moved in it was a nest of rats," he said, "but my dog broke their necks. One by one."

She gave him another glance. Either he was trying to scare her off or this was him upgrading his house from humiliating to petrifying. She went on smiling. She was dedicated to being absolutely charmed so she ignored the rats and leapt at the fact that he had a dog. "What kind of dog?"

"Mutt. Part beagle." The bull's-eyes were fading.

"Can I see him?"

"*Her.* Yulia."

"Can I see her?"

He frowned, and she thought she'd been too pushy again. "She has a problem," he said. "When she meets a new person she barks like crazy and then her eyeballs, they sometimes do—" he flung open his fingers in front of his face—"pop out and hang."

"Pop out?" she said.

"And hang by the nerve." He shrugged. "She lets you put them back in. She is gentle with people she knows."

"Wow," Marcy said.

"But it is like you said about Miss Torg. Pretty disgusting."

In his tiny, cabbage-smelling kitchen she watched him kneel before a roly-poly, pus-coloured dog with an ugly bat face and a bunch of tits drooping to the floor. "Yah, yah," he cooed, and the dog, who a minute earlier had been yapping furiously and attempting to bite the bobbing yoyos that were its own eyes, now sat still and silent while Ziggy first wet both hands in a bowl of warm salted water and then carefully lifted the right eyeball up into its socket, tucking in, as he went, the purple elastic band that Marcy presumed was the nerve.

"Why do you go and get so excited?" he said. "It's just a girl. She won't hurt you."

Marcy was reminded of Gary and Cedric. Did every loner have a repulsive creature waiting at home for him? Or was this just the case with the loners *she* loved? With the boys she loved, because when she thought about it, even Al, her popular boyfriend, lived in the same house as a blind, cranky aunt who peed in her chair, and maybe he didn't clean up after her but he read her the newspaper. Heal the sick, cleanse the lepers, Marcy thought apprehensively, wondering what it meant that she found herself surrounded by them.

When its eyes were back in, the dog waddled out of the kitchen, piggy tail churning, toenails clicking on the grimy red-and-green linoleum, and Ziggy carried the bowl of water to the sink. A big, pink-skinned boy, his shapely little ears like the handles on china teacups. Her beloved. What was he doing in this filthy kitchen? Right up from the floor, grease spattered the pea-green walls so that her first impression had been that they were papered in a modern design, similar to her family's green living-room drapes whose flecks she believed to be real silver.

Oh, that she could offer him a robe of her living-room drapes.

He turned on the tap. A thin wail issued from the water pipes, a sound that seemed thrown from her throat. She took a step toward him. Another step. With one finger she touched the small of his back.

He froze. Like a guy with a gun in his ribs he went dead still, hands half up. So she froze, too. Not a single word occurred to her and no conceivable next move until the pipes started clanging and he reached to turn off the tap. She stepped back, a prickly sensation paring down her skull. What had she done? In Germany did you never touch the boy first? "Verily, verily," she said to herself. Tears scalded her eyes. She turned to see where she had put her homework books and as she did he spun around and grasped her upper arms. Pure fury was what she beheld, his jaw working in such a way that she thought he was preparing to spit.

It was a dry, closed-mouth kiss, a hard push of his lips against hers.

"Is that what you came for?" he asked sharply when it was through.

"Yes," she whispered.

He kissed her again. Lips slammed shut, pinching her gums against her teeth.

That night she demonstrated the kiss to Joan, who wrenched her face away. "Well, how do you think *we* felt?" Marcy asked, insulted. Joan resumed humming. Like melting, came her unspoken response. Marcy sighed, remembering, and Joan sighed. "He's so passionate," Marcy explained dreamily. "He's the jealous type, though," she said after a minute. "We're going to have to be careful."

She yawned. Joan's yawn was the echo, not tiredness. In a few minutes they would go to bed to continue the conversation there, but Marcy would immediately drift off in the midst of a romantic fantasy about her and Ziggy trapped in the school basement following an atomic-bomb explosion.

(Joan, meanwhile, would lie with her eyes wide open behind her sunglasses, expectation eventually causing her legs to make small trotting movements.)

———

Some nights Marcy wakes up and goes into her mother's bedroom to watch from the window. "You shouldn't even be out of bed," her mother will say if Marcy says she wishes she could go out to play, too. Years ago her mother said, "Pretend it's a dream," and in the mornings Marcy often wonders if it was. It's a bit scary. Her father wanders into the edges of the yard and vanishes. Out of almost any glint or arrangement of shadow she can assemble him, but it's usually where she wasn't looking that the man shape re-emerges.

Whereas Joan, by her hair and pyjamas, is always visible. Joan is a pearly light. Her arms are white wands. The ball she catches and throws is not a tiny dove but is the white part of her red-white-and-blue rubber ball. She hops and wiggles and thrashes around, you'd never know it was the same person.

Joan is the little piano player of whom Marcy's dreams foretold. In front of whom "balling"—whatever that means—is like "balling in front of the dog."

# THIRTEEN

FOR YEARS NOW Sonja hasn't needed to look down or add up. It's all in her fingers, a sensation, as certain as anything she knows, of having clipped exactly two dozen bobby-pins onto the card.

If that sounds hard to believe, watch her knit. The needles crackle. Before your eyes, scarves descend like foreign banners in primitive zigzag designs and garish colour combinations. Pink, purple, turquoise and orange. Black, red, peach and yellow. "I just grab a bunch of balls" is her stock response to why those particular colours? "Huh!" she says, appraising a finished product as if it had just dropped from the sky into her lap. In one evening she can turn out two scarves and a hat.

Family and friends are welcome to take whatever they want, and the rest she stores in cardboard file boxes to be collected, come Christmas, by the Salvation Army for distribution among the poor. Over the course of a year that's approximately eighty boxes, or five hundred scarves and three hundred hats, all told. That's a lot of poor people's heads and necks, so many that it's not unusual for Gordon to be driving downtown and spot a bum wearing one of her creations.

There's no mistaking it—the blinding colours, the long dense fringe on her scarves, the colossal pompoms on her hats. He tells her that his heart swells when this happens, but the truth is it sinks. Not for her sake or even for the bum's, it sinks over the clash of bum and hat. It sinks over every preposterous, well-intentioned coupling of which this one seems to be the wretched gist. Once he saw half a dozen drunks sprawled on a subway grating, all of them wearing her hats and scarves, and it was like coming across a flock of tropical birds crash-landed on an Arctic shore.

This is not to say that he isn't proud of her. Naturally he's proud. Of her charity, her generosity, but more than that of her talent. It turns out that she is clever after all! Slow-witted, there's no getting around that, but a wizard with her hands. At work he keeps his eye out for young men he can picture falling for a good-natured, overweight, slow-witted girl who is a wizard with her hands. So far there have been four prospects: Bernie, the chinless short-order cook who works in the cafeteria; Ed, the pock-faced proof-reader who wins speed-typing contests; and the Bowden brothers, tubby bookbinder twins who give away the punch lines of each other's cornball jokes. Homely bachelors all of them but with kind hearts and narrow horizons, and not a queer bone in their bodies as far as he can tell, although you never know. He invites them home for dinner and they come. They talk to Sonja, they admire her five-foot-high "I'm Tops at Schropps" bobby-pin, they act bowled over by her scarves and hats, they leave wearing a scarf and hat.

But do they ask her out?

"If she'd only wear some lipstick," Gordon frets to Doris one evening over their rum-and-Coke nightcaps. It is the end of July and they are standing at the living-room window to watch a lightning storm. "Or do something with that hair of hers," he adds.

"She'll meet somebody someday," Doris says, rapidly patting down that hair of *hers* but taking no offence. She is too fired up. This morning in the Dominion store line-up she met a beautiful dusky woman who could have been Harmony La Londe, right down to the nurse's uniform, gold tooth and smoky laugh. Her name was Cloris Carter. "Hey, we rhyme!" Doris said, and that laugh of Cloris's, that first gust of it, left her feeling all golden brown at the edges. When she suggested that the two of them have coffee one afternoon, Cloris clutched her by the wrist and said, "Yes, yes, you come to my place." It was something else, the look in her eyes. Bloodshot, boiling, as if she were letting Doris see right into her arteries. They arranged a date for Saturday at two o'clock. Doris would bring her shortbread cookies. Walking home, pulling the bundle buggy in a state of dread and rapture (in case she hadn't read Cloris right, in case she *had!*), Doris noticed three small bruises on her wrist.

Now, watching the storm, she finds herself bringing that wrist up to her lips and sensing from the bruises the slightest emanation of heat. "Somewhere there's somebody," she says to Gordon, "who will love Sonja just the way she is."

"Where will she meet this somebody?" Gordon asks as lightning—three, four flashes—stutters across the sky.

"Five Mississippi, six Mississippi—" Doris counts. When the thunder claps, she jumps and spills some of her drink. "Where?" she asks. "On the doorstep." She swipes at her wet blouse. "He will suddenly appear on the doorstep!" she says in a starry-eyed voice (she is now thinking of Robin the Avon Lady). "You'll see." She pats his arm. She clicks her fingernails on her glass. She makes an unconscious leap from Robin to birds and says in her English-accented stage voice, "It was the nightingale and not the lark that pierced the fearful hollow of thine ear. Nightly she sings on yond pomegranate tree." She dashes to the corner and pulls the cord to open the drapes wider.

Gordon wouldn't call Doris brain-damaged but he does secretly suspect that six years ago she suffered a small stroke. From reading all those neurology books he knows that changing suddenly from a relaxed person to a jittery, distracted one can be the aftermath of spastic paralysis. Poor Doris. His good, neglected wife. Despite her ambitious plans for his career, has she ever complained about how he failed to measure up? Not once. What she did instead was get them out of debt with that *Queen for a Day* haul and then go on to make a career out of entering every contest going, sending in box tops by the bagful, composing little ditties. Is it her fault that all she has won since *Queen for a Day* is second prize in a toilet paper contest? First prize would have been something. First prize was five thousand dollars. Second prize was getting your photo printed on each sheet of ten rolls of toilet paper. For the heck of it Doris mailed in a photo of Bill Cullen (the host of *Name That Tune,* a TV game show that never replied to her dozens of letters begging to be a contestant) and—who knows? maybe they liked the joke—back came ten rolls of Bill Cullen's head. Which Gordon couldn't bring himself to use because he had a crush on Bill Cullen at the time. He sighs. It seems odd to him now, falling for someone that old.

"What?" Doris says.

He looks into her bright little eyes. "You were a fine actress," he comes up with.

She laughs, pleased. She pecks at her wrist.

"Damn fine," he says, meaning it now.

"Well, Sweetie," she says, touched by the quaver in his voice, "let's just say I was an actress."

She wasn't even that. The closest she got, professionally, was palm waver in a summer-stock production of *Antony and Cleopatra,* and Gordon knows this, not because she slipped up but because for no reason he has ever been able to put his finger on, her oldest lies have grown transparent to him. (He finds it extremely poignant that they have, as if a sad but natural aging process has ravaged some part of her that was once beautiful.) "I wish Sonja had something like that," he says. "A stimulating outside interest." Then he remembers that she did have one, once. "Say, why doesn't she take up dancing again?"

Doris laughs. "Gordon, she weighs two hundred and fifty pounds."

"Okay, that would give her the incentive to go on a diet." But already he can't see it. He sees those hippos from *Fantasia,* the ones in tutus.

"Don't worry about her so much." She taps at moths dithering on the other side of the pane. Fly to Cloris! she silently bids each one. "Sonja's the happiest person I know," she says, and perks up a notch because she realizes that that's the truth. She starts bobbing to the song in her head.

"I wonder," Gordon says.

"Is that rain?" Doris sets her glass on the arm of the chesterfield and races out of the room. A moment later he hears windows slamming shut.

When she returns he says, "What's she going to do? Live with us all her life?"

"Well, why not?" She alights on the edge of the chesterfield and drains her glass.

"Go to her grave a virgin," Gordon says.

Doris looks at him, a clear, blank look like a mirror he is meant to see his blunder in.

"Oh, Geez," he says. "I don't know why, but I never count him. What was his name? Some joke name . . ."

"Yours. Remember?" She springs to her feet. "He said to her, 'Call me Yours.'" She shivers. "What a creep. All done?"

She snatches his glass as the sky is splintered everywhere and they both feel a surging, a kind of arterial tug.

———

It is two days later. Saturday. Day one of the record-breaking continent-wide killer heat wave that before it is over, eighteen days later, will pick off Grandma Gayler and a slew of other retirees as they lug home groceries and mow lawns despite the radio and newspaper warnings. Across two nations, cans of prunes and consommé from dropped paper bags will roll down sidewalks. Unmanned power mowers will charge through hop-scotch games and into busy intersections.

It is July thirty-first, 1965, the twenty-seventh anniversary of Gordon and Doris's first date, not that either of them remembers. It is ten years to the day since Gordon quit smoking and he doesn't remember that either. From his own life only three anniversaries have ever stuck with him: his birthday, the day his mother died, the day Al Yothers walked into his office.

After today, make that four anniversaries. The fact that July thirty-first is also day one of the 1965 killer heat wave he'll keep forgetting, year after year, unless there's an item about it on the news, and then if they say that twelve people died that first day he'll think, Thirteen. Meaning including himself. Not his near-fatal heart attack but the death of the flimsy idea he had of himself up until then as a Man Doing No Real Harm.

That Saturday in 1965, during the part of it that he still considers himself harmless, he is nevertheless paranoid, suffering one of his regular onslaughts. So it isn't just the heat he's sweating from. Sonja, sitting across from him at the card table and affixing her bobby-pins, is *raining* sweat, but look at her go!

At least there is a breeze out here. Here, under the aspen, there is a breeze and some motley shade and the pleasant hay smell of freshly cut grass baking in the sun. (Unlike the doomed retirees Gordon doesn't mow the lawn, Doris does. Because of his heart murmur she says, but really because the roar outside their bedroom window at seven o'clock in the morning is her already at it.)

There is a pitcher of pink lemonade. Doris brought it out before she ran off in short-shorts and a halter top. From between their house and the house next door Gordon caught sight of her wavered by heat and the jiggle of her flesh and maybe by his own disbelief that she would go out in public half-naked. What with his being in a state of acute apprehension anyway, he allowed the idea of another man to rear into his mind. "Where is your mother off to?" he asked Sonja.

Sonja, her mouth full of peanuts, said, "She's taking shortbread cookies to a Negro woman she met who just came to Canada and doesn't have any friends yet. She has a gold tooth, though."

That odd bulletin was an hour ago. It is now just after eleven o'clock. Joan is playing the piano. Bach, her new passion. Out of the opened window of her bedroom (they've moved the piano in there) her clipped version of the *Goldberg Variations* marches like ants. If Gordon wasn't feeling so paranoid he'd find it heartwarming listening to his youngest girl doing her imitation of Glenn Gould while he reads a manuscript in the company of his oldest girl who is likewise working at her trade, such as it is. If he wasn't feeling so paranoid and this Wild Bill Hickok manuscript wasn't so awful and if he could come up with a title for it. On Friday his big inspiration was *Hard on the Saddle*. He was patting himself on the back until his secretary, Margo, in her customary deadpan, said she didn't think it would wash.

"Jesus," he said, suddenly seeing it. He was flabbergasted. "I need a vacation," he said with a feeble laugh.

"Or something," Margo drawled. Ever since, he has been fretting that she is on to him. That everybody is on to him. He hasn't had a lover in over three years but the desire is there like a compounding debt. Like owing the Mafia, there's no getting around it, cough up or die. Who *can't* see the cocks in his eyes is what Gordon would like to know.

So every few pages he finds himself glancing at Sonja and wondering if in her guileless way she has sensed something fishy about old Dad. A far more diabolical possibility is that she knows because Joan knows. That Joan knows and has communicated it to

Marcy, and that Marcy has consulted her older sister. Who has consulted Doris.

But hold your horses, *does* Joan know? Even if he has let a few things slip to her, she wouldn't understand, she's only eight, for Christ's sake. She's sharp, though, sharper than she lets on. He had better watch himself, stay on the ball. Maybe he shouldn't lie down, but he's usually so beat at the end of the day. What is it about lying on that floor? Is it some chemical in the carpet? For a year or so she's been humming the whole time he's there, and he finds that really soothing, hypnotically so. Is it her humming, then? No, he has *always* had an urge to pour his heart out around her. Why? And (here's where it gets out of hand) why can't he distinguish between what he's said out loud and what he's only been thinking? Dead-giveaway words—"lover," for example, or, worse: "queer," even "Al Yothers"—will suddenly seem to be booming off the walls, and he'll jerk up and gape at her alert little face in the back of the closet while the words, whether he spoke them or not, settle like nuclear fallout. "Did Daddy just say something?" he might ask. She'll nod or shake her head. Or moo. Or click her tongue. Or just go on staring. He gets the feeling she's giving him the response that suits some rigorous, unfathomable purpose of hers because never in her face has he witnessed reproach or shock. Never, not under any circumstances.

Now take Sonja . . . He extracts the soaking handkerchief from his shirt pocket and dabs his hairline as he studies her. In *her* face, ever since she quit school anyway, he hasn't witnessed anything other than contentment. He'd love to be able to believe that look. He used to believe it, not any more. Partly it's her shooting up from plump to fat. He can't believe that, simple though she is, she doesn't care. He can't believe that you can be a twenty-four-year-old woman who has never gone out on a date (okay, you've gone out on *one* date) and not be suffering. He can't believe that a contented person has only one friend and that friend is a snarky, go-go-booted doughnut glazer with a laugh like a pneumatic drill. He stands in the doorway of Sonja's bedroom, and that almost everything in there is something she made herself—the poodle-patterned bedspread and matching curtains, the shellacked and framed jigsaw puzzles of the Royal family, the pompom trim around the vanity, the fake fur cover that turns the jewellery box into a poodle, the container of glued-together acorn caps from which burgeons a bouquet of reconstituted china dolls' heads on candy-apple sticks—this, to him, is the really depressing part. When you consider that she dreamed these things up and poured time and effort into them! Maybe it's just bad taste. There's a possibility that what we have here is purely low I.Q. married to craft, but what he sees when he looks around is purely misery. The livid scabbing over of secret mayhem, another configuration of which is her good cheer.

What *is* the mayhem? Getting pregnant at fifteen springs to mind, usually. Now, today, he wonders if it isn't him. He doesn't mean her *knowing* that she has a strange father, what he's suddenly wondering is, if a queer father, by unconsciously failing to emit certain normal masculine impulses, plays havoc with his daughter's temperamental development. Her *intellectual* development! Jesus, what if she's slow because he's queer? No, that's nuts. He lifts his glasses and wipes his face with the handkerchief. Just let her be genuinely happy is all he asks. If blowing his brains out would guarantee her happiness, if his torso on a spit were Yahweh's price . . . Let him tell you, those cut-and-dried Old Testament deals, more than the miracles they're what he regrets you never hear about nowadays.

"Dig in."

Her voice startles him. He puts his glasses back down and sees that the elastic neckline of her flowered muumuu has slipped, revealing one sweat-spangled shoulder as sloped and fleshy as a breast.

"You need to eat plenty of salt when you're perspiring," she says. She yanks the neckline up before helping herself to a fistful of nuts.

"That's right," he says, overly impressed, as always, when she knows anything. He fishes out a single nut, pops it in his mouth. "Wow, is it a scorcher," he says boisterously. Like an ordinary father in a lawn chair he leans back with his fingers laced behind his neck and looks up at the sky. To the east it is marbled by dense grey-mauve clouds. Straight overhead the aspen leaves shiver, effervescent. He hopes another thunderstorm is on the way. Some water on this fire. It's too hot to even breathe but people are out doing things. The amplified purr of a manual lawnmower. A screen door banging. Screams of little girls. Or of seagulls.

His own little girl, the one who has never screamed, is playing "Take the A Train" now.

Not for the first time he wonders if Joan was drawn to the piano because you can get ten notes out of it at once. He himself doesn't play an instrument, but if he did it would be the piano for how it is capable of simultaneously reproducing the pitches of an entire orchestra and as such is the instrument that comes closest to resembling the life of the mind, the only life that allows you to live so many other lives. He listens to her. He thinks of how Doris is always saying to people, "You can be a genius in one part of your brain and still be brain-damaged in another part."

"I wish you wouldn't say brain-damaged," he tells her.

"What do you want me to say?" she asks.

"I don't know," he says. "Nothing, preferably. Not brain-damaged."

"But she *is* brain-damaged."

"According to the neurologists certain functions appear to have suffered some degree of injury, yes. But whether or not these injuries are permanent has yet to be established."

"That's what I said. Brain-damaged in a part of her brain. Sweetie, let's call a spade a spade."

They've had this conversation, verbatim, a hundred times.

He drains his glass of lemonade and glances at the bedroom window. The poor kid must be sweltering in there. She's got the electric fan, but an air-conditioner is what she could do with. He sighs, and Sonja says, "A penny for your thoughts."

"Oh, just wondering what mountains I'd have to move to afford an air-conditioner."

"I'll buy you one," she says. "I'm Miss Moneybags."

He sits up straight. Joan's deliverance might be a lost cause but Sonja's has just been revealed to him. "Listen," he says.

"Hmm?"

"I want you to use some of that money and go on a trip."

"A trip?"

"To Europe. Or around the world. Around the world! Why not? On a ship, first class. I'll tell you what, I'll arrange the whole thing for you, the whole shebang! All you'll have to do is pack."

"Mommy says the money is my nest egg for a rainy day."

"Ah, to heck with that. You can build it back up again. You're young, you don't have any responsibilities. Now's the time to see the world."

She grabs a bunch of bobby-pins.

He puts his hand over hers. "Hold on a minute."

She swipes her tongue along her upper lip. She smiles, but her hand under his is not still.

"I'm serious, honey. You could see Buckingham Palace, the Eiffel Tower, Paris, French poodles—" He thinks of her bedspread and jewellery box—"*real* French poodles! And you'd meet all sorts of interesting new people. A trip around the world! It could change your life."

"Oh, I don't want to change my *life*," she says.

They blink at each other. "Well," he says, "think about it, just think about it, okay?" He has lost his steam but he adds, "Monday I'm going to check with a travel agency, get some prices." He gives her hand a pat and instantly she is back to her pins.

The sun beats down. He moves his chair a little to the left for more shade. Charred is how he feels, in cinders. That black thicket of bobby-pins, that's him, in cinders. He picks up his pencil, puts it down. Pours himself more lemonade and stretches and flexes his bum leg. Bellowing "D" words—"Degenerate! Depraved! Deviate! Dystopia!"—he wrapped the convertible around a tree and shattered his femur in three places. His suspicion is that when his leg stops seizing up, on that day so will his heart. "Do you know who I am?" Al said. "Yours," he said. "Daddy, I'm yours." If somebody says what you've been dying to hear without knowing it, it's like the countdown on ether, you can't resist.

Yours. Daddy, I'm yours.

Gordon sets the glass on the table as steadily as he can, but his hand is shaking too hard and lemonade splashes out.

"Oops," Sonja says, and then, squinting at him, "Are you okay?"

"Fine." He can only mouth it.

"You're white as a ghost," she says pleasantly.

He clears his throat. "Sonja."

She drops a completed card of pins into the box beside her chair. He clears his throat again. What he is thinking is so fantastic, so evil, that it should have occurred to him at all has already given it intolerable substance. "Honey," he says.

"Hmm?"

"What—" He takes a breath and glances around. One last look at the world intact. "What did Joan's father look like?"

He has never before asked about Joan's father, and neither, he is almost certain, has Doris. Right from the beginning the guy was out of the picture—what was the point? So you'd think that Sonja might register surprise at his question. Think again. She chuckles. Still clipping pins, not missing a beat with the pins, she chuckles! And because in the marrow of his bum leg Gordon knows what she's going to answer, her chuckling sounds mad to him, the implacability of her serenity is what strikes him, in the second before she speaks, as the true mad thing.

"All I ever think of is his nostrils," she says. "He had the hugest nostrils I've ever seen. Like this." She circles her thumb and forefinger. "That huge. But he was just huge all over, gigantic, way over six feet. In a million years you'd never think he was related to Joanie. Oh, jeepers, I almost forgot! He was a carrot top!" She beams at him. "Honest. He asked me to guess his nickname and I said Red, of course . . . "

Her voice fades into the sound of a tennis game, the sound of popping champagne corks. The light dims. There goes the light, all concentrated into a single ray that burns through the pocket of his shirt. "Court-jester shoes," Sonja says, and it sounds as if the volume is being turned up and down. "Daddy!" she calls from the deck of a ship already out to sea, but the ray has whipped into a flaming lasso that binds his arms and he cannot wave to her.

He is in the hospital two weeks, in a private room paid for by his company's insurance plan. The saver of his life, through mouth-to-mouth resuscitation and a tire-screeching drive to the hospital that flattened his own cat, was his neighbour to the north, Harry Jolley. Harry's wife, Mabel, bakes a cake for Harry to take to the hospital. It is in the shape of a cat with chocolate-stick whiskers, a tail extending into a halo and with the words, in pink icing on the body: GET WELL SOON! Harry reads the inscription aloud to Gordon, whose glasses shattered when he toppled over in the lawn chair. "She really means it," Harry says apologetically, setting the cake on the window ledge among the flowers. "She doesn't blame *you*." He smacks his lips. He and Mabel are childless. Harry sells asbestos insulation and every summer makes a new building for the thigh-high turn-of-the-century toy village he is constructing in his back yard. The village is called Tibbytown, after the cat. The signs on the stores are Tibbytown Feed and Grain, Tibbytown Dry Goods and so on.

"The old girl came down with bladder failure last year," Harry says. "*That* was no day at the beach, no siree bob." Gordon thinks he is speaking of Mabel until he says, "So how I'm looking at it, she's out of her misery." He smacks his lips, he keeps smacking his lips. He is the spitting image of Charles Laughton, the bloated head, the blubbery lips. In three years the first male lips to touch Gordon's turn out to have been Harry Jolley's. During Harry's visit this is Gordon's only thought. He feels neither gratitude nor sympathy nor repulsion. He feels the chill of a perfect irony, compared to which the chill of his near death is nothing.

When Doris sees the cake she says, "What nitwit gave you this?" Behind his closed eyes Gordon comes close to smiling. "For crying out loud," she says, "you don't give chocolate cakes to heart-attack victims!" He hears her tasting the icing, sucking it off a finger. "Well," she says, "Sonja will make short work of it. I'll bring it home if it's all right with you."

Gordon goes on pretending to be asleep. Since there is no dissuading her from showing up three times a day and since he has nothing to say to her, he fakes the exhaustion she is so certain he must be suffering anyway. She races around, watering the flowers, dusting, moving the electric fan, searching through the stations on the transistor radio, giving his nails a fast clipping, pumicing the soles of his feet (which overhang the end of the bed), dry-shampooing his hair, opening the window, opening it again when the nurses slam it shut, shaving him, feeding him . . . her frenzy tracing occult intaglios around his body. Occasionally he yields as if to an incantation and then, even while she's scraping a razor over his face or shovelling food down his throat, he really does doze off.

In the evening, when she brings Marcy and Sonja, he keeps his eyes open. He hardly speaks though, and this is no act. Marcy's thin, scared face, her myopic eyes peering into his, is an occasion he can't imagine ever having the wherewithal to rise to. Sitting on the edge of the bed she twists his fingers. Her fingers are hot, in the hearth of each nail her chipped red polish a flame. Every night her first order of business is to deliver a message from Joan. "Joanie went outside all by herself last night." "Joanie says to keep the radio for as long as you like." One evening she arrives lugging Joan's tape recorder because she and Joan have recorded, especially for him, Joan playing "Mister Sandman."

"Remember you used to have this record?" Marcy says as they're listening to it. "Remember?" Pulling on his thumb, she sings along—"Please turn on your magic beam . . . "

"That sounds great. I wonder why Bunny wants another one," Sonja says.

"Another what?" Doris asks.

"Another thingamee there, another tape recorder," says Sonja, who bought Joan this one for her seventh birthday. "Last night she handed me a picture of a big expensive kind. She cut it out of the newspaper."

Sonja, during these visits, squeezes into the chair in front of the electric fan and does her knitting. The clicking of the needles is louder than at home, or so it seems to Gordon. And her body odour—a chicken gumbo soup smell—is stronger. He wonders if his other senses are overcompensating for his blurred vision. He can't make out her face. In her muumuus and with her knitting she is a rampage of colour that outdoes the flowers hands down. At the end of her first visit, when she bent to kiss him, he whispered, "Honey, I'm sorry." Meaning about Al Yothers, not that she'd know that, but meaning also that the heart attack didn't finish him off. Not that she'd know that either.

"I just thank my lucky stars I was there," she replied. "And that Mr. Jolley was at home. He did artificial respiration on you for, oh, jeepers, ten minutes! To tell the honest truth, I thought you were a goner and so did Mrs. Jolley, but Mr. Jolley, he wouldn't stop, uh-*uh*, not him. He puffed up his cheeks"— a display here

—"and kept on blowing." Out came her breath in a peanut-scented gust. "Blowing and blowing and blowing."

Gordon has worked out that Al Yothers seduced Sonja while he and Al were lovers. He has gone further: he has worked out an interval of not more than five hours between penetrations—Al's of her, and his of Al—because he is certain that he and Al saw each other that same night. It was the night Al wouldn't shut up about virgins. "Like taking candy from a baby," was his threnody. "Candy from a friggin' baby."

"You enjoy taking candy from babies?" Gordon asked.

"Depends on the baby," Al said, throwing him a sneaky look that, given Gordon's assumption they were talking about virgin *boys,* pointed to the cherub Gordon had seen him lighting a cigarette for outside the Chinese restaurant where he and Al rendezvoused.

He has worked out that it isn't his fault. How could he have guessed the stunning wattage of Al's vindictiveness when he was so blind he didn't even know the lights were *on?* Writing AL WAS HERE on his back was more than a flicker, he can see that now, but by then the affair was over and you could argue that that was only Al's lame idea of a joke or even Al's way of ensuring that Gordon wouldn't want to come back, wouldn't turn up again and tempt him. As Gordon keeps telling himself, to know that somebody doesn't love you is not necessarily to know that somebody lies awake nights mentally poking you all over for where the knife will go in.

No, it isn't his fault. It isn't even a tragedy. It's a blessing. It is how Joan entered the world. Gordon has worked this out. Now all he has to do is buy it. He can't stop thinking about when he was six or seven, how after his mother had kissed him goodnight he would make her look under his bed and in his closet. "All clear," she'd say. "No murderers." He never bought that either, although he believed her. Some nights he didn't sleep until dawn, and he is

still persuaded (irrationally, you don't have to tell *him*) that by refusing to fall for her version of "all clear" he saved his own life.

Saving his life is the last thing he's interested in these days. Except that he has to plug on to pay the bills. What are the odds anybody will sell him a decent life-insurance policy now? One
evening, after Doris and the girls left, he felt so bleak he climbed
out of bed and stretched his arms heavenward because the doctor
had said that one of the most dangerous things he could do during
the next few months was to stretch his arms over his head. Why
that should be, Gordon couldn't imagine, but he tried it. He stood
there with his shirt riding up and his fingers near enough the overhead lights to feel the heat. Down by his shins the breeze from the
fan flapped his pyjama leg, a derelict sensation. With his arms still
stretched high he walked over to the window and wondered if this
was one of the most dangerous things you could do because the
cardiac ward is on the top floor and the windows are big and easy
to open, so once you're locked into position what's to stop you
from diving into the parking lot?

Back in bed he wept. And wouldn't you know that's when the
minister from the Presbyterian church, the one that Marcy used to
go to, made his appearance. As if he'd been lurking outside the
door all week, waiting for his big break. To make a long story
short he ended up jerking Gordon off. Throughout the chitchat
and the prayers Gordon put on his exhaustion act, but when the
minister said that as a boy he'd spent a year in an iron lung Gordon opened his eyes and said, "Geez, you poor kid."

The minister shrugged. His name was Jack Bean. He resembled a child made up to play an older man. Silver hair and lots of
it, slight build, caramel freckles saddling a button nose, slender
damsel fingers strumming the Bible. A prematurely greying thirty,
Gordon put him at. The shrug surprised him. On a platter Gordon had offered him an opportunity to talk about God's mysteri-
ous ways, but instead he appeared bewildered, resentful even. "It

was torture," he said, moving Gordon to pat him on the knee, pure fatherliness.

At which Jack's leg shot out and kicked the bed. They both jumped, Gordon lifting his hand. A look passed between them, unmistakeable. Over Jack's knee Gordon's hand hovering like a benediction. Letting the hand drift back down was the most natural thing.

"Why were you crying?" Jack asked. He glanced at the door. It was shut, he'd shut it. He shifted from the chair to the edge of the bed while Gordon, simply by keeping his hand still, found it halfway up Jack's thigh.

"I don't remember," Gordon answered.

Jack walked his fingers under the sheet. On Gordon's thigh they halted. "What about your heart?" Beads of sweat like braille across his forehead.

"Strong as an ox."

Jack nestled into his shoulder. "God forgives everything," he whispered.

# FOURTEEN

S ONJA'S FRIEND, Gail, glances up from her magazine and says, "You're eating it! Oh, you pig, I can't believe it! What a fat pig!"

There is only the head and halo left. The rest Sonja ate last night. She selects a melting chocolate-stick whisker and quickly nibbles it down to nothing. "If *you* don't want to get fat," she advises, "you'd better not have any."

Gail turns to one side, exchanging blank looks with an invisible witness. "Well," she says, turning back to Sonja, "thank you very much." She has two voices: disgusted and—this one—sarcastic. "Thank you for that truly fantastic helpful hint."

A fond smirk from Sonja. *She* knows when her leg is being pulled.

It is about two o'clock in the afternoon, another scorcher. For the seventh day in a row Sonja is doing her pin clipping in the back yard. Doughnut glaze turns to water in this heat, so Gail has the day off from her job (again), and since she lives in an attic room with no air-conditioning and "there was nothing better to do" now that she has broken up with her boyfriend she came over to work on her tan. She is wearing a madras bathing suit with a lacy bodice that gives the impression she is developed. A matching madras bow is in the crease where her bangs fringe off from the rest of her hair, which when she and Sonja first met—at Schropps, where Gail was a clipper herself for a total of three days—was egg-yolk yellow but is now silver-white and crackly looking, reminding Sonja of that stuff you put in the bottom of Easter baskets. Her toenails are painted skin colour, the colour of the skin-colour crayon. Her feet are so thin that when she took off her shoes Sonja mentally counted toes, doubtful that there could be five across. This was when Gail was sitting in the other lawn chair and had her feet on the table . . . before Sonja described Gordon making a sink-draining sound, then keeling over in the chair. "Not *this* chair," was Gail's reaction, and she held her arms aloft as if the arms of the chair were splattered with manure, then she got up and spread her towel on the grass, ordering Sonja to do the back of her legs.

Sonja hauled herself out of her chair and lowered herself onto her hands and knees. "You're one skinny minny," she said as she applied the suntan lotion.

"Go suck eggs."

"Go jump in the lake," Sonja shot back cheerfully. Does Gail ever remind her of Sniffers, the hamster she used to have! Every time she tried to pat Sniffers or even slip food into his cage, he bit her. Eventually she had to flush him down the toilet.

Gail, likewise, isn't thrilled with the arrival of food. When Doris brought out the cat cake, what was left of it, Gail said, "Oh, barf."

"Don't charm me to death," Doris said, setting the cake on the table.

Gail sighed. "I'm sure it's delicious, Mrs. Canary. It's fattening is all I meant." She had to shout the second part because Doris was already over at the clothesline, yanking the sheets off. "By the way, Gail," Doris called, "could you babysit Joanie tonight? Just for a couple of hours while we're at the hospital?"

"Gee, I'd love to," Gail said. "But I have a date."

This wasn't true. Only a few minutes ago she'd been moaning about having nothing to do that evening.

"Isn't Mrs. Jolley going to babysit?" Sonja asked.

"She can't," Doris called. "She's picking Tibby up from the taxidermist's."

When Doris was gone, Sonja asked Gail why she had lied, and Gail said, "'Cause your little weirdo sister gives me the creeps."

"Huh," Sonja reflected after a minute. She couldn't fathom it. It was like a rose giving you the creeps, like a bunny. "It takes all kinds," she observed, knowing this to be the truth. Knowing the truth to be only aversion.

"Shut up and listen," Gail said. "'Thirty-two ways to beat summer boredom.'" She was reading from her magazine. "'One, have an anti-boredom party. Picket around a pool, along a beach. Best placard wins a prize.'" She looked up, her face all horror and disbelief, exactly like a person having a heart attack (Sonja could now appreciate). "Who comes *up* with this retarded b.s.?"

Now, while Sonja wolfs down the cake before it melts, Gail is making her do something called a "Miss Sophisti-quiz," the topic of which is, "Are you in step with the sixties?"

"'He's very impressed with Bob Dylan,'" Gail reads. "'Do you say Bob Dylan is, one, a terrific comic? Two, a protest folknik to be reckoned with? Three, an exciting Welsh poet?'" She squints up at her. "You better know this."

"An exciting Welsh poet?" Sonja tries.

"You are so *stupid!*" Gail screams. She slaps the magazine shut, rolls onto her back. "I can't believe how stupid you are." She writhes. She appears to have burst her appendix. "I don't even know what we're doing this quiz for anyway. As if anyone would ask *you* out."

"For your information, Little Miss Know-it-all, I've been out on a date or two in my life."

Gail laughs, that laugh of hers that always makes Sonja want to grab anything breakable. "Oh, yeah?" Gail sputters. "With who? Mr. Schropp?"

Mr. Schropp, Sonja's boss, is over seventy.

"That," Sonja says, "is for me to know and you to find out."

———

By "date or two" she means three. All with Hen Bowden. (*She* doesn't count Yours.) They took place on consecutive Saturday afternoons almost a year ago, and up until now they have been her secret. Not even Doris knows. The first date, which was more like a pick-up, was toward the end of September. She was standing at the bus stop, on her way to Schropps with her shoe box of no-good pins. The way it works at Schropps is you buy your own pins and cards, and on the last Saturday of every month, if you can be bothered, you have the opportunity of returning any no-good pins (the ones without plastic tips) in exchange for a cent a pin. Sonja can be bothered. In a single month she goes through so many cartons of pins she can make an extra ten dollars on the no-good ones.

The only person in on Saturdays is Mr. Schropp. He hates it when clippers show up for a refund. Handing over the money, he wheezes pitifully, as if you were killing him. But Sonja wasn't dwelling on what was in store for her. As she often does when she's waiting for a bus and there's nowhere to sit down with her knitting, she was envisioning the secret adventures of the poodles in her bedroom, what they get up to when nobody's looking. There are fifty-seven of them not including Mimi, the jewellery-box poodle. Mimi is the leader, she communicates by doing semaphore with Kleenex tissues. The rest of them, the bedspread-and-curtain poodles, stand on each other and form a pyramid to see out the window. Because they love Sonja they become living dusters and clean her room. Afterwards they dance on their hind legs. Since Sonja was going to be gone for several hours that Saturday the poodles were getting into mischief. "Behave yourselves!" Mimi signalled. But the poodles burrowed in Sonja's underwear drawer and played skipping with the laces of her old saddle shoes and, oh, no! now the little rascals were having sword fights with the bobby-pins!

It hardly needs pointing out that when the horn beeped, Sonja was a million miles away.

A white Volkswagen. The driver—a man with reddish-brown curly hair and a big, happy face—leaned over, rolled down the window and said, "Jump in, Kiddo."

"That's okay," she said.

"It's Hen Bowden!" the man bellowed. "What? You've forgotten me already?"

"Oh, Mr. Bowden," she said, remembering the twin brothers her father brought home for supper about a month ago. She laughed as she approached the car. The Bowden brothers! What a pair of kidders.

"Do me a favour, drop the Mister, sister . . . Gimme that—" He reached for the box. "I'll throw it in the back." She was trying to squeeze into the passenger seat but couldn't fit with her box. "What's in it?" he said, giving it a shake. "Ant bones?" He laughed, a single, blared "Ha!" that caused her to jump. His brother had had the same laugh. When they came for supper, between them their separate "Ha's" had sounded like one person laughing normally but at slow speed.

Hen twisted around to put the box behind her. When he sat forward again his weight settling in the seat caused it to whoosh. "What'd ya say?" he addressed the seat. "Diet, you fat slob!" he answered in a growly voice. He looked down and yelled, "All right already, I'll dye it but what colour? Ha!" He turned to her, his bursting mole-splattered face as friendly as a raisin pie. "Where to?" She stopped laughing and gave him directions, and he said,

"Down by the train station, right where I was headed. Say, what time does the next train leave?"

"Jeepers, I don't know."

"Two, two, two."

She checked her wristwatch. "I hope you're a fast driver."

"Ha!"

All the way to Schropps he wisecracked. "What's that on your collar?" he asked, When she looked down to see, he flipped her nose with his finger. She asked how his brother was and he said, "Len? Len's home playing strip solitaire. Ha!" Then he said, "Poor old Len, thinks he's a deck of cards."

"Really?"

"Went to a shrink, shrink said, 'I'll *deal* with you later.' Ha! I know a guy, now this is a true fact, I swear, I know a guy thinks he's a pair of drapes."

"Really?"

"Went to a shrink, shrink told him to pull himself together. Ha! 'Course I think I'm a goat, been thinking that ever since I was a kid. Ha!"

By the time she got the joke, if she did, he was already on to the next one and she had already laughed at his laugh. He was the funniest man she had ever met, way funnier without Len giving away his punch lines. Come to think of it, maybe it had been *him* giving away Len's punch lines. Her father had said that nobody could tell the two of them apart, that they had driven their wiener dog crazy by seeming to be in two rooms at once. What a ball it must be at their house. She pictured them bumping bellies as they had done that night at supper, pretending to fight, saying, "Why you no good . . . Why I oughta . . . "

At Schropps, when she was out of the car, Hen called that he would wait. She bent down to the passenger window and pointed out that it was almost twenty-two minutes after two, he'd better hurry, and he said, "What am I going to do with you, Kiddo?"

"What?"

"Ha!"

When she was back in the car he said he knew where they served the best chicken and dumplings in the city, how about they go and treat themselves? Figuring that he had given up on catching his train, she said, "Sure." Don't forget, this was a friend of her father's. "You won't be sorry," he said, licking the drool from the corner of his mouth. She licked her drool. She was suddenly hungry—everything was food. His brown-checkered pants, waffles. His hair, caramel corn. Her drool kept on coming, and so did his jokes. The reason he and Len were bookbinders was that they were *bound* to do well. He used to be engaged but now he was footloose and "fiancée free." He wanted lots of kids, and he intended to help with the feedings, since a baby had to have a bottle . . . "or bust." "Bust" embarrassed her—although she couldn't help laughing—and she looked out her window. They were driving along the lake, the strip of park and beach east of downtown. Meringue-crested waves. Brown-sugar sand, gingerbread boys. She thought of a joke. "Do you like Chinese food?"

"Man oh man, do I?"

She pulled back the corners of her eyes. "Eat me," she said.

He gave her a startled glance.

"Eat me. Get it? I'm Chinese."

"Oh, all right. Sure, you're Chinese food."

She sighed and said, "Brother, I just can't tell jokes," and he said, "Let's keep this to ourselves."

"Keep what?" Her joke?

"This date."

"September twenty-sixth?"

He smiled. "Why do you suppose you never got a call from Len or me?"

"Um—" She tapped her finger against her chin. "Don't tell

me." Phone, she thought. Dial. Hen. "Because a hen doesn't call, it clucks?"

"Because we *both* fell for you. Had a fight over you, if you want to know what it came down to. Darn near strangled each other with those scarves you gave us."

Nothing could be further from her mind than that he was serious.

"Anyhoo," he said, "we made a deal. Neither of us could ask you out. Hands off the merchandise. But, man oh man . . . " He shook his head and smiled over at her.

It took her a moment to realize that his hand was on her knee. She looked at it clamped there, freckled and puffy, a kind of starfish. Except that it was a man's hand. On her knee. She looked out the window again, sucking her fingers and trying to register how she felt. Not swept off her feet. The truth of the matter was it could be anything on her knee. A poodle. A banjo.

In the restaurant he was a riot. The waitress—Vicky, it said on her uniform—asked if they wanted their chicken smothered in gravy, and he said, "What the heck, Vicky, kill it how you usually do." He told moron jokes non-stop. Sonja knew a moron joke herself—"Why didn't the baby moron fall off the cliff? Because he was a little *more on*," and she got a laugh out of him but she could tell he'd heard it before. Vicky, however, cracked up. As Hen later explained, Vicky was an albino. Dead-white skin, hair like candy floss, matching pink eyes, which blinked a lot. She had a moron joke, too—"Why did the moron walk around with his fly open? In case he had to count to eleven." Sonja didn't get it and she guessed because the moron's fly was open that it was rude, but she laughed to be polite. "Whoa, Vicky, Vicky," Hen said. "Sonja here's a nice girl." Vicky gave Sonja the once-over, then, sighing, pouring them coffees they hadn't ordered, said, "I was a nice girl once, but when you get pregnant after being more or less raped, excuse me I should probably say 'forced against your will,' and then the father runs out on you so you have to give the baby up and then you find out that the baby is brain-damaged, well, excuse me for living, but 'nice' has a tendency to fly out the window."

Hen whistled. "Man oh man, hey, Vicky, that's too bad." He slipped an arm around her waist. "Anyhoo, who said you weren't nice? Show me the dirty rat that said that! Let me at him! Why, I oughta—" He turned to Sonja. "Vicky's the nicest waitress we've ever had, what do you say?"

Don't look at Sonja. Her heart was racing, her palms were dripping. *Now* she felt as if a man's hand was on her knee. Vicky had been talking about *her*, that's what Sonja thought. Or maybe . . . was Vicky related to Joan? That white hair, the white skin? What she meant was, had Vicky and Joan been related in a former life? She watched Vicky roll her pink eyes and laugh at Hen, then write up their bill, then angle around the tables and into the kitchen. In her left ear she heard Hen say, "Two's company, three's the result." Feeling frantic, feeling like a train trying to make it up a hill, she shovelled dumplings into her mouth, her eyes welded to the swinging kitchen doors.

It was the darndest thing. She'd forget all about Joan being reincarnated and then something like this would happen. A sign. The last one was two years ago. She was down in the laundry room going through the rag bag in search of velvet to sew hats with for her china dolls and she found a man's white shirt that had ALI WAS HERE written on the back. Instantly she knew it was a message from Callous Alice—or Ali for short—the woman everyone at Dearness had said Joan used to be before she was born. She dropped the shirt and screamed. That is to say her throat discharged a sound that Doris, up in the kitchen, thought was somebody reeling in the outside clothesline. "Was that *you?*" Doris laughed. "Sweetie," she said, "what are you up to?" because when Sonja brought her down to the laundry room to show her the shirt, it was gone!

Meanwhile, in the restaurant, Hen told more moron jokes, and what Sonja took for streetcars rumbling by outside turned out to be herself laughing—her lungs and chest carrying on like a car still chugging after you switch the engine off. Huh! she thought when she realized. She glanced down at her hands, half expecting them to be knitting. You never knew with this body of hers, it had a mind of his own! By now she was breathing easier and repeating to herself, "Joanie was Alice, Joanie was Alice," to show whoever had sent the Sign that she hadn't forgotten, although she more or less had.

---

She was grateful that on the drive home, for the first half of it anyway, Hen didn't talk. He flicked a toothpick in the corner of his mouth and belched, so Sonja allowed herself a few burps as well. When he finally spoke it was, coincidentally, to ask about Joan, who of course had stayed in her bedroom the night he and Len had come for supper but he had heard her playing the piano. "How's Mozart?" he said.

"Funny you should ask," she said. "Because you know what? Vicky reminded me of her. I've never seen anybody else with hair that white and with such white, white skin."

"What!" His eyeballs seemed to dangle at the end of springs. "Joan's an albino?"

This is when he explained what an albino was. No pigmentation, the pink eyes.

"Joanie's eyes are green," Sonja said.

"Green, that's good, that's good. She's probably just one of those really blonde blondes. Albinos don't live long, you know."

Sonja's heart staggered. "Oh, I'm sure she's not an albino." She looked down. There was Hen's hand on her knee again.

"I'm sure she's not, too. Hey, if you want to *di-late*, become an optometrist. Ha! Listen, speaking of trysts, ours are going to have to be restricted to Saturday afternoons. That's when Len has his oil painting classes. I tell him, I say, Len, artists are born . . . which is the problem. Ha! Anyhoo, we're only going to be able to see each other once a week, Kiddo."

"That's okay." When had it been settled that they would see each other at all? He patted her knee and said don't worry, he'd get around to telling Len about her before the wedding but in the meantime—"We'd better keep mum about this, and I mean from daddy-o." They were now pulled over in front of the bus stop where she had been standing almost three hours ago. He spit the toothpick onto the floor. "Same time, same station?"

"I guess so."

He kissed her, her first kiss. It reminded her of the time a horse nibbled sugar cubes from the flat of her hand. When it was over he looked at her from eye to eye. "We're going to have to work on that," he said.

She settled, walking home, that if he had been serious about the wedding she would come right out and tell him she wasn't a virgin, and that should put an end to that. She *wasn't* a virgin, was she? Did it matter whether or not you'd had a climax? She was fairly certain there had been no climax. She *had* had a baby, after being "more or less raped," although she had never thought of it that way.

She stopped walking and pressed her palms to her temples. Recalling Vicky's astonishing disclosure made her feel as though her head had been clanged between a pair of cymbals. She tried to think straight. You can't have a baby and be a virgin, not unless you're the Virgin Mary. Okay, that made her not a virgin.

It wasn't as if she hadn't worked this out before. She was twenty-three years old. It wasn't as if she hadn't thought about a husband before, either. Plenty of times she'd tried imagining how a husband would fit into her life, and what it boiled down to was, he wouldn't. Who would babysit Joan when her mother was off gallivanting? What would Schropps do without her? And even if her husband moved into her house and let her go on working, where would he sleep? By herself she took up the whole bed.

And yet . . .

And yet she remained open to this one possibility—Being Swept Off Her Feet. Weighing 250 pounds and working as a pin clipper had afforded her a taste of it. The buoyancy, the lightness. The bubble feeling, as she thought of it. Call her sick (Gail did), it didn't change the fact that the bubble feeling was why she couldn't wait to get to her pins in the morning. If a man could offer her anything close to that kind of pleasure, well, now that there was a man in the picture, she figured she might as well give him a whirl.

Although, judging by the kiss and by his hand on her knee, she and Hen weren't off to a flying start.

---

The following Saturday it's sunny and warm, in the mid-seventies. An Indian summer day as Hen points out and then he fires off a million Indian jokes. For the first few minutes they were Chinese jokes in a Chinese accent, inspired by the five bags of Chinese food in the back seat. When Sonja climbed in the car, not seeing the bags, she said she smelled garbage. "I've never minded the smell of garbage," she said truthfully after he drew her attention to the bags and told her about his plan for a picnic at Edwards Gardens.

"Ha!" Right in her face, like a blast from a tuba. "You clack me up, Round-eye."

On the fringe of that blast she smelled alcohol and was flattered because she knew that sometimes your date needed to screw up his courage with a few stiff belts. Before, when he had leaned over to kiss her cheek, she had smelled his Old Spice aftershave, the same as her father wore, and had felt a bit apprehensive, she couldn't have said why. A moment after that she noticed the $14.99 price tag hanging from a thread on the back of his shirt collar and she was amazed. Had he spent all that money just to impress her? The shirt is white cotton knit, short-sleeved. He is dressed entirely in white—white sailor pants, white loafers, which also look new. He is going all out. But, then, she should talk.

For the occasion—for the First Annual Pin Clippers Luncheon was the story she'd handed her parents—she is wearing her mother's Evening in Paris perfume and her lipstick (the same and only tube Doris has owned going on fifteen years now). She is wearing her best dress, the red empire-line. She has taken up the hem.

She has shaved her legs. Hence her slashed knees and ankles. (Hence the pinkish bathtub ring that, right about now, Doris is pondering.) It was such a long bath that it turned her the colour of bubble-gum. "Wow," she said looking at her naked self in the mirror afterwards, something that she never did. When she grew accustomed to her hue, another spectacle hit her. "Wow," she said, "am I ever fat!" She felt no repulsion, no embarrassment. She was entirely in awe, the same feeling people get in the presence of a stupendous natural wonder that all the photographs have impoverished. After a moment she plumped up her high round breasts. She dabbed at the moles on her breasts and belly. Look at all those moles! She enumerated the biggest ones and came up with thirty-two. Then she slid a finger between one of her belly's scallops and felt the finger clasped tight. She turned sideways for that view, shook her arms and laughed at the wobble, patted her hands over the alluvium of her bottom and thighs, the miles of it! Then back to the moles. They reminded her of someone's face.

"Holy moly!" she said, realizing.

Now, here in the car, it is hitting home that she can never be completely bare naked in front of him. What if he saw it, his own face blown up on her stomach? She can picture him laughing his head off, as she laughed off hers, but she can just as easily picture him saying, "Whoa," and backing away with raised hands, hands off the merchandise.

So here is another reason not to get married. As if she needed another reason.

———————

At Edwards Gardens the roses gape like water lilies. All the trees are still dark green but along the gravel path there are drifts of yellow leaves, and every now and then a yellow leaf saw-tooths down. There are black squirrels with their tulip heads and doe eyes. They leap out of the aluminum light. Up on hind legs they hold a paw to their heart.

Sonja carries four bags of the Chinese food, cradling two in each arm, and Hen carries the other, a cooler and the car blanket. He walks in front of her and bellows words over his shoulder—"Nicotiana!" "Cosmos!"—speaking in a foreign language, she thinks, impressed, until it's "Nasturtiums" and then "Marigolds."

He leads them down a secluded slide of lawn to a stream. By now she is pouring sweat and has a stitch in her side. After setting down his load he spreads the blanket right at the verge of the water and kicks off his loafers and sits. He yanks off his socks, shouting at her to do the same. "Don't peek," she says as she lifts her skirt to undo the fasteners holding up her nylon stockings. What she doesn't want him to see is her slapdash sewing job—the length of white elastic that at the last minute she attached to this old garter belt (using black thread because black was handy) to get it to stretch around her waist.

"Hen no peek." He's back to his Chinese accent. "Hen shy guy." On his knees he is opening the bags and removing the containers. "Hope Round-eye not on diet. Confucius say, Diet is for person who is thick and tired of it. Ha! What is Round-eye's plef-lence—Seven-up or beer?"

Thrilling herself (she is a teetotaller) she answers, "Beer."

"*Now* you're talking," he says in his normal voice.

With their feet in the water, their beer in paper cups and with their paper plates balanced on their laps, they eat. Shrimp fried rice, chop suey, sweet and sour pork, egg rolls, chicken balls, beef chow mein, piling up their plates three times each, and anything that falls into the stream is instantly constellated by minnows. The water is cool. The breeze wrinkles the water in places, but by the end of her third beer Sonja isn't certain that those wrinkles aren't the scales of big fish almost breaking the surface. She doesn't ask Hen what he thinks because he is telling her about himself, it would be rude to interrupt. He is telling her about himself and Len, to be specific. They are thirty-one. They grew up on a chicken farm outside Windsor, no brothers or sisters. What goes peck, peck, peck, boom! is a chicken in a mine field. Their mother is a squeaky-voiced, anxious-to-please woman who wins blue rib-bons for her pies. Their father is a pessimist. He breaks mirrors just to make sure he'll live seven more years. He could never tell them apart so he called them Tweedledum and Tweedledee or just Hey Fatso. When they left home at eighteen they tried their hands at a variety of jobs. Gutting fish, house painting. For a while they were garbage men but they were always at other people's disposal. Then they worked in a lumber yard where the business was "come see, come saw." Getting jobs as apprentice bookbinders was a lucky break. Now, nine years later, they make good money, enough for two Volkswagens, their own house. They have made a deal—who-ever marries first, the other moves down to the basement.

Hen looks at her when he says this about marrying, and she tries to keep a straight face but all she sees, looking back at his mole-covered face, is her naked stomach. "Come see, come saw," she chuckles, pretending that that's what's so funny.

"Now you, Kiddo." He runs the backs of his fingernails along her cheek. His fingers smell of soy sauce.

"Now me what?"

"It's your turn to tell me the story of your life."

"Oh, okay." She sets her empty plate on the grass and leans back on her elbows. The sun falls like pins on her head. Her head feels oversized. Her bloated, slightly upset stomach is a fish bowl teeming with minnows. "My name is Sonja Canary. I'm twenty-three years old. My dad, Gordon Canary, is a book editor." She clicks her tongue. "You already know all this."

"Go on." He seems very serious. He is pulling on a coil of her hair.

"Um. Let's see. My mom's name is Doris Canary. She teaches school at home to my sister Joanie. So does my dad, at night. He just started. He teaches her English, history and geography. I have two sisters. Marcy, who is fourteen, and Joanie, who is almost eight. Joanie's such a little bunny. She's . . . well, the doctors say brain-damaged but my dad says that's a bunch of baloney because she's a genius. Not just at playing the piano but—" She stops, disinclined to talk any more about Joan in case he starts making brain-damaged jokes. "My sister Marcy," she continues, "is also very smart. And a real skinny minny. She wears a padded bra called Little Fibber. Isn't that cute?" He nods. "So, anyways," she says, "my mom—" She rifles through her mind for what else to say. "She doesn't bake very much. She . . . oh, I know! She enters contests, hundreds and hundreds of contests every year, and the very first one she entered she won two fur coats, a colour television, ten bushels of beans, two wheelchairs. Just oodles of prizes! She—"

"Tell me about Sonja."

He has let go of her hair, allowing her to lie on the grass and close her eyes. "Well," she says, "I've only had the one job. Clipping for the Schropps Pin Company. Some people can't hack the clipping profession, but I have a ball. I don't know, maybe I'm a born career girl." She opens her eyes at this last part to see how he'll take it. His face hovers above her, startlingly red and puffy like a face balled together out of Plasticine.

"Has Sonja ever had a boyfriend?" he asks.

"None of your beeswax."

He traces his finger along her lower lip. And then he's kissing her.

How does the kiss make her feel? Not, this time, as if a horse is nibbling at her hand, more like she's a baby bird and he is feeding her juicy worms. Even the taste is wormy. It's not bad. It's not being swept off her feet, though. It goes on for so long that her mind drifts to the knitting she'd be doing if this was a normal Saturday, and her fingers begin to crave and twitch.

"You're not kissing me back," he says at the end of it.

"Sorry."

"Whoa, Kiddo, Kiddo. Sorry has nothing to do with it. Don't you *feel* anything?"

"Sure."

"What?"

She thinks hard. "Nice?" she says hopefully.

"Nice!" He shouts it to the world. He sighs, shakes his head. Looks back at her. "Kiddo," he says sadly. Then he says, "Would you let me . . . " He bites his lip.

"What?"

"Feel you up?"

"Feel me up?" Her brain is lagging behind the conversation. She is still at him shouting "Nice," so she speaks without comprehension.

"Touch your breasts," he says.

*Breasts,* she hears. Her face burns. She crosses her arms over her chest.

"Hey, don't tell me you're the kind of girl who would rather repulse advances than advance pulses."

This flies by her but she says, "Maybe I am, maybe I'm not."

"Ha!" Half-hearted, running his thumb down her neck. "Ah, let me touch you. I want to make you feel good."

She looks to the right, where she has heard children calling. There's nobody there. Sunlight threads through the trees. "Well, I guess it would be all right," she says and drops her arms to her sides. Because he bought all the food. Because she doesn't want to hurt his feelings. Because him feeling her up might get her off the ground.

He starts with her left breast. Circling his palm, a gentle rub. Since that's where he's looking she is free to study his face. It's a kind face, she thinks. Too red, maybe, but kind. All those moles, one as big as a bean. Before she knows what she's doing she's counting them. That's just her. Whenever she is at the dentist's and gazing up, what does she do but count the holes in the ceiling tiles.

"You're so beautiful," he whispers, switching to the other breast.

"Thanks." Without losing count. Fourteen, fifteen. His face comes closer. Seventeen—

He is kissing her again.

She closes her eyes and orders herself to concentrate. She tries to imagine that she is a balloon, but she falls, she falls like a lead balloon. She tries to dredge up the glimmering feeling that precedes the bubble feeling, but there is only her indigestion, a thousand more minnows in the fish bowl. She sticks her finger through the loop of thread on his collar. He'd better hurry up. Any second now she's going to burp.

Just in time his mouth lifts, and she turns her head and lets out a beery belch. "Excuse me," she says.

"Kiddo," he says.

Sonja isn't somebody who dwells on the unpleasant side. Neither is her mind a steel trap. So when she thinks about Hen she doesn't remember that defeated "Kiddo" or that her finger stayed caught in the thread or that his ears lit up baby pink when he realized that the price tag had been hanging from his collar the whole time. She doesn't remember that on the drive home his jokes were all about suicides. Another kiss, which caught her in the ear because she happened to turn her head just then, might as well have never happened as far as she is concerned, and her recollection of their date the following Saturday is so blurred she isn't sure she didn't dream it. A trip to a country fair, a ride in a paddle boat that sunk, and the owner in so many words blaming their combined weight, saying, "All I know is, there's no holes in her." A ride on a Ferris wheel that got stuck with them upside down, her vomiting into her hair. And then, even after that, him kissing her but she brought up again down the front of his shirt. About the drive back into town she forgets everything. She forgets him confessing that in the story of his life he left out the year he was married to a nag named Dot who left him for a dentist named Ernest. She forgets the one about the worms who were so hungry they fed in dead earnest. You'd have to hypnotize her to get her to remember him saying, "After Dot ran off I swore I'd never again settle for a frigid woman."

She *does* remember that on those dates he told a hundred hilarious jokes, but can she come up with a single one? And she remembers what they ate. The home-made fudge and foot-long hot dog, the chicken and dumplings, the Chinese food . . . that entire scrumptious meal. She remembers, or imagines she remembers, that he was "all hands." In her opinion this is why they stopped dating. "He was all hands," she says to herself and feels perfectly justified as well as like somebody not born yesterday.

What about Vicky? Yes, she remembers the waitress, Vicky. She remembers the Sign. Ten months later on the seventh day of the killer heat wave when she informs Gail that she has had a date or two in her life, it is on Vicky's confession (which she recalls as having found fascinating rather than hair-raising) that her mind catches. And while she's on the subject, she wonders when and where the *next* Sign will show up.

The answer (talk about coincidence) is: (a) now, and (b) in front of Grandma Gayler's house.

# FIFTEEN

FROM Grandma Gayler's grocery bag three cans of Campbell's beef consommé, a can of Carnation evaporated milk and a can of Chef Boyardee ravioli roll down the sidewalk. Of the half-dozen small grade "A" eggs, at least one oozes out of the box and starts frying. The Milky Way chocolate bar squashes and liquefies under her shoulder. The bottles of Tab and Pepto-Bismol shatter, the pink fluid going stringy where it comes into contact with the fizzing brown.

Grandma Gayler lives long enough to take stock of the damage. She hopes that the other eggs aren't cracked. That will make it an even dozen in two days if they are. On Thursday she dropped her bag of groceries while trying to open the screen door, and there went all six eggs, what an awful mess it made, and the peaches were bruised as well, of course. "Isn't that the limit," she thinks as her heart pumps itself out. She imagines she is speaking but she is not. She has no idea she is dying, otherwise she'd be preparing her soul for its embrace in the arms of the mother who illegitimately bore her eighty-four years ago, her senility having progressed to the stage where, by mother, she means Queen Victoria.

She does not die alone. A girl she is presumably acquainted with (but cannot place) crouches next to her and fans her with a magazine while the girl's mother phones for an ambulance. The girl is a chatterbox. Grandma Gayler tunes her out and yet does hear this full sentence: "I'm going to take a commercial course so I'll have something to fall back on."

"Very sensible," Grandma Gayler thinks she replies. She is not in pain, she feels no pain at all. How lovely to be basking in the sun on such a gorgeous day in the company of this sensible girl who she now believes is Doris thirty years ago, Doris wearing odd shoes. Who, a minute later, her gaze having come to rest on the girl's white latticed stockings, she believes is the rose trellis behind her old house on Robert Street. Who, in the final seconds of her life, she believes is a light in her eyes, a benevolent interrogation. "Mind the frogs," she tells her interrogators, or thinks she does. Her last imagined words.

---

Her last *spoken* words turn out to have been, "Oh, no, not again!" Cried out when she dropped her grocery bag and heard by the girl, Cynthia, and her mother, Alma. Mentioned, in their lowdown, to Doris. Overheard by Sonja.

All four of them are on the lawn of the funeral home, a half hour early. Sonja immediately makes the connection to Callous Alice, to reincarnation . . . to Grandma Gayler already starting to reincarnate in the throes of death! What a thought! It buckles Sonja's knees. "Mommy," she says and clutches Doris's arm.

"Are you all right, Sweetie?" Doris thinks the heat is getting to her.

Sonja, speechless, just gapes. "Excuse us, please," Doris says to Alma and Cynthia, and she hustles Sonja over to a bench in the shade where for some reason Joan is sitting by herself. "Where's Marcy?" Doris asks. Joan shakes her head, keeping her hands over the lenses of her sunglasses and continuing to imitate the cicadas. Doris turns to Sonja. "Are you all right?" she asks again.

In a whisper so that Joan won't hear, Sonja explains.

"Oh, for crying out loud!"

"But Mommy—"

Doris plants her hands over her ears. "I don't want to hear another word about it!" she says, her voice winging to a breathless, ecstatic timbre, which Alma and Cynthia (the only mourners to arrive so far) hear as a crack . . . poor Doris cracking up under the strain. Sonja hears it for what it is. A slam. Case closed. Stymied, and still flabbergasted by the Sign, Sonja covers her mouth with her hands.

(So to Marcy, who is keeping an eye on the bench from the far side of the parking lot where she's flirting with the car-park attendant, the three of them seem to be putting on a see-no-evil, hear-no-evil, speak-no-evil monkey act. "What's going on?" she murmurs, and the attendant looks where she's looking and says, "You *know* those people?")

Back at the bench, Doris says, "I have enough on my plate with your father in the hospital." She springs to her feet and peels one of Joan's hands from her eyes. "Now come on, both of you, let's go inside and face the music. Where's Marcy? Marcy!"

It is an open casket. Grandma Gayler believed that the soul hung around in the body until after the funeral and should therefore have the opportunity of seeing everybody file past. Her other argument was, "What if I'm not really dead yet?"

What if she isn't? Doris wonders and resists the urge to get out her compact and hold the mirror at her mother's mouth. They've put pink lipstick on her mouth. Her mother would have been scandalized. It's nice, though, Doris thinks. Really, her mother was a pretty woman . . . for whom prettiness was a cross to bear, a scourge in the eyes of the Lord. When Doris was growing up there was an ugly, bad-tempered girl named Arlene living next door, and every time Arlene had a tantrum, Doris's mother reminded her that Arlene was homely, which was not an appeal to

Doris's sympathy, as you might imagine, but to her respect.

"Well," Doris says. She rips expired petals from the white lilies in her mother's folded hands. "These aren't the calla lilies I ordered, but what the heck. She looks peaceful, don't you think?"

"She doesn't look like *her*," Marcy says. She is whispering, although nobody else is in the room, only the four of them. This is the "Private farewell between the immediate family and the *diseased*" (as Sonja thought the funeral director said).

"You know who she looks like?" Sonja whispers now.

"Who?" Doris says.

"Queen Elizabeth. An old Queen Elizabeth."

Pause.

"No, she doesn't," Marcy whispers.

Doris suspects that Sonja said this only because it was the nicest thing she could think of. Her poor, batty mother. "You hear that, Mother?" she says. "Queen Elizabeth!"

"It's her hairdo." Sonja really does see the Queen. "The way it's curled up like that."

"She just looks so white," Marcy says and glances at Joan to compare pallors.

Across the room in a huge brown-upholstered chair Joan imitates the low roar of the air-conditioner. This makes for stereophonic sound at the casket. "Shouldn't Joanie come and say goodbye?" Marcy asks. She doesn't like how Joan is teetered rigidly to one side with her twig legs sticking straight out like a doll somebody left behind.

"No, she's too young," Doris says sharply. "It'll spook her."

But Joan has already climbed off the chair and is walking over. Her at-home walk—arms trailing, fingers strumming.

"No, you don't," Doris says.

Joan dodges by her. She grips the edge of the casket and stands on tiptoe. Very faintly, she continues to roar.

"Okay, you win," Doris says. "Can you lift her, Sonja?"

"Upsadaisy," Sonja says, plucking her up by the waist.

Joan leans right in. Her hair has come loose of its barrettes and brushes Grandma Gayler's face.

"Don't hold her so close," Doris says. But when Sonja pulls her back a bit, Joan thrashes and her sunglasses fall into the casket.

"Oh, cripes," Doris says, going to snatch them. Joan beats her to it and puts them back on.

"I think she wants to smell her," Marcy says.

"For the love of Mike—"

"She does," Marcy says. "Look, she's sniffing."

"Okay, that's enough," Doris says. Before she can say "Put her down," there is a loud crash outside.

"What was that?" Marcy runs to the window and parts the brown velvet drapes. "Uh-oh!" she says as Doris and Sonja come up behind her, Sonja still holding Joan, who shuts her eyes and plants her hands against the glass, baby-like.

Right outside the window, there has been a collision between a hearse and a blue car. The hearse is only dinted, but the front of the car is balled up like paper. "Oh, great," Doris says when the driver of the car opens his door. "It's Reverend Bean."

"He's bleeding," says Marcy. She means the hearse driver. Blood runs down his chin. He is the boy she was flirting with, she must go to him.

"If this doesn't take the cake," Doris says, rushing out of the room after Marcy. So Sonja sits Joan in a chair and goes out, too.

A quarter of an hour later, they return with a gang. Alma and Cynthia, Reverend Bean, the usherette who lived upstairs from Grandma Gayler and a loud, drunk butcher named Alf whom nobody has ever heard of but he claims to have been a very close friend of Her Ladyship, as he calls Grandma Gayler. "To me," he shouts, "she was a duchess!" He spirals his hand in a courtier's salute. He has no thumb. He is a large old man with ears like telephones and desperately sad eyes.

"Wait'll you see her," Sonja says, taking pity on him. "She looks like the Queen now."

It was only a small cut on the hearse driver's chin, and although Reverend Bean has assumed complete blame ("Never pray at the wheel . . . you can't resist closing your eyes"), the funeral director is going to cover the damages. Marcy sees him give Reverend Bean a stack of business cards and say, "Maybe you'll pass them out to your elderly parishioners."

Marcy is the first to enter the room. She wants the funeral to hurry up so that she and the boy have time to meet at the Dairy Queen later. "Hey," she says, "somebody closed the lid."

"Where did Joanie go?" Sonja says, coming through the door.

A chair has been moved in front of the coffin. "Don't tell me," Doris murmurs. With a queasy, tranced sensation she recalls from when she used to walk onto an audition stage, she goes to the casket and lifts the upper half of the lid. It's as heavy as rock. When she has it opened a crack, enough to see in, it slips from her fingers. Bang!

Reverend Bean is there in a second. He quickly lifts the lid back up. For a little man he is strong. "Oh, dear," he says, opening the lid all the way.

Joan is squeezed in along the nearest side, on her back. Her wrists are crossed over her chest, her head turned toward Grandma Gayler and the end of one of Grandma Gayler's curls between her opened lips so that the curl looks like a little horn Joan has drunk from, died from, that white curl the same white as Joan's hair, Doris notices with particular horror. "Get out," she hisses. She snatches Joan's hands. They are are ice cold. When Doris pulls her up, her head flops.

"Here, let me," Reverend Bean says. He has already opened the lower half of the lid. He reaches under Joan and scoops her out.

"Joanie!" Marcy cries.

"What do we have here?" the butcher shouts.

Joan's arm dangles as Reverend Bean turns this way and that for a place to put her.

"The floor!" Doris says.

He lays her down. He grabs a cushion from the chair and tucks it under her head. On each side of her Doris and Marcy kneel. "Snap out of it!" Doris says. She pushes the sunglasses up. Blows on Joan's face. Joan's eyelids don't even flutter. "Come *on!*" Doris says.

"She's probably just napping," Sonja says to calm her mother down.

"Her hand is freezing!" Marcy says, terrified.

"What seems to be the problem?" shouts the butcher.

"Could you please move away?" Doris says to him and the others. "She's afraid of crowds!"

He stumbles back. By now the funeral director and more mourners have come in. Reverend Bean corners the funeral director to explain. Alma whispers to the butcher, who bellows, "Ah, a cretin!" In front of the casket the usherette paces.

"Joanie, wake up," Marcy says, shaking Joan's arm. It wobbles like a rope. "Joanie!" She has an idea. She brings her mouth to Joan's ear and clicks her tongue three times—"Tsk, tsk, tsk."

It works.

"Tsk, tsk, tsk," Joan echoes, then opens her eyes.

Doris sits her up while Joan puts her sunglasses back down. "What was that all about?" Doris asks in a high, trembling voice that sounds like she's tittering.

The butcher's face breaks into a wild-eyed smile. "All's well that ends well!" he bellows.

"We were hiding," Marcy says. In her agitated state she doesn't realize that she is speaking of Joan in the plural. "The crash scared us and we needed to hide."

"Don't you ever do a thing like that again," Doris says to Joan.

"We're getting warmer!" Marcy says. She hasn't let go of Joan's hand.

"Poor little tot!" shouts the butcher, striding back to them. Before he reaches them, Joan pulls free of Marcy and scrambles to her feet. She runs to a chair, climbs into it and covers her ears. A few seconds later, she is back to imitating the air-conditioner.

An hour later, in the car, Marcy silently grills her. Wasn't Joan scared in the casket?

No.

"Why did it take so long to wake up?"

We didn't want to leave.

"We didn't want to leave the coffin?"

No.

"Where, then?"

Where we were.

"Yeah, but we mean, where was that?"

Asleep.

"We mean, we didn't want to wake up from our dream?"

Yes.

"What was the dream about?"

A silver place. All cold and silver.

"*Gold* and silver?"

No, cold.

"She had a *dream* she was cold!" Marcy says to her mother and Sonja in the front seat. (At the funeral home Doris had said that Joan's skin got icy from lying next to Grandma Gayler.)

"I'm not surprised," Doris says now.

That night in bed Marcy asks Joan about the dream again, but all she hears is that it was cold and silver; it was a cold, silver place. Finally she thinks, "Just don't do it again."

Silence.

"Promise," she thinks. She touches her forehead to Joan's. Her eyelashes brush the lenses of Joan's sunglasses. "Promise!"

No.

"Okay, we won't take us to another funeral, then," Marcy

thinks, turning away. And figures, that settles that. It never occurs to her (why should it?) that Joan doesn't need to climb into a coffin to imitate a corpse.

———————

A little later that night, in her bed, Doris thrashes and sweats. She can't get used to Gordon not being beside her. She can't stop seeing Joan in the coffin.

The pediatric endocrinologist they took Joan to last year warned that if her smallness indicated a certain rare type of dwarfism (Doris has forgotten the name for it) she might not live to see her twentieth birthday. The tests were inconclusive, and the endocrinologist said that the odds were she *wasn't* this type of dwarf, but Doris now realizes that ever since then, in some quarantined precinct of herself, she has been expecting Joan to suddenly drop dead.

She kicks off the sheets. Think about something else! she orders herself. The butcher, think about him. Well, what a boor *he* was! She can't imagine her mother having given a man like that the time of day. She wonders why he called Joan a cretin, what Alma whispered to him. Then she remembers Alma and Cynthia saying that her mother's last words were, "Oh, no, not again!" and is startled because she completely forgot about it until now.

"Oh, no, not again!" Why would her mother say that? Not *what* again? And Sonja is absolutely right. "Oh, no, not again!" *is* what Aunt Mildred and those superstitious crackpots at Dearness claimed Joan was born screaming.

It's a coincidence, all right. Enough of one to make Doris wonder if Harmony is messing around with voodoo dolls. Look who's calling who superstitious! True, but this much is also true: the coincidences have been piling up since Doris fell for Cloris Carter in the Dominion store line-up, and the message appears to be: Don't.

A week ago Saturday. She is sitting beside Cloris on Cloris's sprawling chesterfield, which is upholstered in a silvery fabric like whatever ironing-board covers are made of. Cloris herself is adorned in pounds of silver jewellery. Gigantic hoop earrings, an incalculable number of necklaces. Wire-thin bracelets segment the length of her arms, those at her wrists jingling like sleigh bells. All that silver. So queenly, so dazzling. In comparison Doris feels like the unworthy palm waver she was in *Antony and Cleopatra*. How dare she? But she can't resist. She lays a hand on the tea-coloured flesh of Cloris's knee. And as if a siren has been tripped, the phone rings. And it's for her. And it's Sonja saying that Gordon has gone off in an ambulance.

Then this past Saturday. She phones Cloris for the first time since Gordon's heart attack. The line is busy. She hangs up, and *her* phone rings. It's the news that her mother has died.

And not only died but, according to the latest bombshell, died wailing, "Oh, no, not again!"

Why not again? What has happened to Doris that she wouldn't have happen again and gladly? Would she marry Gordon? The lyrics that have just popped into her mind are, *All I want to see is the back of your head, getting smaller, and smaller, and smaller,* but she mentally smacks them away as being ridiculous and thinks, "You're darned right I'd marry him again." Would she have kids? If it were up to her alone she'd have a litter of them. What about Sonja getting pregnant out of wedlock? Well, that all turned out for the best, didn't it? What about her father dying at sixty-seven, twenty years before her mother? From the day he retired, her father did nothing but suck on a bottle of Canadian Club and listen to his scratchy polka records. So, guess.

Would she give up the stage? She'd even do that again, although that was a hard one.

She's on shaky ground here, thinking about the theatre. It has always hurt and mystified her why she never got a foot in the door.

Why didn't she? She had what it took—moxie, she could do any accent. And she wasn't bad looking in those days, either. How long ago was it? Nineteen thirty-seven. So twenty-eight, twenty-eight years ago.

She was nineteen, working in the typing pool at Nesbitt Insurance. A good job for a girl during the Depression. For another girl. In her last year of high school Doris had brought down the house playing Eliza Doolittle in *Pygmalion*. Standing ovations. Flowers at her feet. Her drama teacher, Mr. Waldorf, had urged her to go to London, England, and pursue his theatre connections. As if he had any, she thought, but this was years later. At the time she had said, hopelessly, "My parents could never afford to send me." Which, of course, he would have known.

"Whatever you do," he said, "don't waste your life in some dreary office."

Words that echoed.

Back then there was a magazine called *Centre Stage* that listed where auditions were being held across the province and just south of the border. When a part sounded promising Doris pretended to get a blinding headache so that she could leave work and go to the try-out. (Her boss, who really did get blinding headaches, would become almost hysterically sympathetic.) Some days Doris rode the train as far as Buffalo and back.

She told nobody about these trips, not even her parents. When she finally won a role, then she'd tell them, knock their socks off. The typing pool already thought she led a shockingly glamorous life. She had bought a tiny picture frame for the photograph it held of a handsome, curly-haired man wearing glasses, and she carried the photo around in a locket, saying that the man was her beau.

"He's a famous playwright," she said. "Dean Lowell." (Her mother's brother's name.) "You might have heard of him."

Some of the girls in the typing pool said they thought they had.

"He's very tall," Doris said, opening the locket. "I call him Lean Dean."

The girls oohed. They said how smart he looked.

"He's a genius!" Doris said. "He writes entire plays in his head. Of course, he's very absent-minded. He's always bumping into things and breaking his glasses. You see there?" She pointed to the arm of his glasses where there was a spot on the photo. "That's cellotape. He can't be bothered to go to an optician and have them properly fixed. He hasn't time for the everyday things." She kissed the photo. "He knows all of Shakespeare's sonnets by heart. The first thing he said to me when we met was, 'Let me not to the marriage of true minds admit impediments.'"

One of the girls waggled her ring finger. "So when's he going to pop the question?"

"Oh, he doesn't believe in marriage. We'll probably live in sin."

The girls shrieked.

It gave Doris a charge, scandalizing them. Some mornings she pretended to be hung-over from a wild night out with Dean and his actor friends. "I'm blotto," she'd groan. "Stay back, kids." She made up stories about these friends. Their dire love affairs, a suicide. She said that a local actress ("I'm not naming names") went to New York for an abortion. "And the next day she was still bleeding so badly she had to sit on phone books. I brought her ours from home and she bled through to the S's."

The typists ate it up. There was nothing Doris told them that they didn't believe. In fact, the more unbelievable she was the more devoutly they believed her. It was unbelievable. Growing up she'd had a horror of lying. Now she lied all the time, without guilt, without ever weaving a tangled web. There were tricks to lying, she realized. Or not tricks so much as rules. Look people in the eye, remember your lies, stick to your lies, never back down from a lie, salt your lies with the truth, respect lies, know that there is no such thing as a simple lie.

Very quickly she had all this down pat and working for her.

So it isn't exactly true to say that she didn't get a foot in the door, because she could talk her way into any audition. It was talking her way into a *part* that she somehow loused up. That silence as her last line died in the rafters like an electrocuted bird, and then, from a back row, that English-accented "Thank you, Miss Gayler," which meant she'd blown as much as a dollar on train fare . . . it was not an experience she ever got used to or entirely over.

Afterwards, instead of going straight home from Union Station she usually consoled herself with tea and a chocolate éclair at Fleming's on King Street. The set-up of the restaurant was in the form of a daisy, five petal-like counters surrounding a central preparation area, and at one of these petals she sat across from a young man who looked so much like the man in her locket that she opened it to check.

No, it wasn't him. The mouth was wrong. And the chin. Dean's had a cleft, this fellow's didn't. Still! He was tall, very tall and lean. And the right arm of his glasses was held on with tape! *Masking* tape, but that's splitting hairs. *And* he was reading *The Complete Works of William Shakespeare*! The same edition that Doris owned! The sonnets were at the end of that edition, and he was concentrating on a page somewhere near the end, looking up every few seconds and then down again, as if committing the words to memory.

Several times he glanced at her. Finally he said, pleasantly, "May I help you?"

"Let us not to the marriage of true minds admit impediments," she said. "Am I right?"

He smiled. "When in disgrace with fortune and men's eyes."

"You don't say. Well, I would have tried 'Shall I compare thee to a summer's day' next. *Then* 'When in disgrace.'"

"You're an actress."

Were she not already in love with this man from having more

or less invented him and therefore knowing all his dear, irreplaceable quirks, she'd be head over heels now. (So much for Ed Metzer.) "Give the man a cigar," she said. "First guess."

(Ed Metzer had been her high-school sweetheart. He had called her Pancake and kissed her for hours without going further. A fine young man, he joined the British navy, he always said he would. The night before he set sail he took her to his aunt's empty house and they lay fully dressed on a bed and kissed while he panted like a dog and slapped her all over, not too hard but almost. "Wait for me, Pancake," he said. "I will," she said, half believing she would, half thinking, "Fat chance.")

——————

She continued auditioning for parts she never got while spinning Gordon the line that she was taking a vacation from her exhausting stage career. A few weeks before their wedding she announced (and she wasn't kidding) that she was giving up the theatre for good. Because they would never see each other otherwise, she said. Because the pay stunk. Because she was tired of lying to her parents about it. And so on. The real reasons were: there's a limit to how much rejection a person can take, and the cost of train fare.

"I've had it with the limelight," she said, and Gordon kissed her as passionately as a man whose hands don't stray can.

Like Ed before him, Gordon respected her virtue. To her relief, to her disappointment. She was the type of young woman who had been raised to take baths in the dark. On faith she accepted that she must have been seen naked in her life but when she imagined her mother changing her diapers she imagined a photographer changing film—using a box, doing it by feel. Added to which Ed's idea of romantic bliss had hardly toppled the walls. When she and Gordon kissed, her body yearned. When she thought about what her body was yearning for, she cringed. Yearning and cringing, her seizured rumba to the altar. Which turned out to be the flower stand in her parent's living room. Her father hadn't worked steadily since the start of the Depression, so it was only a small family ceremony in the living room.

Afterwards, after the cold cuts, sandwich squares and lemonade punch, Doris and Gordon drove through pelting rain to the waterfront and drank half the bottle of bootleg whiskey that was the best man's wedding gift. Doris had never been inebriated before. She had assumed it would relax her, but it made her so jumpy she screamed at every clap of thunder.

She screamed when Gordon picked her up and staggered over the threshold of the decrepit Victorian apartment house that was their new home. He carried her up the three flights of stairs. She covered her mouth so as not to scream and wake the other tenants. He put her down to open the door, then picked her up again and carried her into their little furnished loft. Earlier in the day she and her mother had cleaned it, you could still smell the Murphy's soap. He kicked the door shut behind him, wove over to the bed and dropped her. She let out a pure, high, steam-kettle scream, and was applauded it sounded like, but it was the rain pattering into the room. Around the bed was a canopy of drips. He fell down beside her. "I can't see," he said. Her response was to remove his glasses, a liberty she had never before taken.

She carefully put them on the bedside table. She felt very calm now. More than calm, she felt a cold formalness, a peculiar expertise, as if her job were to dismantle this very long man feature by feature, limb by limb, and spread him on the bed for the sake of science. In her head a German-accented voice sang, *Ze shin bone's connected to ze ankle bone, ze ankle bone's connected to ze foot bone, now hear za verd of za Lord.* She was all set to undo his tie when he turned toward her and began to pull out pins that held the soggy garland of pink roses in her hair.

With her help he succeeded. He patted her head and murmured, "The bride." He kissed her. Still kissing her, his hand slid down her hair to the front of her neck and then lower, to her collarbone, and she demolished into the flesh that surrounded her breasts, she was all breasts on a pillow of flesh, but his hand lifted, and where it landed next was stretched along her waist. "Small," he said, giving her occasion to appreciate the yardage of his fingers. Then he rolled onto his back and closed his eyes.

"Sweetie?" She shook him. Shook him harder. "Sweetie." Gave up. Let's face it, for all her brave readiness she was mostly relieved.

The next evening was the first time. It wasn't her plan but she ended up wearing the Saturday-night nightgown her mother had sewn and wrapped in a Weston's bread bag and left under her pillow two days before the wedding. Thick flannelette, high-collared, floor-length, a pattern of tiny strawberries . . . a flap, midway down the front, that you unbuttoned. Doris knew what it was, what it was for. How many Sunday mornings had she seen her mother's plain white Saturday-night nightgown laundered and drying on the basement clothesline? (Never the outside line.) The strawberries, now those were a surprise. Risqué for her mother. Would Doris wear it? Her reaction when she opened the bag was an embarrassed, insulted snort. Crumpling it up and stuffing it back into the bag.

But she packed it with her trousseau, didn't she? And that second night, when Gordon set the tone by emerging from the bathroom in grey cotton pyjamas *and* a housecoat, all her nerve slithered off and she made her entrance in "the contraption," as they would eventually call it. She caught him squinting at the flap as she climbed into bed. "Don't laugh," she said.

"I'm not laughing," he said and switched off the light.

Eight months went by before she had the nerve to touch him down there. It was February. She remembers, because earlier in the day Ed's sister had telephoned to say that Ed's ship, HMS

*Exmouth,* had been lost at sea and that Ed "had gone down defending the Empire against the Nazis."

"Oh, don't tell me," Doris said, although somehow the news seemed like old headlines. She pictured Ed slapping the waves as he sunk.

"You were almost a war widow!" the distraught sister gloated, as if by dumping Ed, Doris had thrown away her one shot at glory.

When, hours later, Doris wrapped her fingers around Gordon's penis, the impulse was to have something to hold on to in the world. And to verify that being the receiver of this thing was all the glory she or any woman needed. That wasn't verified, not overwhelmingly or lastingly, but the sense she'd had for months that his penis was no carrot was.

She wasn't completely innocent, she'd heard that a man's thing was supposed to feel hard, not be so droopy. His *worked* perfectly fine, he ejaculated, it was just that it took a lot out of him. Sweat so torrential she sometimes held out a hand to see if it wasn't the roof leaking. His feeble heart banging away. When he paused for a breather she could never tell whether it was that, or he was having a heart attack, or he was through.

That night as on every other night she awaited the warm drool between her legs. She was the one who cried out then, she was so happy for him, so happy for herself, her drawn-out pleasure. As usual her climax had happened way back from all his fiddling around trying to get himself erect and inserted.

In other words his penis was no disappointment. Far from it. The other payoff was that intercourse was painless. Nice and easy, for her it was anyway. At her end it was rather luxurious while being so driven at his end that it was, really, a heartwarming event. Most women have to be pregnant before they experience that rush of protective love that a blind little invader of their body is capable of arousing.

By the time she *was* pregnant she was so moved by his penis—

its helpless pluck—that she was pitching in: rubbing it on her bare breasts ("the contraption" had long since been torn up for rags) and planting little kisses on its German-helmet-like head. Somehow she wasn't surprised that her lips had what it took to make him erect. Which is not to say that her feelings weren't hurt. He found her private parts unsavoury—this was the conclusion she drew—and she started washing them in a vinegar solution that seared her numb and within a few days lent an orange tinge to her pubic hair. For a while after that she wouldn't touch him, but eventually she couldn't resist. Back to the rubbing and squeezing. The little kisses.

When he ejaculated in her mouth for the first time she spat the semen all over his stomach and groin. She would have sworn there were quarts of the stuff. She was horrified. But even as he was apologizing and pawing at the fanned-out strings of semen linking her lips to himself, even as she was watching his dumb play on this harp, a pulse was drumming between her legs and she was like a bomber of Berlin, gaping down from the stratosphere at the splendid aftermath, saying to herself, "Look at what I just did!"

Did he ever kiss *her* down there? Seventeen years later Harmony would put the question to her. "Are you crazy?" Doris would answer. She could imagine almost anything but she could not imagine Gordon nuzzling her like a dog. Until Harmony came along, she had thought it was pretty far-fetched that any woman was loved in this way. She wasn't even sure that it was legal. It had to be slightly demented, she thought, the desire for somebody's lips on your private parts. Yet there it was, sideswiping her during sex with Gordon, springing up in her dreams where nine times out of ten the kisser was a woman. In one of the first of such dreams the woman was her great-aunt Beatrice! The sleeping Doris thought, "Oh, well, Aunt Beatrice is dead," and decided to enjoy herself. She woke up aghast, climaxing.

These dreams continued all her life, once or twice a week.

She'd be at a home-and-school meeting or at the beauty parlour, and suddenly she'd be in a clinch with a woman. As in dreams where you're naked in public, nobody paid attention. Furthermore, the climaxes that rocked her awake made the ones she had with Gordon feel like minor aftershocks. So she wasn't talking about nightmares. A lick of shame maybe as she emerged from the smoke of the dream, but shame wasn't inevitable. Could she help what she dreamed?

Could she help what she *day*dreamed? About the time that Gordon stopped making love to her (it was before then, but here's the version she lives with) she would be attending a home-and-school meeting for real, no dream, and find herself staring at Harriet Barker and imagining her ironing or cleaning her oven in a see-through black negligée. Harriet was the tall, thin, sophisticated type. Only if Doris dressed her in a sexy nightgown and stuck a cigarette in her mouth could she conceive of her doing housework. When Harriet wasn't there, Doris gazed at Libby Burt, who was trim and perfect, a little Dresden doll smelling of Jergens lotion. Libby she liked to imagine hanging laundry in white underpants and a white lacy brassiere. Pouty, sighing Libby, bending to pick up a towel, standing on tiptoe to peg it to the line.

For at least a year that was as far as it went. Visions of beautiful women doing housework in their underwear and nightgowns. And then one day she put herself in the picture. Showing up unexpectedly, being invited in. (No wonder when Robin knocked at her door, she knew what to do!) And then her dream women weren't even ones she was acquainted with. Women on the bus, receptionists, nurses, women she spotted as she tore through magazines for coupons. Women who were only drawings! The ScotTissue woman in her tight zebra pants and red sweater with the white fur collar. The Hertz rent-a-car woman! "She's Got the Hertz Idea," the ad said. What did that mean? Stupid with longing, Doris tried to decipher the caption, as if the woman herself might have been the author, but the message was impenetrable. The woman had the Hertz Idea, that's all that was clear, and because of this idea the woman's lovely forehead was perspiring, and her mouth was wide open, and her tongue—red as her lips—was sticking out as if to catch raindrops.

Whether she could help them or not, Doris's daydreams did shame her, though not to the degree that she put up much of a fight or was tormented. A rictus under her heart was all it really amounted to, a few seconds of adjusting to the evidence that she was one way and the world was another. She might have fretted more than that but there didn't seem to be any point. Daydreams like hers were comparable to seeing crazy shapes in clouds—Winston Churchill wearing a poke bonnet, say. What was the chance that that mile-wide Winston Churchill head up there was going to start bellowing, "We shall fight in the fields!" and terrorize innocent bystanders? Until she met Harmony she would have said that she was more likely to win a million bucks than she was to kiss another woman even on the lips let alone below the neck.

So Harmony was a miracle. The absence of shame and guilt was a miracle. There was fear, but only afterwards and only of being discovered. Under Harmony's hands, Doris's body turned to bells. She could just lie there, blameless, as Harmony instructed her in the declension of her own flesh. "What's this?" Harmony asked, touching Doris's nipple. The nipple chimed.

"My breast," Doris said shyly.

"Your nipple," Harmony corrected. She cupped her hand over Doris's crotch. "This?"

"You know."

"Lie still, Baby Lamb. What? What is it?"

"It's . . . down there."

"Cunt," Harmony said.

Doris gave an embarrassed laugh.

"Say it," Harmony said. She meant business.

"Cunt," Doris said out loud for the first time in her life.

Harmony stroked her with one finger. "This?"

"Beats me."

"Lie still. I never knew such a jittery woman. You don't know what this is?"

Doris shook her head.

"That's your labia. Your labia majora, to be specific."

"Labia majora," Doris said, feeling like Tarzan.

"Labia minora," Harmony said, moving on.

Sex was something else altogether. Slithery, equatorial. For Doris it almost restored her belief in God, because the lyrics that entered her head as she approached orgasm were from her old Sunday-school hymnal and because after her orgasms she found herself inspired to sing them (with Harmony humming along in a loose vibrato), feeling that at last she really understood "glory on high" and "joy divine," and what it was to be hallowed and unburdened. On the train home the phrase "abomination of desolation" kept occurring to her. She couldn't sleep. Come dawn she'd be standing between cars watching the endless basting of the sky by wires and poles while every love song ever written got an airing in her brain. Harmony had told her that lesbians were not as few and far between as Doris had thought, and maybe so, but Doris doubted the same could be said of women who decorated your breasts with gold leaf. She wondered whether, if she bought some gold leaf, she could talk Gordon into plastering it on her. "Well then, Sweetie, what about drizzling me with honey and licking it off? After the kids are in bed, I mean."

Unlikely scenarios were Doris's specialty, but this one was out of her league. Anyway, Gordon wasn't Harmony, even if you drank too many rum-and-Cokes and kept your eyes shut. By the same token, Harmony wasn't Gordon. Nobody was anybody else, although people resembled each other and linked hands like paper dolls.

If she knew this, then why after all these years did she persist in thinking of Cloris Carter as another Harmony La Londe? As Harmony but with Robin's urgency? There was harm in that. And harm in thinking of herself as herself nine years ago. No roaring heck in the looks department, but a big draw for Negro women. The afternoon of Gordon's heart attack when Doris pressed her hand on Cloris's arm she may have felt she was overstepping the bounds but at the same time she believed that Cloris felt nothing of the kind.

# SIXTEEN

BILLIE HOLIDAY on the portable record player—"Gimme a Pigfoot and a Bottle of Beer." On the silver chesterfield Doris and Cloris drinking iced tea and taking another stab at the shortbread cookies Doris brought over almost six weeks ago now. Talk about stale. Cloris cracks them like nuts between her front teeth. "Hmm-mmm," she says. She is kind. Stupendous. Wearing mauve slacks and a short-sleeved yellow blouse today, and the countless silver bracelets that make cyclones of her arms.

It's a half hour since Doris arrived in her black mourning dress. The dress is for Cloris's sake, to milk the loss. (That still makes it a loss. Doris has wept as much as anyone would for a mother who in the last year of her life went through her photo albums cutting out her daughter's head wherever it appeared and substituting Queen Elizabeth's at an appropriate age, which didn't always guarantee a match in size.) Doris is now regretting the dress. It's too tight under her arms and it's sticking to her like tar because the heat wave may be finished outdoors but not in Cloris's bachelor flat above Hollywood Dry Cleaners. A laurel of beads at her hairline seems to be the full extent of Cloris's perspiration, whereas Doris feels like an irrigation system. She's been thinking of getting the show on the road, asking whether Cloris would mind if she took the dress off and hung it in the bathroom to dry, except that what if two seconds later the phone rings and somebody is dead? One of the girls this time? You don't have to be superstitious to acknowledge that things happen in threes.

No, here's what's really holding her back. What if Cloris isn't game? A month ago she would have sworn that Cloris was. Why? She can't remember why she was so sure. She can't believe she was that trusting. A wide-eyed kid reaching for a sparkler when the odds are it's a blowtorch. Careful, she's telling herself now. *Careful* is the lone lyric in her brain, so paramount it doesn't need a song.

She is still thinking of Cloris as another Harmony but she's taking into account that Harmony was starting her menopause before she woke up to women, and Cloris can't be much over thirty-five. For the sake of describing Doris's state of mind you could say that she is keeping three running tallies: Looks Good, Looks Bad, and Can't Tell. Under Looks Good is Cloris at the door crying, "Doris!" as if they were sisters separated for years, and then hugging her so hard her spine cracked. Cloris laughs and says, "Lord, I snapped my husband's rib that way," and this (the husband, not the injury) is under Looks Bad for the second or two it takes her to add that she ditched that bastard in Detroit. The photograph on top of the TV turning out to be her brother goes under Looks Good. As does Cloris seeming fascinated with whatever Doris says. Under Can't Tell is, does she look at everyone like that? (Like Joan does, come to think of it.) The whites of her eyes are webbed with red veins. Is that genetic or from suffering? Under Looks Good is that when Doris loses her train of thought for the second time because of Cloris staring at her and she blurts out, "Your eyes are something else," Cloris laughs with her mouth opened as wide as the Hertz rent-a-car woman's.

A moment later Cloris's face is all sadness and sympathy. She wants to tell Doris how sorry she is about her mother dying. A beautiful crooning in the back of her throat as she clutches Doris's hand (Looks Good). She says she can't even think of *her* mama dying. "That woman is my rock of ages," she says. For a moment this Looks Bad—she's a church-goer—but it turns out that, like Harmony, she lost her faith because God is a man and she's had it with men. "They're all lowdown snakes." Looks Very Good, although Doris feels obliged to point out that there are exceptions.

"I'm talking about white mens, too," Cloris says. She frowns at the floor and then her eyes swivel back up to Doris's. "*Mainly* white mens."

"Oh, white mens can be SOBs," says Doris, adopting Cloris's plural as obliviously as she adopts other people's accents. Her tone suggests that she has a personal anecdote or two up her sleeve. She doesn't really, but she could easily invent a few on the spot.

Cloris declines to ask. "Amen," she says, reaching for a cookie. She shakes her arm and the bracelets start up like a field of crickets. "You got a fine man by the sounds of it," she says.

"Gordon? They don't come any better than Gordon. Our girls just adore him . . . " She sighs. "But, you know . . . " Sighs again and looks straight at Cloris, jamming desire into her eyes.

Cloris looks back, looks hard. Telegraphs red lightning. It goes on for so long that Doris believes they must have crossed the line and she is this close to saying "He *is* a man" when Cloris says, "Seems there's not a man alive doesn't have some *but* trailing after him. He's a good provider, *but* he's one mean jackass. Oh, he's handsome, Lord knows, *but* is he lazy! More buts than a damn ashtray." She laughs. Boulders moving underwater. She has the one gold cap, no fillings that Doris can see. What white teeth.

Doris pretends to laugh along. She fans her thighs with her skirt. Then, suddenly fretful, she stands and starts moving around, saying, "Don't mind me, I've got ants in my pants." She fingers the starched collar of Cloris's nurse's uniform hanging on the back of the bathroom door. Goes over to the kitchenette and taps a line of boxes on the counter. Cheerios, Frosted Flakes, Ritz Crackers, Pillsbury cake mix, Dash detergent. The trouble is, she needs Cloris to make the first move, but if Cloris is new to this then it's up to her and she just doesn't have that kind of nerve.

"That's for damn sure," Cloris says. She is talking about having come to Toronto for the better pay at Sick Children's Hospital— she's a pediatric nurse—and to start her life over, but the prejudice up here is going to take some getting used to. It's not the hateful kind, it's the plain, dumb, happy kind. Her superintendent calling her "Jemimah." The whole hospital taking it for granted that she and the one black intern on staff must be messing around like a pair of dogs. Doris shakes her head, clicks her tongue, half-consciously registers "black" for "Negro," all the while breathing deep to ward off the fit she feels approaching. Some kind of convulsion, could be sneezing. It's an oven in here. Now she's panting. Maybe it's a stroke, the third calamity turning out to be *her* dead.

"Sit down, honey," says Cloris. "You look hot as a griddle. By the window. Here, I'll turn the fan on you."

Doris sits, the "honey" working on her like a shot of whiskey. It's been so long since a woman called her honey. Is it a pass? What does *she* think? Make it a pass, she nevertheless prays, already dying for another one, more sweet talk. Cream Cheese, Baby Lamb, Mango Juice, Honey Baby—Harmony's names for her were a gourmet meal.

"Honey, you all right?" says Cloris, and her hand is on Doris's thigh. A smaller hand than you'd think, and older, corrugated like tree bark. Is *this* a pass? Doris knows that she's being way too impatient, vulgar is more like it. Even most men would have the decency not to try anything so early in the game. But she can't help herself. She could cry. She has a better idea, and given that her heart is going like a troupe of tap-dancers, it's not completely an act. She half rises out of the chair and then collapses into the stage faint that she taught herself almost thirty years ago and that, at last, has come in handy.

Except that Cloris's crowded little apartment isn't a stage. Instead of hitting the floor, Doris's head hits a horse-head book-end she hadn't noticed sticking out from under the chair, and she really does black out. For a good half hour, she'd swear, because while she is unconscious she dreams that she and Cloris make love.

The dream starts with her curled up on a bed between orange sheets, exactly like the ones Harmony used to have. She lifts the top sheet to verify that she is naked and sees how the orange makes her flesh look peachy and slender, years younger. She'd like to know where you buy these sheets. Another thing: how did Cloris manage to lug her onto the bed? Well, Cloris is a nurse, Doris reminds herself, nurses are strong. She lets the sheet waft down.

And hears breathing. Then registers the warmth of it on the nape of her neck. And something brushing her upper back. Nipples. She knows that feeling. In exquisite slow motion she feels the nipples press, give way to the breasts, which flatten on her back as her rear end is cupped in a belly, flesh arriving and spreading over her in waves.

She doesn't move in case she's dreaming and wakes up. No, she can't be dreaming! You don't see colours in dreams! A leg parts hers and starts a gentle pumping. A hand skims down her arm to her hip, barely touching. She hears the bracelets. That settles it, she must be awake. In a dream like this would she think to include the bracelets? What's more, if she was dreaming, Cloris would be wrestling with her by now. All Doris's dream women tend to be on the rambunctious side. They would *roll* her over. They wouldn't ask, as Cloris just has, "Can we kiss, Honey Baby?"

From here on it's *like* a dream, which for Doris is only more proof that it isn't. During sex with Harmony, Doris always hallucinated that the two of them were some kind of marine life. What she and Cloris have become are starfish. Her albino, Cloris inky.

Their tongues entwine in impossibly long helixes. Doris's jaw seems to unhinge, it opens so wide, until she has Cloris's entire chin in her mouth. Cloris then sucks Doris's chin into *her* mouth. They feed over each other's bodies. A seashell pink underwater light. When Cloris slides on top of her, their mouths lock onto each other's cunts as if driven by tides and the principles of physics. Whatever Cloris does, Doris does, this synchronization a natural law. Doris rolls her lips over Cloris's labia, she makes her tongue as soft and fat and wet as Cloris's labia, she nurses Cloris's clitoris with more tenderness than she kissed her own sleeping babies. And though her mouth is full, she keeps saying, "Cloris," and Cloris keeps saying, "Doris," in voices very clear but far away, as if they have lost each other.

"Cloris."

"Doris?"

"Cloris." And there is Cloris's face, upside-down above her own. How did that happen? Who turned on the lights? Cloris is dressed. That was fast. Doris goes to touch her own temple, and touches Cloris's hand. What is Cloris doing? It hurts like the dickens there. "Mama may have," sings Billie Holiday, "and Papa may have . . . "

"How do you feel?" Cloris asks.

"How long was I out?" She scours her beloved's eyes for some aftermath. Okay, she was dreaming, but it's not inconceivable that Cloris had the same dream. Look what happened with her and Sonja on the train back from Vancouver!

Cloris glances at her wristwatch. "Almost four minutes."

She must be kidding.

"One more minute," Cloris says, "and I was phoning for an ambulance."

"Four minutes?" Doris is still aroused, her cunt throbbing along with the song in her head (*If you get me going, you get what's coming . . .* ) and with the pulse in her temple, which Cloris is pressing an ice pack to. "What the heck did I fall on, anyway?"

"A book-end. Lord, you've got a bump to beat the band."

Doris swallows hard.

"You aren't nauseated, are you?" A cool, alert look, her pupils contracting. Her nurse's look, Doris thinks, and feels so bereft she releases a little whimper. "Let's sit you up," Cloris says, starting to lift her.

Doris resists. "No, I'm fine. If I can just lie here for a second."

Cloris eases her back down. "Well, sure you can."

"Only four minutes? Really?"

"Shush. Don't talk now."

Doris gazes at her. Her gorgeous mauve lips that a minute ago—unbeknownst to them!—were kissing her. The eyes that saw her stark naked. Upside down, Cloris's eyes are reptilian, unreadable. What Doris can't get over is that Cloris missed the whole thing! It is all Doris can do not to roll over and sniff Cloris's crotch for that nut smell. Why doesn't she? The point of the faint was to end up in Cloris's arms, better still her lap.

Doris thinks about this and can't quite believe it. Gradually she is appalled. What was she trying to pull? An old bag like her taking advantage of this beautiful woman. She thinks of Cloris saying, "You're my first white friend in Toronto," and feels stunningly corrupt. She feels like a sack of garbage somebody dropped in Cloris's lap. She sits up—too quickly—and groans.

"Take it easy," Cloris says.

"I'm okay." Although there's a bowling ball tumbling around inside her skull. "Let me hold that," she says about the ice pack, and when her fingers touch Cloris's she gets aroused again. She can't shake the sensation that she and Cloris actually did make love. She feels blessed by it. Except that because only *she* knows that they made love, she also feels slimy and forlorn. And protective. Wanting to shield her new lover from the sex-starved housewife on the loose in this room.

"Can I get you a glass of water?" Cloris asks, coming to her feet.

Doris looks at her way up there. "A glass of water?"

Cloris smiles, a wise, loving smile so exactly like the one Joan beamed on her that time in Grandma Gayler's basement that her face seems to drain of pigment and age.

"Or would you like more tea?" Cloris says.

Doris can't speak at all now. Cloris's smile has stupefied her.

"*Iced* tea," Cloris says.

"Um—" Doris gets out. Her stopped heart generates a thicket under her breast. What does it mean, a smile like that? How can you tell if it's for you alone or for the idea of someone like you? Or if *you* are beside the point? If you have waned into a transparency through which the real cherished thing is being seen?

"You say," Cloris says.

"*You* say." One thing she's figured out—all the decisions from now on will be Cloris's.

"Iced tea." She walks to the kitchenette, sandals slapping, bracelets ringing.

"Then I'd better be going," Doris says, but not so that Cloris will hear.

# SEVENTEEN

ROLLED UP under the rose-coloured carpet in the closet that Joan calls home is the white shirt Marcy wrote AL WAS HERE on. The day that Sonja found this shirt, Joan was watching her from behind the sofa and under the laundry tubs. She had been curled up on the old bath mat there, softly imitating sounds at the farthest rim of her hearing: a hum of traffic two streets away, a train whistle, a collision between a car and the train at a level crossing, sirens, a yapping dog whose eyes had just popped out and were dangling from their nerves (not that she knew this, although she knew about that dog from Marcy). Despite the damp she was drawn to the laundry room because it doesn't have windows and because she had discovered that in basements the sharper sonorities are tempered. (In Grandma Gayler's basement, sound was so velvety it burst into the open as mould!)

When Sonja started fishing through the rag bag, Joan switched from yapping to echoing Sonja's aimless hum. There was no resisting it. To a decibel Joan had registered the hearing range of each member of her family, so she was able to stay just outside of Sonja's. The beat of her own heart she retarded to keep time with the slow two-four rhythm of the hum. Sonja's yell, which was like the scraping of gears, she mimicked with enough volume to give

179

away her whereabouts had Sonja not been so alarmed. Joan herself was alarmed, all sudden or loud noises affecting her like firecrackers. Normally she would have run for cover, but here she was already under cover, and the noise, after all, had come from her darling Sonja. Who was now backing out of the room.

With the soles of her own feet Joan reproduced the thumps of Sonja ascending the stairs. Then, curious, she crept over to the shirt that Sonja had dropped.

She saw the letters. Quickly she smoothed the shirt out, and what *she* read was ALL WAS HERE.

All was here. It rang a bell. For at least four of her six years she had been aware of how close at hand everything was, of how whatever she wanted tended to be wherever she was. "Come out," Marcy said. Why should she? What was in the bedroom that was not in the closet? All was in the closet. All was there.

Joan is no pack rat, but she decided to hold on to this shirt.

---

She has never once removed the shirt from under the carpet. She doesn't need to. She is supremely conscious of its pacifying vibration, which is so like Sonja that it is a surrogate Sonja.

For Joan, the whole world vibrates—objects, people, weathers, shades of light and season, and sounds themselves emanating their signature amplitudes and oscillations. At least half of all frequencies, no matter what their amplitude, hurt, especially when they are new to her, but it is not out of the question that if she is subjected to a painful vibration enough times it will turn into a pleasant one.

Too bad this hasn't been the case with light. Light continues to hurt, sunlight more so than artificial light. Sunlight sounds like the dentist's drill and assaults like needles in her eyes, whereas the dentist drill, turned off, has a bearable thrum, as does the dentist,

Dr. Jhar. When the drill is turned on, within its torturous buzz is a soothing resonance veering on that of darkness. Darkness purrs. Similar to basements, it softens all vibrations. White paper also purrs. Green paper tinkles. Licorice Allsorts, the shower curtain and a girl named Gail tinkle like a lady's laugh.

As far as Joan can tell everything vibrates like something else. The exceptions are corpses, music and herself. She doesn't vibrate at all, she knows from her reflection. The mirror vibrates but not her in the mirror, even though other people's reflections sound exactly as they themselves do. She believes that this absence is why she is beautiful. Having heard all her life how beautiful she is, she believes that what people are talking about is her dead stillness, her hollow hush, and that they find it as pleasing as she does.

She had always thought that corpses wouldn't vibrate either. Or that they would boom like old cheese—too loud, too deep and slow. But the vibration of Grandma Gayler's corpse was so fast that it levelled into one long, silky tone from which glowed a glorious silver light that didn't hurt Joan's eyes. Heavenly light, she guessed it must be.

There was no heavenly music, however. She wishes there had been. Would it have vibrated like anything else? Earthly music vibrates only like itself and causes Joan to quiver along with it . . . because she herself is hollow, that's what she thinks. The quivering is lovely when the music is good but like an electric shock when the music is off key or crude. Bad music coming from the television is the worst. Even turned off, the screen discharges a sickly, descending ruffle that she takes for granted must have inspired canned laughter. After hearing bad music she used to listen to her circulation and digestion while picking up the most distant sounds she could, back and forth, that long systole of the near and the remote working as a pain killer. Now what she does is play the piano, and this is literally a shot in the arm, in each arm, high and low frequencies flowing from the keys up her fingers, up her arms and pouring over her skin until the frequencies are in balance, at which point the pain wisps away.

Print is the opposite of bad music. Print is a sight for sore eyes. She reads three books a week from the lending library (this doesn't include the one or two a month that Gordon reads to her) and she has close to a hundred books and twice that number of magazines of her own.

She has been reading since she was three, a year before Doris set up the classroom. Because Doris is her darling she pretended for another year to be illiterate so that Doris would think she was teaching her.

Everyone asked why she wouldn't write. Why she wouldn't talk. She couldn't have told them even if she could have. At the time that they were asking, she was still years away from articulating to herself the perception that words have colour in her head but not outside of it, or that the draining of colour is not a reduction of the word so much as it is a transformation she finds too eminent to tamper with.

She will write numbers, though. Numbers are different, they are almost always colourless. Unless they are blue. Certain numbers are a shade of deep blue that is the blue of everybody's breath in her dream where people are crowding into the closet. She has another recurring dream, the one where she's talking. "I hate you," she says in this dream. And then, "I'm so sorry." No, she doesn't! No, she isn't! She hasn't the faintest idea what hate and sorry feel like.

She eventually learned that these dreams were nightmares, and that nightmares are evil spirits that oppress people while they sleep.

The word "nightmare" is not listed in the "General Information" section of *Pears Cyclopaedia,* which is where she first looked for it. It is not listed in any of the sections, as she found out when she read the encyclopedia straight through, a page a day from

January first, 1961, until February eighth, 1963. In the autumn of 1965 she learned of the genetic tie responsible for her being disposed to such an undertaking. That September, a few days after returning home from the hospital, her darling Gordon told her that the man Al Yothers was her real father.

"I wish Al could hear you" is what he said. "Imagine having Glenn Gould for a daughter and not even knowing she's alive."

"Mister Sandman is Al Yothers" was Joan's first thought. (She's fast.) When she was three, Sonja said that she and an orange-haired giant named Yours were her real parents. Later, when Joan first heard the song "Mister Sandman," she got it into her head that Mister Sandman was Yours. This was around the same time that Gordon told her about a man named Al Yothers who liked to read the encyclopedia cover to cover. So her immediate response after putting together Mister Sandman and Al Yothers was that it made sense. She may not *look* like Mister Sandman's daughter, but what do you know? They both read the encyclopedia!

Her response upon reflection was to adjust her name from Joan Yours to Joan Sandman and to double-check the word "queer" in the dictionary because she remembered Gordon having used it once in connection with Al Yothers, as well as with a bar. Considering that Gordon often hinted at what amounted to his own "sexual desire toward a member of his own sex," namely Al Yothers, she supposed that Al Yothers (Mister Sandman) was likewise queer in this fashion. She did, however, wonder if on top of that he might be "eccentric" or "mildly insane."

Mister Sandman. Her darling. He is so fascinating.

But then, to her, who isn't? *What* isn't? Even pain, even her nightmares, even indexes and tables of contents are lit up like sparklers—unforgettable! For many years she assumed that reading and memorizing were the same function. Once, after she had finished investigating a little book about card games, Marcy gave her a memory test, which at the time Joan thought was a mind-reading test since Marcy had been right there to see her read, and therefore memorize, the book.

Marcy flipped through the pages. "Okay," she said, stopping at a page in the middle. "Here's a good one. How many possible poker hands are there in a deck of fifty-two?"

That number was blue. Joan couldn't write it. She touched the pencil to her lips.

"We know what we're thinking," Marcy said.

"Two million, five hundred and ninety-eight thousand, nine hundred and sixty," Joan thought.

"We're thinking if we give the right answer, then everybody will know what an incredible memory we have and they'll say we're so smart we have to go to school."

Was Joan thinking that? She assumed she must be, if Marcy said so.

"We won't tell anybody," Marcy said.

Joan wrote, "52."

Marcy sighed. "Fifty-two. Oh, sure." She slapped the magazine shut, and Joan was driven to swat her own thigh to echo the slap. "We never give a straight answer," Marcy said. "We're so exasperating."

When Marcy left the closet Joan looked up "exasperating" in the dictionary. It was another way of saying "causing irritation or annoyance." She already knew what irritation and annoyance were. They were like loud noises. She knew that a straight answer was a single answer you stuck to. For instance, "Are you happy?" Yes. "Really?" Yes. "You're not just saying that?" No.

But there are so many answers to a question like that—sometimes, maybe, yes, no, yes and no. Which is the straight one? Gordon is always asking her if she is happy, and to tell him the truth she moos one time, clicks her tongue the next. Shrugs. He only wants to make her happy. That's why he gave the CBC radio producer the tape of her playing the piano. "I only wanted to make you happy," he said.

He then said, "I really put my foot in it, didn't I?" and this was a question to which she was able to give a straight answer.

———————

Supper time, November 1965. Spaghetti and tomato sauce, white bread stacked on a plate, margarine so blindingly yellow that Joan can't look at it until Doris turns off the overhead light.

"A nice, soft dinner," Doris says. (Soft dinners are ones that eliminate the blare of chewing.) "Unlike last night," she says, referring to the undercooked carrots. She nudges Joan, and Joan blinks to acknowledge her while looking at her face in the new aluminum salt-shaker. She is so transfixed by her slightly warped reflection that she misses Gordon reaching over to switch on the radio. The click gives her a start. She imitates it with a click of her tongue.

There is music, the last bars of what she recognizes as Bach's Prelude and Fugue No. 5 in D Major played by Glenn Gould. Then a man says, "What you are about to hear will astonish you." His voice is a windy bass like the sound of blowing over a bottle but the frequency within it is as high as a mosquito.

"Self-taught," he says. And, "Just eight years old when she made this recording." Between her face in the salt-shaker and that mosquito hum Joan is too distracted to hear more than these words. But one note and she twigs. All it takes is that first note.

Her heart skips and races. This syncopation makes her gasp. Involuntarily her mouth opens so wide she has the impression that the word she won't speak is there in the cavity, hardened into block letters wedged between her molars.

"Gordon, turn it off," Doris says. Before he can, it turns off by itself. So do the hallway light and the refrigerator motor, all in the same instant. So do the streetlights, but only Joan realizes this because only she is aware of the sudden silence from the electrical transformers. She covers her ears with her hands. Slips off her chair and runs down the hall, the blackness directing her like a thousand hands. On the closet floor, behind a stack of books, she curls up.

Time passes, she has no idea how much. Maybe she falls asleep, and her darlings wake her up. They talk just outside the closet door. Gordon says there's been a blackout. Doris says, "I guess you don't have your mom's taste for the limelight." Sonja says, "Poor bunny, poor little bunny." Marcy says, "I *told* them not to."

Joan keeps her hands pressed to her ears and yet still hears everything they say. Above the underwater squall of her circulation their voices are clear and thin, like dead children calling. She wonders if her being on the radio—that terrible frequency—is what caused the blackout.

Later that evening she hears over her transistor radio that the whole northeastern seaboard suffered a power failure. She still wonders if it was her. By then five people have telephoned to say they caught the beginning of the broadcast. From Doris's half of the conversation Joan gathers that the last two callers are inviting her to perform somewhere. She covers her ears again at the prospect of evaporation. Too many strangers around her—too many strange, human vibrations—and she will break apart like a cloud and be the air they breathe. Wouldn't that be something! But it scares her. Not for the first time she is grateful for all the barrettes and ribbons that, she takes for granted, Marcy fastens to her head to keep it from flying apart.

From that night on she stops playing the piano when the window is open or people visit the house. She does not seek fame. She cannot afford to, she cannot ever again tape record herself playing the piano. Not that she has done so more than three times. All those stacks of tapes in the other corner of the closet, they aren't her.

Despite what her darlings presume. "You're building up a sizeable record library there," Gordon says, and she can hear the desire in his voice. How he would love for her to play him a couple of tapes!

He'll have to wait, she hasn't even played them for herself yet. One day she will, she'll summon the whole family and all of them together will listen to selections from the tapes in their entirety. When that day will be and how she will choose the selections she isn't sure. Meanwhile, the tapes are her private property.

———————

She has forty-four full tapes in four stacks and is eleven years old when she reads an article in *Maclean's* magazine about a composer named David Rayne who makes music out of recorded conversations. He does this by extracting individual words and speeding them up or slowing them down to produce the desired pitch and tempo, and then stringing the pitches together to produce a melody. On a separate tape, repeated words or phrases and sometimes entire sentences serve as a rhythm-and-bass line. For the finished product he plays the two tapes together and records that.

"It's a tricky business," says Mr. Rayne, "because all the way through the process the melody tape and the bass tape have to be perfectly synchronized with each other."

In one fast reading Joan not only grasps his technique, she imagines a way to adapt it to a composition of her own. Her heart races. She checks her wristwatch to monitor the acceleration and for a moment is absorbed by how thrilled she evidently is.

Mr. Rayne's latest record is called *Transonic Express*. Those two words ripple down Joan's spine, spiralling, a vibration echoed by the photo of "David Rayne at work in his studio." In the picture there are three upright reel-to-reel tape recorders that could be the same model as her newest one, her Philips. She looks up from the magazine and scans the closet. Maybe if she moved all her books out. No, there's more room in the basement. A long table like his, a stool . . . She studies the picture. Earphones, she'll need earphones for privacy. What else? How about she leaves that part to Gordon, who only wants her to be happy? And how about she let Sonja, "Miss Moneybags," foot the bill?

On the evenings that he is home Gordon still reads library books to her. This evening, when he comes to collect her from the closet and says, "What'll it be, Bates or Beckett?" (they alternate between two novels at time) she extends the magazine to him, folded back at the article on Mr. Rayne.

"You want me to read this?"

She nods and stands on tiptoe for a better whiff of his face. From certain things he has told her during his before-supper visits as well as from the coincidence of his body odour at those times and from reading an article about semen in *Scientific American,* she has figured out that an alcohol-bleach-armpit odour indicates he has recently ejaculated with a man, a man who (you never can tell) might be Mister Sandman. Not since Christmas has she picked up that combination of scents on Gordon. She closes her eyes and breathes it in like fresh air—that smell!—the closest she might ever get to her real father.

"Are you sure?" Gordon says.

She opens her eyes. How sure is she? Absolutely? Fairly? *Is* she sure? While the prospects strobe across her mind, she tries to elicit the faint frequency of the queer whom Gordon ejaculated with. (Occasionally, if you've touched somebody, his or her frequency will ring on your body for a while afterwards.) A hum is what she longs to hear. Over the years she has convinced herself that Mister Sandman discharges a thin, honeyed vibration exactly like the hum of the tape recorder.

No, there's nothing, but while listening for a hum she has been struck by such a good idea that she beeps.

"I'll take that as a yes," Gordon says, and they start down the hall to the basement.

She continues to beep over her idea, which is this: Mister Sandman can be in her composition after all! He can be the hum! She doesn't have to listen to the tapes to know that on all of them, in the background, is the sound of herself humming to the hum of the tape recorder. So if her humming stands in for Mister Sandman, the voices of all her darlings will be in the music!

# EIGHTEEN

I N THE SUMMER of 1968 Marcy informs her family and friends that from here on in her name is Marcia. The paranoid girl who dated fuzzy male shapes with erections she grabbed on to like a white cane, *that* was Marcy.

Marcy was a girl who unhooked her bra and writhed herself out of it faster than Houdini, then leaned forward and crossed her arms to give the impression that her breasts were as full as they had appeared to be under the padding, and to her boyfriends this was just her so swept away by passion she couldn't wait for them to fumble with the hooks. As far as she could tell, her boyfriends never figured out that her bra was padded. None of them (and this includes Chuck, the old guy) ever fondled her with the finesse that would have led her to believe they were doing comparative measurements.

*Marcia* on the other hand is no escape artist. She doesn't have to be, her life is sharper, calmer, narrower, down to a single boyfriend named Paul. Whereas Marcy only saw her boyfriends clearly from six inches away and then only in their fine-lined, follicled parts, Marcia, through her new contact lenses, sees Paul all at once and at a distance. As for wearing a padded bra, she came right out and told him she did. On their third date they decided to live together in Vancouver after high school and maybe even get married eventually, and she couldn't see hugging herself for the next fifty years to manufacture cleavage. That was one of the reasons, anyway.

Telling him wasn't easy. Confessing that she was a murderer or was dying of cancer would have been easier. Saying that she wasn't a virgin, which she did on their first date, was way easier. Breaking his heart fifteen months later, even for that she wouldn't have to smoke two joints to work up her nerve.

She smoked them sitting on the toilet, lighting one from the butt of the other. Then she sprayed some of her FDS to freshen the air. In her stupor she left the FDS can in the bathroom where Joan, who'd been waiting outside the door to empty her potty, found it and a few minutes later was caught by their mother spraying it where you were supposed to (as if an eleven-year-old recluse needed an outdoor-fresh-scented crotch). At this point Marcia happened to stagger back to the bathroom, and she was pretty stoned, but what she remembers is her mother snatching the can from Joan, reading the label and then noticing Marcia and asking in a strangely perky voice, "Is this yours?"

"No," Marcia lied without expecting to get away with it. *Who else* would a can of feminine deodorant spray belong to in this family?

But her mother said, "I guess *I* must have left it here," and gave a little laugh.

What? Her mother used FDS? Her parents still had sex? While the bathroom went into orbit Marcia braced herself in the doorway and tried to act normal. "Hey, maybe Angela left it," she joked (Angela was her mother's new best friend, a glamorous redhead divorcée who sometimes slept overnight on the living-room chesterfield when she'd had a few too many), and her mother threw her a sharp look and then dropped the can, whose slow-motion roll under the toilet produced a hollow, scraping sound that Joan made a good stab at imitating.

———

Later, around midnight. Down by the expressway in a derelict parking lot, Paul's beat-up fifty-nine Dodge convertible, its shattered seats and a hole in the floor big enough for Marcia to hang her bare foot through and caress her instep on dandelions.

They've smoked a joint. She has jerked him off (being too nervous for intercourse). She has told him. It's an aftermath of watching cars stream by on the expressway, cars becoming cars across the windshield. His left hand drums the dashboard, his right saws the bobby-pins in and out of her French-roll hairpiece. The last thing he said was "Mercy." This was back when he ejaculated, and although it's what he usually says after he comes and is, she appreciates, less a play on her name than a hangover from when he used to listen exclusively to rhythm-and-blues, she chose to interpret it as a divine message that he was in the proper, compassionate frame of mind to hear her news. (She no longer believes in God but she is like somebody who speaks a new language and dreams in the old one.) "I think you should know I wear a padded bra" is how she put it.

Now, in the long, long silence she is envisioning every conceivable outcome, from him wanting his fingernail peace necklace back (his mother's red fingernail clippings glued in a repeated peace-sign pattern onto a suede strap) to him slicing open the bra and grooving over the fibrefill. Finally she can't stand it. "Well?" she says.

"Well what?" Lazily. And then he shouts "Ahh!" as her hairpiece comes off in his hand. "Shit!" he yells and throws it out of the car.

They search for it in the sword grass and thistles. He says he thought it was a dead bird.

"Every girl I know wears a fall," she says, on the verge of tears. Two girls she knows do. But it never occurred to her that falls were deceptive, any more than false eyelashes are. God, does he think her eyelashes are *hers?* She swallows around what feels like a nest of hornets. She can see herself coming apart, she means literally, a child's fat ruthless hand plucking out her eyes, her nostrils. In kindergarten they took pipe-cleaners, buttons, wool, scraps of fabric, stuck them on potatoes and made dolls. When the potatoes started to rot they pulled the buttons and things off and returned them to a shoe box. The potatoes they set on the window ledge to watch grow mould.

"Hear birdie, birdie," Paul calls to her hairpiece. Hunched over, he sweeps his pole-vaulter arms through the grass. The grass is brownish, the margarine lights of the parking lot having bronzed the scene. *His* hair is long and blond for real. Gleaming like tin. Seeing—at that angle and in that light—a better girl than she thinks *she* is, she just gives up. "Do you want to break off with me?" she asks.

He straightens. "Huh?"

"It's okay if you don't want to go out with me any more," she says, irritated at having to repeat it.

He cocks his head this way and that. "Why wouldn't I want to go out with you?"

She unhooks her bra, wriggles out of it. "That's why," she says, flinging it at him.

He paws it off his head. "What about it?"

"It's padded, okay?"

"Yeah?" he says. "Like, so?"

It's as if she leapt out of a high-rise and landed on a soft mattress. She is alive. She stands there breathing, waiting for the relief.

Which seems to be held up by a kind of sludge. Suddenly clogging her heart, a thickening bloat where a hallelujah choir should be. She presses a hand over her heart, and the surprising sensation of her own unpadded flesh there seems to be why Paul shouts, "Hey!"

He's right, it does look like a dead bird. He holds it aloft, her bra dangling from the wrist of the same hand.

---

After that night, when they're making out, she feels free to leave her bra on or take it off, he doesn't care. If it is going to be only the two of them by themselves she can dispense with the false eyelashes. Marcia is a girl who wears a fall and contact lenses, but alone with him she doesn't *have* to. "Do your own thing," he says. He has the hair to get away with saying.

Boys at her school used to make cracks about his long hair, but even when it was calling him "Sweetie" or "Girlie" he just nodded in his easy-going, half-impressed way and after a few months some of those same boys were growing out their Beatle bangs. There's no question he's popular. Besides owning a convertible *and* a motorcycle, he's a star pole vaulter, six-foot-two and lean. As the school's first real hippy he should be an outsider. As a hippy who is also a jock, he's more like an ambassador from a place that might not be so twisted after all. A big draw for Marcia, the big initial draw, was that she hadn't grown up with him. With most of the cute boys in her class she shared a humiliating sexual history. Spitting into each other's mouths and thinking they were French kissing, to give an example. Now here was a boy from three thousand miles away. He'd never been her boyfriend, he had never ditched her, he didn't hate her, he had no reason to kick an ugly freak dog in the head and then mail her a snapshot of the corpse with "Whose Fault?" scrawled on the back.

He was nineteen. In her grade because he had failed but not in her class, so from September until May he was little more to her than a mop-like blur in the hallways. She wore her glasses only in the classroom, and then only in the manner of a lorgnette, whipping a frame up to one eye when it was imperative to see the blackboard. In May she bought contact lenses. There went her life savings. The day before she wore the contacts to school for the first time, she and her friend Pammy were about to cross the street when Paul zoomed by on his motorcycle, so close that if Pammy hadn't yanked her back onto the curb she would have been hit.

"Didn't you see him?" Pammy cried.

No, Marcia hadn't. Tomorrow she would. Standing there, squinting at his blond hair streaking afterjets, she knew who the first boy she was going to lay her twenty-twenty eyes on would be.

As she put in the lenses on the morning of that big day she had an old, slightly creepy sensation of miracle. The finger of God, not her finger, daubing her eyeballs. She walked to school gasping at every little leaf and blade of grass. When she walked up to Paul before first period his sub-atomic clarity made him seem embarrassingly vulnerable, as if she were seeing him naked through x-ray glasses. Behind her, Pammy squealed into her hands. A minute ago, when Marcia had said she was going to ask him for a ride on his motorcycle, Pammy had squealed at even the idea, the nerve.

"It's not nerve," Marcia had said.

"What is it?" Pammy said.

"I don't know. Not nerve." Instinct, she thought, although of course she couldn't tell Pammy that.

It was seven hours later smoking her first joint in a field surrounded by poplar trees and scattered with lambs that the prospect of being completely honest with a boy first entered her mind. She and Paul lay back in purple clover under little balls of white cloud that she took for the innocent thoughts of the lambs. White butterflies, like an evolution of those thoughts, flickered in the intricate distance and bloomed before her eyes, one alighting on her hand when she reached for the joint. Does life get any sweeter? Set down in this crib of trees she and Paul were pure, new beings.

There was all that, and there was his long blond wavy hair. One day years from now, looking at a photograph of the two of them, she wouldn't rule out the possibility that she confessed and then devoted herself to him alone based entirely on his resemblance to Jesus. But maybe it was only his showing up in her life when she happened to be going through a stage of flirting with truth and monogamy anyway. "I'm not a virgin," she said, starting big, and the field and sky seemed to enlarge, as if to accommodate an audience.

"Virgins are nowhere," he croaked through an inhalation.

"I'm a brain," she said. "I pretend to be barely passing, but the lowest mark I've ever had is seventy-nine percent."

"Far out," he said. "You can help me with my homework."

"I don't talk like it but I have a dirty mind."

"Far fucking out," he said, rolling her way while, with the joint between her lips, she quickly wrangled herself out of her bra.

They had sex, another distinction in that to keep her reputation on this side of slut she had never before gone all the way with a boy from her school. Two days later, moved by him cupping his hand to light a cigarette in the wind, she told him she loved him and said she had a feeling he loved her, too, and he cocked his head this way and that and then drawled, "Yeah," sealing it with a couple of slow nods.

But back up. She has loved all her boyfriends, from Dug on. Not necessarily loved who they are, who they are counts, but she is capable of overlooking no personality. Before a boy speaks to her, her heart is pretty well loaded up anyway . . . on him lounging at his desk, for instance. It doesn't take much more than that. The swoons she used to go into over boys with hands like shovels doing the fine woman's work of taking down notes while every now and then looking through the window to size up the world out there. As if he were being frisked, a boy stood with his hands pressed up against the window of the history classroom, gazing out, and he was no longer Michael, not to her, he was Beloved.

A boy named Norman she fell in love with for his hairy, Roman-centurion calves. Hair on calves and forearms can make her feel just lost. An Adam's apple can hypnotize her. She would like to ride her finger on it. How can she *not* think of his penis, bobbing up the same? There's hardly a boy alive she isn't already a bit in love with for his penis. Just the idea of a simple little penis (simple when compared to the brain, little when compared to a leg) having the power to pull the whole boy along, lug him like an ant carrying a hundred times its weight. When a boy drops her, usually for a prettier girl, she mentally kisses him off with "Al was here" (this phrase having mutated from meaning "beware" and "bruise" to expressing a state of stoic wistfulness) while consoling herself with the knowledge that there are more Beloveds where he came from. In the palm of her hand are usually two more.

Until Paul, her pattern was to have a school or public boyfriend (a boyfriend she brought home to meet her parents) and a couple of secret "back-door" boyfriends. The school boyfriend tended to be straight, a bit shy. If he tried to paw her below the waist he was apologetic to the point of wanting to smash his car into a brick wall when she shoved his hand away. The other boys she met at dances held in other schools. She met them on the Broadview bus, in stores. Last summer she picked one up at a free clinic where she pretended she was a runaway in order to qualify for the birth-control pills they were handing out.

In their cars and houses she had sex with her back-door boys. They were dangerous in that they seemed to walk a fine line, although they were usually still in school and law-abiding. A gearing-up for danger is closer to what she saw in them, some quality like that apparent in a man arranging his shoulders before striding through saloon doors. Gloomy boys also excited her, as did a look (provided that it was not directed at her) that could kill. In the same vein she was a sucker for a sneer, imagining it to be the tail of a black streak. Not once was this the case. Far from it, her back-door boys no matter how evil-eyed turned out to be a mess of soft spots. They were the ones who spent their own money to feed a bald, bony cat that collapsed into walls and went into gymnastic twitching fits. They shared a single bed with an uncle who blew apart half of his brain after first attaching balloons to his gun so that it would float away from the corpse and give the impression that somebody (namely his business partner) had murdered him. But before hearing the full story Marcia would simply see the weirdo and think, "Not again."

The boyfriend who slept with his brain-damaged uncle was Ed Oates. Both Ed and the uncle muttered out of the corners of their mouths like spies, and like a spy Ed operated a short-wave radio in his basement bedroom. When she told Ed about her other boy-friends' deranged uncles, cats, brothers, etc. and wondered what the story was here, he muttered, "You're like a short-wave radio operator up in Alaska. You're picking up the only signal that goes as far as you are."

---

What does she pick up from Paul? From the boy for whom she dropped Ed and two other Beloveds? That he was born cool and that he and Sonja are tied for the most contented people she has ever met. "Blissed out," he'll announce when he's doing nothing except standing there. She has seen him mad, though. Short blasts of rage so unexpected and out of place in the otherwise laid-back conversation she thought they were having that if she hadn't heard the swear words she would have thought there was something stuck in his windpipe. The blasts happen only when he's talking about his father.

On Paul's fifteenth birthday his father died of cirrhosis of the liver. "A small planet" is how he describes the size of his father's gut by then, and he says that what made it such a drag was that his fa-ther couldn't keep his pants up. At one time or another everybody in Paul's neighbourhood had seen his father on the street with his pants around his ankles, bawling and staggering, and "Everybody goes, poor guy." This is Paul, still mellow. "All they see," he says, "is like a pitiful lush panhandling for brain surgery in England. That was his pitch . . . he had some rare type of brain tumour. And half the cats fall for it or, hey, maybe they don't fall for it, but they dole out the bread to good old Jim who used to fix their cars. What does good old Jim do? Buys a mickey of rye, goes home and beats the crap out of my mom." Paul looks nothing but reminiscent. A shake of his head shimmies his hair before he says, "Fucking sadistic piece of human-shaped shit," in that choked, enraged growl. Returning to his normal voice he adds, "If he hadn't croaked I'd have iced his ass, man."

So half of the weirdo at *his* house is dead, and it's not as if he was anybody Paul ever loved blindly. That honour belongs to the other half. His mother.

"Call me Brandy," she tells Marcia when they meet. She sounds like a gangster. Then she has a coughing fit.

During the fit (it goes on and on) Paul leans across the corner of the kitchen table to thump her thin back between pointy shoulder blades that have their only-slightly-larger counterpart in the old-fashioned bra she's wearing. When she's down to puttering noises that might be a bitter laugh she sucks her cigarette then smacks her way through the smoke to clutch Marcia's wrist. "You're all skin and bone," she growls. Then, "Hell of a lot makeup." Again, look who's talking. False eyelashes thick as hula skirts, purple eye shadow, blood-red lipstick, orange foundation cracked on her cheeks in a brick-wall pattern.

Her eyes are Paul's, but a paler blue and filmed over. To try to drum up some friendly feeling within herself Marcia imagines the crap being beaten out of her and thinks, "Poor lady." Out loud she says, "I'm so glad to meet you."

"Are you a thingamajig?" Brandy shoots back. Her red spiky fingernails gnaw at Marcia's wrist.

"A what?" Marcia glances at Paul, who goes on beaming like a matchmaker.

"You know . . . ," Brandy says fretfully. She releases Marcia and pokes a finger through the shellac of her yellow bouffant. Way down in there she scratches. "A . . . a . . . a . . . ah, shit." She twists to glare at Paul. "A thingamahooey," she barks at him. "You know, untouched."

"A virgin," Paul offers. He helps himself to one of her cigarettes.

"A virgin!" Brandy barks at Marcia. "Are you a virgin?"

Marcia nods. She doesn't look at Paul.

Brandy's eyes narrow to slits. "Don't mess with me," she growls and slides one hand under the table.

Marcia shakes her head—no, she wouldn't mess with Brandy. When Brandy's hand comes out from under the table without a gun, Marcia starts breathing again. "So," Brandy says, "did he tell you we're a team, him and me?"

"A team?"

"We're like this." She crosses her fingers. "Where he goes, I go." She skewers back round to address Paul. "Right?"

"That's right, Brandy."

Brandy grunts and returns to giving Marcia the once-over. Put 'em up, her eyes say. Spread 'em, sister. She stubs out her cigarette and clears her throat for a spell while crumbling a corner of the yellowed newspaper that is spread all over the table. Marcia looks at Paul. Paul holds up two fingers in the peace sign. Brandy's spiky little fist nudges Marcia's forearm. "What do ya think of that?" she says.

"Of what?"

"Paul and me being a team."

"Oh!" Marcia says. "Fine. I think it's really great."

Brandy nods. A slow wise-guy-eh? nod. With a wave of her hand to include Paul, she mutters, "Go play in traffic."

"I wasn't kidding," Marcia whispers to Paul out in the hallway. What she means is, Brandy is no one that she hasn't made allowances for years ago. She means, where her boyfriends go, hasn't a Brandy usually gone with them? At least Paul's mother isn't a retard who tortures you with endless Jack Benny imitations. But what about Paul's American draft dodger friends, the three guys

Paul says they'll be sharing a commune with out in Vancouver?
Won't *they* mind him showing up with Brandy?

Marcia doesn't ask, not right away, maybe because the whole
commune–draft dodger idea still seems unreal to her. When she
does ask, by then her visions of the future keep forgetting to include him and she has reached the stage of slapping together a left-
over future that he can pick at after she's gone.

(His answer will depress her. "Are you kidding?" he'll say. "Another chick to do the cooking?" That he imagines she *can* cook she'll
find touching, that he imagines Brandy *will* cook she'll find pathetic.)

———

After knowing him a few months she realizes that not once has she
seen Brandy at the stove. Paul's the one who makes all the suppers,
alternating between broiled steak and chile. Two portions, two
plates, but only for show. Because eventually he blows the cigarette
ash off of Brandy's portion and eats that, too.

Brandy, meanwhile, goes on reading the *Toronto Star.* Sitting at
the kitchen table, she reads it start to finish, every word including
page numbers. The weekday paper can take her three days to
complete, the Saturday edition takes five. When Marcia first
meets her she is still working her way through 1966, barking out
headlines about the Watts riots and the first artificial heart.

In response to which Paul says "Bummer" or "Far out." De-
pending.

"What the hell are you talking about?" Brandy sometimes
snaps at him. "This is ancient history." And a minute later she'll
read that steak is on sale at the Dominion store and mutter that
she should pick up a couple of sirloins.

It seems that Brandy got into reading the newspaper about a
year before Paul's father died. "Hey, it's her bag," Paul says. "Keeps
her spaced out." He is prone to mentioning how spaced out she is,

"what a spaced-out lady" eventually becoming his entire contribution to any conversation about her. From his admiring tone you'd think he was talking about her cherry pies. In Marcia's opinion Brandy is more out of her mind than spaced out, but she lets it ride until Paul meets Joan and says about her that *she* is spaced out. Marcia goes rigid as sticks. "What do you mean by that?"

"Truly weird," he says.

"What do you mean?" she says again.

"Living on the outside."

"Joan doesn't live on the outside. She never leaves the house."

"I'm talking about where she's at in her head, man."

He puts his arm around her. She jerks away. "How would you know where she's at?" she says.

"It's right there." Tapping under one eye. "You can see it."

"What do you mean, you can see it!" High in her throat something flaps in a tight little circle. "Joan wears sunglasses! It was dark down there!"

"Not that dark."

"What are you saying?" she cries. "That Joan is the same as Brandy?"

His face tries that on, likes it. "They both read stuff cover to cover. Right? You said Joan reads indexes, right?"

Marcia swallows.

"Copyright page to *the* end," Paul says with relish. "That's weird, man."

It is, Marcia thinks for the first time. For the first time concerning Joan's reading habits, that is. Otherwise it isn't news to her that Joan is weird. That Joan might be a weird*o* is the black-edged telegram. She wonders . . . and here they come, popping up like Indians on the horizon—Cedric Short, Ziggy's dog, Ed's uncle, Paul's father, Brandy. That whole gang of weirdos. Gingerly, she dips Joan into the middle.

Immediately snatches her back out. Joan isn't one of them! Is she? *Is* she? In her mind she holds a salt-shaker-sized Joan just above the babble, the lolling. She takes a breath and gives the group a closer look. Are they really so awful? Tuck in a few eyeballs, straighten up that head, pull up those pants. That's it. That's better. Feeling almost chipper now, she tells herself that even in so-called perfect families there are webbed feet and kleptomaniacs, perverted gerbils, some loony genius ancestor.

She thinks this but she can't do it, she can't not draw a line. "Well, *there* the resemblance ends," she says to Paul.

"Right on," Paul says. "Two spaced-out chicks."

That he has laid eyes on Joan is an inaugural event. Of all Marcia's friends only Pammy has met Joan, and that was only the one time. None of Marcia's other boyfriends ever met her. Usually they weren't even aware that she existed.

But with Paul, for the first year anyway, the ideal of no secrets is more of a drug to Marcia than drugs. She wants him to know everything about her and her family. With a kind of thirst she hauls out the photo albums. She opens underwear drawers, her own and Sonja's. "Look!" she urges him. Always on her lips, not "love" as much as "look!" Look at her pimples, her fillings, her ear wax, the period blood on her underpants. He cranes to see. He says, "Wow." In his bed she can just lie there like a starfish, limbs outflung. Up until him, lying naked on her back like that would have been unthinkable because of how it wipes out her breasts.

(She admits to herself that getting into position for an orgasm was tricky in the old days. And as for telling her old boyfriends what she wanted them to do to her, are you crazy? If she had smoked dope back then it might have been a different story. Give her a few tokes and she'll ask for anything, say anything, there's no shutting her up. Stoned, she is convinced that marijuana might even make Joan talk. Now is as good a time as any to mention how she tried to get Joan to take a puff. Joan accepted the joint, she rolled it between her fingers, sniffed it, but no way would she hold it to her lips. "Maybe when you're a bit older," Marcia said, finding herself relieved. Joan was only eleven, after all. When she was sixteen, seventeen, who knew? Because for all that Joan digs in her tiny heels, she can change her mind like that.)

About meeting Paul she changed her mind after a whole year of mooing "No." Shutting herself in the closet and closing the door when he dropped by, despite loving the sound of his motorcycle—from far off, anyway. In fact, how Marcia knew that he was about to arrive, and arrive on his motorcycle rather than in his convertible, was that Joan would climb onto the desk and press her ear against the curtained window, and a minute later Marcia would hear the hum that could have been any motorcycle but never was and in another minute would be a roar in the driveway. By that time Joan would be back in the closet.

For a whole year Joan resists meeting the driver of that motorcycle and then, in seconds, she capitulates over a strand of his hair. It is wound round a button of Marcia's yellow cardigan, which is hanging from the closet doorknob. On her way into the closet Joan spots the strand, stares at it, frees it. Glancing up from her homework and catching this meticulous extrication, Marcia says, "That must be Paul's."

Joan reads the length of the hair like ticker tape. She switches on the penlight that is attached to her visor and strokes it with the beam.

"There's more where that came from," Marcia says. The beam hits her in the left eye. "We could bring him around," she says carefully, awning her eye with one hand. "We could feel how silky his whole head is."

Joan clicks her tongue.

"Really?" Marcia says, quietly so as not to startle her into a moo. "We're not kidding?" The beam holds steady. If Joan isn't shaking her head neither is she nodding. "Tomorrow afternoon," Marcia suggests in her softest voice. That is, she thinks it.

# NINETEEN

M OST AFTERNOONS you'll find Joan working at her editing bench down in what used to be the laundry room. The bench is a long, toddler-height table that Gordon constructed out of a door. The seat is a bar stool whose legs he amputated halfway up. He shaded the bulb and hung it from its wire about six inches above the bench, but a few weeks later, apparently because it got in her way, Joan had him remove it. By then she had purloined his high-powered penlight and fastened it with wads of masking tape to the brim of his green visor, the one he wore in the thirties when he was a proofreader. First, though, she cut and shortened the strap at the back and then sewed it together again using red thread and a perfect cross-stitch that Sonja said *she* hadn't taught her.

Strange about Joan going to so much trouble over the light considering that she hardly ever turns it on. Upstairs she occasionally does, but downstairs, except for the odd times she refers to the manual Mr. Rayne mailed to her (fifty type-written pages) she sits in virtual darkness and tracks through the tapes. Listening, stopping, rewinding, listening, stopping. Since she wears earphones and has made it clear that the tapes are her private property, nobody could swear on a Bible as to what they contain, but even Marcia takes it for granted that it must be Joan playing the piano.

Four years of playing for herself when she was alone. What else could be on them? It isn't as though her old tape recorder was ever seen out of the closet more than once or twice. It isn't as though she was capable of carrying the thing around. The family figures that what Joan did was open the closet, sit at the piano and record from across the room, and if that made for less than perfect quality it hardly matters now. Because they also figure that her aim is to pull the pieces apart, note by note, and rearrange the notes in some modern, dissonant collage inspired by the bizarre compositions of David Rayne.

Once Gordon finally appreciated why Joan was so entranced by this Rayne character, his delicate heart (already swollen and leaping over Reverend Jack Bean) started booming in his ears like cannons. All gung-ho he consulted Rayne himself about the equipment she would need, about the nuts and bolts of sound editing. In Rayne's swanky Rosedale home he listened to Rayne's records, which the old man conducted in the manner of someone trying to wave down a plane as he shouted over the music how his compositions were stories told in the language of pure, arbitrary sound.

"If you think of individual pitches as words," Gordon later explained to Doris, "then, extrapolating from that, a series of pitches is a phrase. A series of phrases, or a tune, is a sentence. And so on. Do you see what I'm driving at? What Joan might be trying to do—and Rayne is with me on this—is come up with a really sophisticated way of communicating with us. A formal language!"

Such was his enthusiasm that he found a collector to buy his bedside table (which was a twenty-year-old, two-foot-high stack of correspondence between him and a has-been author who signed up with another publishing house and became hugely famous) and used the money to have the washer-dryer removed from the laundry room and hooked up under the cellar stairs. He sprang for shag carpet, black (Joan's choice), and for the three top-of-the-line tape recorders that Rayne had recommended.

"Your heart!" Doris fretted.

He yelled, "To hell with my heart!" and carried the old door downstairs to build the editing bench. He hauled gallon paint cans. After blackening the walls and laundry tub, he suspended an oval mirror from the ceiling to hang between two of the editing machines at Joan's eye level, then he affixed a reflective silver strip along the edge of the bench so that she wouldn't bump into it. (As if she would!)

———

When Paul gets a load of the set-up—the shag, the dark, the mirror, the levitating silver band and the tiny creature in earphones and oversized cat's-eye sunglasses, her white hair blooming barrettes and ribbons, her forehead beaming a white horn—he whispers, "Oh, wow," in a reverential voice that, for Marcia, shrivels all his previous raptures.

They stand just inside the door, which was open. The instant Paul speaks, Joan spins around and whacks them with the beam.

"Joanie, this is Paul," Marcia says softly.

Joan stops the tape, then mimics the sound of that. Nails him with her ray. Marcia nudges him to go closer, and he does, stooped over and on tiptoe, bellowing, "How are ya?" With the ray in his eyes he can't see Joan flinch, but Marcia can and whispers, "Not so loud."

"Do you mind turning that thing off?" Paul rasps. Click. Done. A second identical click is Joan's fingernail tapping the earphone. Paul, always happy to join in, *says* click—"Click, click, click." It is like the end of a movie . . . the tape clicking out, the house lights coming on, a grey powder wash whose source is the rec-room windows. "Groovy operation," Paul says, bobbing his head in a half circle. Joan's head tips. As Marcia knows, she is studying his hair. "Groovy dress," Paul says.

It's a white sleeveless sailor dress with a big square collar and a criss-cross of red string at the throat. "That used to be mine," Marcia says. "When I was in kindergarten."

"No kidding," Paul says. Then, "Hey," addressing Joan. "Why aren't you humming?"

"She only hums in the closet," Marcia hisses. This wasn't a confidence but hearing him mention it, it sounds like one. "She wants to touch your hair," she says, yanking his arm. "Crouch down."

"I'm crouching, man." He holds the edge of the table and sinks into a knee bend that brings him and Joan eye to eye. She tucks her stocking feet under the stool's rung, the stool in the crux of his grasshopper thighs. "Help yourself," he says, bowing his head. "Touch away."

First she switches the penlight back on. Click. Click. Over his skull and shoulders the beam skims. Along his part it stops. A white wand there, balanced at a precarious tilt. Her arm, another white wand, she holds straight out and up in a Heil Hitler gesture, then lets it drift down until her hand touches his hair.

"Go ahead," he tells her, "muss it up." She draws strands between her fingers and studies them in the beam. She squishes her palm on the crown. "Yeah, dig in," he says. She seems to consider it but changes to stroking. Slow, gentle. As if he's a sleeping child, Marcia thinks. Then she thinks, a lover. Then, a dying man. His hair lies flat and has the grain of blond wood. Four times Joan caresses the length of it. "Feels great," he says. Instantly she stops and switches off the light.

"All done?" he says. He looks up at her. Their faces are close together, hers half the size of his. Their breathing sounds like people on respirators. She leans even closer and starts sniffing. That scrutiny Marcia knows. To witness him under it, her face prickles. Pure wordless interest—telepathically that is all she is picking up.

Ten, fifteen seconds pass. When Joan suddenly twists around in the stool Paul drops backwards onto his hands.

"That was far out," he says, standing up. "I was seeing doves and beautiful . . . oh wow, like, electric eyes."

Joan turns on the tape recorder. It's over.

"Let's go," Marcia says.

Paul raises one hand. "It was a trip," he says to Joan's back.

"Come on," Marcia says, tugging his other hand.

"So, Joanie, can I come and see you again some time?"

"Leave us alone," Marcia hisses.

"Huh?" He looks at her.

"Leave *her* alone, I mean."

No, she doesn't. She means "us." In Joan's treatment of Paul—complete absorption but only for as long as he was completely absorbing to her—Marcia has seen the blameless playing out of her own instincts. Now, pulling Paul from the room, she is seeing all the boys she has relinquished for monogamy, and a wind is blowing through her ribs.

———————

And yet another three more months go by before she takes a bus to the Village and in front of the Old Folks' Home (longhairs floating by on the sidewalk, whitehairs flopped in wheelchairs on the lawn) picks up a muscle-bound boy named Lance. Eyes that zoom, reddish curls she slips the four fingers of one hand into and wears for a second like brass knuckles. They are stoned on his cigar-sized joints. He bounces on his toes. He is shorter than she is but only every half second. He talks fast. About the war in Vietnam, about revolution, Black power. He mimes pulling the pin from a grenade and lobbing it at a police car. "Pigs!" she calls out to impress him. His gaze whistles down her torso, lassos her hip-hugger jeans. He keeps patting his shirt pocket where the lump of a real grenade might be. Isn't . . . as she learns at his parents' mansion.

On the way there, on the bus, they drop a half-tab each of acid for the moon landing. She pretends it's not her first trip. By the time they get off the bus she is a giantess holding the wee hand of a walking boy doll, and all the trees are upside-down females exposing their crotches. She and Lance go straight to the greenhouses, through the kitchen—where he grabs a jar of honey—and out the back door. It's a jungle in there, flowers going off like fireworks, trees shooting up like fountains, alive vines, exotic smells she will call spikenard and saffard and calamus, shrieks she will assign to scandalized ladies before she sees the birds. He says, "Go like this," and stretches her arms in the crucifixion pose. Her fingers brush fronds, giant green tongues. Her skin secretes crystal studs. For the symmetry and the thrill she stretches out her legs.

Stand like that and a boy might throw knives. Not this time, not him. He takes the lump out of his pocket, rips it open and sprinkles golden seeds from her shoulders to her wrists. Almost immediately aquamarine and peach-coloured birds drop onto the stamens her arms have become. The birds cling and peck like little lovers, tickling. But that's nothing. Next he leads her to torch flowers, opens the jar and dabs the inside of his lips with the honey, and from out of nowhere three tiny helicopters appear. No, hummingbirds! They are hummingbirds! They are kissing him on the mouth.

"Okay, they're revved up," he says, twisting his head away from the next bird in line. With a finger huge as a zeppelin he dabs her lips. The hummingbirds buzz near her face like flies. "They dig your lipstick," he say as the first tongue pokes into her mouth.

"Turn you on?" he says after the third bird.

It does. Why? Their tongues are just toothpicks. But it's an incredibly erotic sensation. By the last bird she is pulsing her body into the thrusts.

When it's all over he kisses her up on tiptoe. Their mouths glue together. She unzips his fly and his penis flips out, long as his legs, white as a root. On the concrete floor, on a bed of bird droppings, he pins her arms and churns up her insides. Then they go into the house and switch on a TV and watch spacemen bouncing on the moon.

———————

Nobody can say that her first time fooling around on Paul was any old roll in the hay. Her second and third times are more along that line. These are with another boy after bird boy doesn't return her phone calls. As far as she knows, neither boy has a weirdo at home, although who knows? Still, that seems to be the end of that phase. Along with her monogamy phase. And her no-secrets phase.

She doesn't out and out lie, she just doesn't tell Paul until he asks. By then, a month later, his refusal to see the clues strikes her as valiant since they must be hitting him right between the eyes. "Nowhere," she answers when he wonders where she was last night. "Some guy downtown," she explains her access to LSD. Her flesh is polka-dotted with hickeys and bruises, she reeks of smells she can't be bothered to wash off—Brute aftershave, sex strong as bad breath.

What a sultry summer that is. It isn't just her. Everybody seems to be drugged out, everybody's an exhibitionist. Her mother tie-dyes T-shirts for the whole family, wears hers without a bra so what you have is a woman whose breasts go from her throat to her crotch. Her mother bleaches her hair platinum blonde. On Saturdays in the back yard she rubs sun-tan lotion on her friend Angela's freckled thighs and back. She slips her fingers under the straps of Angela's bikini. Under the waistband. Alone in the kitchen, she sings "You Give Me Fever," and breaks out into a slow, twisty, snake-armed dance that makes Marcia scream with embarrassment. Her father grows sideburns and starts doing exercises in front of the TV before breakfast. Marcia would die before telling him that when he stride-jumps you can see the shape of his penis flapping under his pyjama bottoms. Her sister Sonja doesn't seem to notice, goes on smiling at the card table across from him. Marcia wonders, does Sonja have any idea what a penis *looks* like? And yet even with Sonja there's a moment that summer when if you didn't know her you'd think she was sitting there having an orgasm. Marcia has just come home from work and she goes into the living room and Sonja is clipping her pins at full steam but she's slid down the chair, she's flushed and moaning and her eyelids are fluttering.

"Are you all right?" Marcia says.

"Hmm?" Sonja says.

"I said, are you all right?"

"I'm a bubble," Sonja says, sitting up straight. "A bubbly, bouncing bubble."

"Are you stoned?" This would be as mind-blowing as her having an orgasm.

"How do you mean?"

Marcia stares at the shrinking circles of pink on Sonja's cheeks. When you turn off the TV you get that same implosion to a dot. "Nothing," she says, but she is entertaining the idea of Sonja as capable of broadcasting who knows what startling programs. "Forget it," she says.

"How was your day?" Sonja asks.

Marcia has a summer job typing and filing at a large employment agency in a renovated Victorian house. The boss, a stocky middle-aged man, greasy black hair, a habit of announcing himself by means of tragic sighs in the doorway, pats her bum and makes her promise never to wear a girdle. His secretary, who is also pushing fifty, and married, takes dictation with one hefty leg hoisted over the arm of her chair. The night after Marcia's first time having sex with the secretary's shy, girlish son is the night Paul asks.

They are lying naked on his bed. It is so soon after his saying "Mercy" that she hasn't spit the semen out yet. Unintentionally she swallows it and her sense is that it acts as a truth potion because before she knows it she is saying, "Yes, I have. Fairly steadily with two other guys right now. Since school ended, though, there have been four, sorry, five altogether."

He is propped up on one elbow, hair falling straight past the bed like drapes. He cocks his head this way and that as he is prone to but for what seems like hours, cocks it, shakes it as if to dislodge a response. Which, after all that, is, "I thought you were, like, too uptight about your breasts."

"I'm not any more." She looks at him, her love a motherly pang. "Thanks to you."

He frowns.

"I love you," she says. "That hasn't changed. You are still my beloved."

"Do you love any of them?"

She nods, pulling the smelly grey sheet up to her neck. She feels translucent with honesty.

"How many?"

"All of them. I wouldn't have done anything with some boy I didn't love."

"*All* four?"

"Not as much as I love you." Here come the lies, she thinks.

Down the hall in the kitchen Brandy snaps the newspaper and hacks. Never in a year and a half has she demanded to know what the two of them are doing in there.

"Man," Paul says. He reaches for his cigarettes, mouths one out of the pack and lights it. "Do I know any of these cats?"

She shakes her head. He knows one.

"Like," he says, "like, possessiveness is nowhere, man, but, man . . . "

With the tip of one finger she touches his forearm. "It doesn't mean I don't want you any more. And if *you* want to have other girlfriends, that's okay."

He glances at her. "Fuck that."

A new tone, it quivers between her legs. She rolls into him but he jolts away.

"You're not even all that pretty," he says. "You're head's too small. I hate the way you talk, like a fucking librarian. And by the way, you look like shit in your glasses."

She laughs, shocked.

"Fuck off," he says and jumps out of bed.

While he pulls on his jeans she lies there scanning herself for the wound. Not a scratch. She watches him doing up his shirt. He is stuck on one button. She thinks of his dead father and crazy mother and her heart starts ripping. Why can't she be true to him? Why can't she forsake all other gods for him, be a nun for him? "What do you want?" she asks. Whatever it is, she'll do it.

"What do I want? You want to know what I want?" His voice is unnaturally high. "I want you not to have told me you loved me. I want you never to tell anybody else you love him because you don't know what the fuck love is, man!" He's shouting. The button comes off and he pitches it at her, then lunges for her neck. "I want this—" He grabs the necklace, jerks it like a collar. She gags. He lets go. "I want you to get the fuck out of my house, you fucking slut!"

She can't take back having said she loved him, but she gives him his fingernail peace necklace, leaves his house and never tells another boy she loves him.

Though she knows what love is. Though she loves him.

# TWENTY

B ACK IN JUNE, Marcia graduated from high school second out of 197 students and won a scholarship to York University. Her parents presented her with a twenty-four-volume set of the *Encyclopaedia Britannica* in its own two-level mahogany bookcase, her father holding her shoulders and standing her back from the case for the panoramic view. "Try to read them before Joanie does," he joked. In July he cashed in a Canada Savings Bond to pay for her textbooks. But in August she tells him that she has decided to keep on working at the employment agency.

"I need a break from school," she says as he prods the ceiling tiles with his fingertips. It is a thing he does when the news is bad. Maybe one of the tiles is a magic door. He will lift her through it and angels wearing mortarboards will haul her off to the registrar's office. "Dad," she says, "I know how proud you are and everything, but I'm tired of being a student."

"You can't help being a student," he says. "You're a natural student." He pulls out a chair and sits across from her at the kitchen table. "I'm going to ask you a question. Are you on drugs?"

"Of course not!" She means, drugs have nothing to do with it.

"Well," he says. He tugs at his new sideburns, which have grown in like balls of cotton batten. "I'm sorry, but I had to ask."

When her mother finds out, her question is, "Is this because of you and Paul?"

Good idea. "I suppose," Marcia says, giving it a try. "I mean, I'm so depressed."

"Sweetie, Paul was a very interesting, very nice boy. I wasn't crazy about his hair, but that's another story. But he's not the only boy in the world! Boys are like buses. Miss one, and twenty minutes later"— she snaps her fingers—"along comes another."

Marcia bites her lips as if she isn't thinking that twenty *seconds* later is more like it. She blurts out a laugh, and her mother laughs and says, "I'm telling you! Buses!" Snap! Snap! Snap!

By playing up the heartbreak angle Marcia reconciles her parents to her taking one year off. That's what *they* think. She is never going to university. What her father doesn't know is that the "natural student" he allowed out on weeknights because she seemed to be one of those lucky people who could get straight A's without studying, that natural student did homework until two, three o'clock in the morning on the bedroom floor in the feeble wedge of light from Joan's closet, and now she's more blind than ever. What he doesn't know is that she needs a steady paycheque so that she can go on surprising her boyfriends with little gifts—cigarette cases, silk scarves, belts, gloves. There's nothing like seeing them all flustered and happy. Or stunned. Scared! Opening the box like a demolitions expert.

Keeping up the heartbroken act requires keeping her two new boyfriends secret, even the one her mother has been pushing at her since she was fifteen. Andy McPhee, the clean-cut Catholic boy who lives across the street and calls women "Ma'am," and went to St. Mike's where he was a famous quarterback known as "The Hands." Whenever he used to walk down the street in his school uniform her mother would say, "If I were thirty years younger . . ." and roll her eyes in Marcia's direction.

"How many times do I have to tell you he's going steady with

Susan Boylan," Marcia would say. Still says, although as she recently discovered that shouldn't have stopped her. "I wish Sooze would do this," he moans when she has his penis in her mouth. He holds her head between his hands and she wonders, Is he thinking of a football or when he's holding a football is he thinking of her head?

Afterwards he worries about having hurt her. He can't stop fingering the bruises on her legs and upper arms. "What kind of guy—" he mutters.

"I bruise easily," she says, but he's convinced she is protecting some thug because *he* doesn't bruise her. (That he never touches her below the head during sex she can't bring herself to point out.)

He tells her that when she was a little girl and her eyes were always swollen, his parents thought that her father was beating her up.

"I had styes!" she says. "Oh, my God, that's terrible they thought that!"

He says, "We prayed for him. Teach Mr. Canary to be a patient and gentle father."

He laughs. The laugh is over the prayer, not the praying. He still goes to mass and is always praying. Before digging into a bag of popcorn he murmurs, "For thy bounty, Jesus, I am truly grateful." Before sex he says, "Forgive me, Jesus." Before he comes it's, "Sweet Jesus!" After he comes it's fingering her bruises and saying a dozen what-kind-of-guys, if-I-get-my-hands-on-the-guys. He's such a throwback. For the wall over his bed she buys him a poster of Ursula Andress in a cave-woman get-up. She buys him a near replica of the hula-girl cocktail shaker her father used to have.

"For me?" he says, awed. "You shouldn't have." He *says* this.

He is studying physical education on a football scholarship. He lives in residence, so they have a place where they can make out, but his roommate is always barging in and there's the risk of Sooze, a nursing student, suddenly showing up. Twice they have gone to a sleazy motel on Kingston Road, Marcia's treat. It's the same motel her other boyfriend takes her to, and as she tells Andy the first time, when he balks at checking in, "You don't call your motel The Seven Year Itch if you're not catering to illicit escapades."

Her other boyfriend, Chuck, isn't really a *boy*friend. He's a married man with three daughters. Thirty-five is how old he says he is, and even if he hasn't knocked off five years she has decided she's interested only in boys around her own age. Baby-smooth skin, small tight testicles. Right out of the package, that's how she wants her boyfriends.

Chuck, though, was her first lover, and when they ran into each other again on the street (he was walking a little white poodle shaved so severely it looked like a poodle twisted together out of balloons) he begged. "For old time's sake," he said. "For me," he finally said, "do it for me," and considering that he once rescued her from what she'd been sure at the time was a lynching, she concentrated on his laugh lines and scraped up some love. Besides, he buys her lunch and is an expert at giving oral sex (he calls it "balling"), which she never would have believed of a steam-shovel operator.

Here's how she met him the first time. She was sixteen. It was mid-July, and she hadn't been able to find a summer job. Then, in a magazine that Sonja's friend, Gail, left in the bathroom, she read an article about how teens could earn extra money over the summer. "Make paper dresses and sell them door to door." "Make vinyl aprons and sell them to restaurants." Were they nuts? In comparison, "Make box lunches and sell them at factories and construction sites" sounded like such a good idea she immediately worried that every girl from her school had already thought of it. Especially since, at the end of her street, there was a construction site.

That same day she borrowed twelve dollars from Sonja and bought two loaves of white bread, three cans each of tuna and salmon, a large jar of mayonnaise, a head of lettuce, a basket of McIntosh apples and another of carrots, two ready-made apple pies, waxed paper and paper bags. The next morning her mother helped her fix the sandwiches. Twenty to start with.

"Let's cut off the crusts," her mother said. "Go that extra mile." It was her suggestion that Marcia write on the front and back of an old white shirt of her father's "Fresh Homemade Lunches. Only $1.00" and wear the shirt over her shorts and tank top.

At eleven-forty-five Marcia carted the lunches up the street in her mother's bundle buggy. The shirt came down to her knees. Her legs were bare, she wore thong sandals and her hairpiece in a French roll. A sex-kitten look except that she suspected her scrawny legs ruined it. What if the workmen laughed at her? Some of them would be foreigners. What if they hated tuna? Her stomach leapt up. "Al was here," she chanted to herself because she had been reminded of that other shirt she wrote on when she was six and because she was hearing the words in an altered and fear-quenching sense—"Al was here, Al was here"—as if an orphan named Al who sold box lunches many years ago under terrible conditions lay down his life.

The site was surrounded by a plywood wall. At the entrance she paused and squinted (this was almost two years before she bought her contact lenses). An enormous pit. Bulldozers, a steam-shovel, a long white trailer. A machine roar that buzzed down her bones, and twenty or so red-helmeted men moving like doomed shapes in a beige haze she tried to blink into focus. She walked in and along a wooden plank, stopping next to a Johnny-on-the-Spot. It seemed to her that a few of the heads turned her way. She smoothed down the front of the shirt to draw their attention to the message.

First somebody wolf-whistled. Then a short, black-haired man (no red helmet) ran toward her, socking the sky with both fists and yelling in a thick accent, "Young lady! What you doing!

Young lady! No sandwiches here!" He came right up to her, so close she was sprayed by his spit.

"I've got . . . I thought . . . ," she stammered, backing up.

"You no business!" he shouted. "No sandwiches!" She backed up, he stepped forward. "I have licence for here!" he shouted. He jabbed his chest. Jabbed in the direction of a small truck—a lunch wagon, she realized, although it was a blur. "Who you think you are, young lady?" She could see right down his throat. His teeth were corn kernels. He shouted, "This private property, young lady!" All the while she was backing along the plank and pushing her bundle buggy behind her but he kept stride like an infuriated flamenco partner.

By now the workers were gathering round, laughing, hollering at him in their language. "I call police!" the man yelled. His rage just kept soaring. "What you say, young lady?"

Nothing. She could no longer even open her mouth or she would cry.

"Leave her alone, Giovanni," a friendly, unaccented voice called.

That was all it took. Giovanni turned like a dreamer toward the voice. The workers parted like the Red Sea and another of their number, only taller, appeared.

When he looked into her face, his jowly, fatherly smile started her sobbing. As she later learned he wasn't the boss, he was only a steam-shovel operator, but he had pull. He took her into the trailer, poured her coffee in a Styrofoam cup. Gave her a twenty-dollar bill for her sandwiches and gobbled down three of them and two pieces of pie. Said, "Honey, you bake one hell of an apple pie." Patted his beer belly. Patted her knee. Patted her thigh. Locked the trailer door.

Four years later, due to a back injury, he drives a taxi. He picks her up a block away from where she works, and either they park for a dollar in an underground lot and make love in the front seat or, if he's had a lucrative morning, he forks out three bucks for half an hour at The Seven Year Itch. Some Saturdays she meets him in the ravine where he walks the dog, Perky, and while Perky keeps an eye out for passersby, they lie back in high grass.

By November she's tired of him. His assets—generosity, kindness, prowess—are lost on her, although she recognizes them and can appreciate them when he's not between her legs. It boils down to, he's too old, a close-up preview of the bodies she might be stuck with twenty years from now. Not a sight you can't get enough of. Anyway, she never was all that crazy about being on the receiving end of oral sex. Lately when he's down there flicking away, she is repulsed and anxious. What goes through her mind is that he is dead except for his tongue, which has gone into fibrillations. She fakes instant orgasms.

"One last time," he begs.

It's a Saturday. They are standing on the sidewalk at the end of her street, Perky leashing their ankles together. As it happens her parents and Sonja are spending the afternoon at a winter fair in Uxbridge where Sonja has donated a hundred of her knitted hats as free give-aways if you contribute to the local Humane Society. So, since it *will* be the last time and it's too cold to do it outside, Marcia says they can go to her house. "I've never done it in my own bed," she says, warming to the idea.

She returns home alone and uses the front door, and five minutes later Chuck and Perky arrive at the back door by way of the woods behind her yard. Perky's toenails tick across the kitchen floor to the hall. At the stairwell Chuck nudges her and points down, his eyes signalling something more than anxiety. She has told him that Joan is in the laundry room. Over the past few months she has corrected the stories (Joan was deformed, a retard) that he'd heard from his daughters. But when he points, it's as if to ask, Is that where you keep the deformed retard? and what's left of Marcia's love drops dead. She could slap his face, if she wasn't suddenly feeling so free of him that it would be like slapping a side of beef. If she wasn't feeling the superiority of her entire family to his family (his stupid daughters, his frigid wife) together with a sense of herself—which somehow exonerates him—as being no part of her family, although she'd kill for it.

"Don't worry," she says at the bedroom door. "She won't come up."

Well, she does come up. Floats up, maybe, because Perky doesn't bark until she scrapes back the piano bench.

Marcia whips the sheet over Chuck. At the foot of the bed Perky yaps and pops in and out of view like a dog on a trampoline, ears sailing.

"What the hell?" Chuck throws the sheet off again. "Shit." Back comes the sheet. Gripping it at his neck, he rolls over and shunts up to the pillow.

Joan is also yapping. An impeccable, faint echo that after a minute or two shuts Perky up. For a few seconds longer Joan stares at him. Then she turns to the keyboard and starts playing the *Goldberg Variations*.

"Get dressed," Marcia whispers.

"She's sitting on my clothes!"

"Shh."

"Shh." From Joan. Otherwise it's as if she doesn't know they are there. What's going on? It took her a year to work up the nerve to meet Paul. "Joanie?" Marcia says softly and is ignored. "Joanie, stop a second, okay?"

"How old did you say she was?" Chuck asks.

"Shh."

"Shh." The echo.

Chuck folds his arms over his chest. "This kid's unbelievable," he whispers loudly.

"I guess we'll just have to wait. She usually only plays it through once."

By the fourth variation Chuck's foot is a metronome and he's stroking Marcia's thigh. In the middle of the fifth variation he ducks under the sheet.

"Don't!" Marcia punches him.

"Ah, come on," he says. "It's like balling in front of the dog."

---

When spring arrives and her father starts pestering her about the university application she hasn't filled out yet, she decides to leave home. He's one reason. The other is needing a place where she can entertain her boyfriends. Lately, in front seats, she wants to break out, smash her foot through the windshield. The Seven Year Itch is all right, but three dollars a time adds up, and those rooms are not paradise. The water is Coke-coloured, the vibrating mattresses smoke and give you shocks.

She'd have left home before Christmas if it wasn't for Joan. The thing is, she still sleeps in Joan's bed. Should she believe it when she hears, "Go"? Never before has she doubted that the voice in her head, when she is looking straight at Joan, is other than Joan's.

"Are we sure?" Marcia says. "We won't miss us too much?" Cupping Joan's small white face in her hands. Skin cool as stone, eyes undetectable behind the dark-green lenses of her cat's-eye sunglasses. All Marcia can see is her own face. There and there. Murky and bigger-eyed, as if floated up from a mind so unselfish that whatever enters it shines back not only improved but twice.

She goes to see about a furnished basement apartment in a house on St. George Street. The landlord is a middle-aged Italian thug named Danny Vitalis who says, "Anybody give you any trouble, I'm here day and night." "Here" is directly above the apartment in a living room of beer-case high-rises and at least ten framed photos of a younger him as a boxer.

"Pretty girl like you," he says, "don't need no creeps hanging around. Nice guys, why not? I got no problem with that. You're young. Live it up."

It's as if he knows her.

There is only a fridge, stove, card table and two rickety wooden chairs, but when her parents finally accept that there's no changing her mind, they ply her with furniture and small appliances. All Grandma Gayler's worldly goods—the maroon wing-backed chair and mouldy carpet and brocade drapes that smell like broccoli, her dresser, her bed with the huge picture of Queen Victoria's head glued onto the headboard, her silverware with the engraved "G" that Marcia used to think stood for "Grandma," her hand-embroidered pillowcases and linen towels, her rusty electric kettle, her electric clock whose face is Queen Elizabeth's, her rusty toaster whose sides open so you can turn the bread, her dented pots and pans. With some ceremony her mother gives her the set of china that used to belong to Grandma Canary. "These were *hers?*" Marcia says. Who would ever think to connect the dainty rosebud pattern with the Battle-axe, as Marcia's mother affectionately refers to the insane-eyed old woman in the photo albums?

As for Marcia's own possessions there are only books and clothes. And her dolls. She looks at the dolls lined up along her bed, pink and frilly, leaning into each other like drunken débutantes. She sees them through the eyes of her boyfriends and says that she's throwing them out.

"Oh, no!" her mother cries. "You've kept them all these years. You'll want to give them to your own daughters one day."

Her own daughters. Marcia thinks about that. The balloon heads of newborns come to mind but burst when she tries to concentrate on them. She looks at her mother and draws back a little because her mother's rabid expression makes her feel like a tube at the other end of which are priceless granddaughters. For the first time Marcia realizes that since Sonja and Joan will probably never have kids, it's up to her or the Canarys will die out. This particular line of them, anyway. They'll be like one of those disappeared countries on old maps.

"Save them," says her mother.

Marcia picks up Little Lovely and puts her upside down in the bag of garbage. A small, pained sound from her mother. "I'm twenty years old," Marcia says. "It's sick that I even still have them." Her throat tightens. "They're *my* dolls," she says angrily. "I'll throw them out if I want to." She snatches them by their heads, by their white shoes. Their rigid limbs graze her wrist as she shoves them down into the bag. A hand rips through, fingers splayed. That's Betsy Wetsy. Her mother sighs and leaves the room. Marcia grabs another bag, tosses in the last three dolls. Out the top, Cindy the Mardi Gras Doll towers, one eyelid stuck shut but she's waving. She's smiling. Marcia takes the bags outside and drops them in the pails. Thunder.

It isn't until the next day when the garbage men have emptied the pails that Marcia's mother says, "Oh, we should have given them to the Salvation Army."

For the move, her father borrows a delivery truck from work. All that morning they load the furniture, Sonja lifting the heaviest pieces, saying "Upsadaisy" as she singlehandedly hoists the solid-oak dresser (to spare her father, his bad heart).

"We'll miss you around here," her father says.

"I'll be home every Sunday," Marcia reminds him. He tugs at his sideburns. "Dad," she says, "I'm doing the right thing."

And he says in a slightly puzzled tone, as if testing this out, seeing if it fits the occasion—"For the children of this world are in their generation wiser than the children of light."

"Honestly," she says, exasperated. She has been through her religious phase.

So has he, forty years ago, and now he's in another. A strange, half-hearted one, it seems to her. He goes to church and is taking private Bible-study classes with Reverend Bean, her old minister, but he confesses that he doesn't pray and doesn't believe in God. "I'm still feeling it out," he says. "Keeping an open mind."

Well, it's his life. None of her business now that she's leaving home and won't have to listen to his quotations from the Bible. They get to her, she hates to admit. It's like hearing him read from her old love letters. It's like being forced to remember what she saw in the guy who wrote them.

---

She adopts a split personality. One for day, one for night. Day is longer skirts and her glasses. Hardly any make-up. Day is the serious young career woman she now half is. She is accustomed to working hard, standing first. She tells her boss that she would like to go places in the company, and he says he'll tell her what—as a reward for not wearing a girdle, she is promoted effective immediately to overseeing typing and I.Q. tests to job applicants. So now she sets a timer and says, "Go."

In November she is given a raise of thirty-five dollars a week, the better to spoil her boyfriends with. First, though, she buys herself a red leather mini-skirt to wear at the Corral, which is a student nightclub decorated to look like a barn. Boys straddle hobby horses and chew pieces of hay. Watch her squint-eyed. Night is padded bras and hairpieces and black false eyelashes. It has taken her years but she has finally figured out that, for boys, the illusion lasts even after it is strewn all over the bedroom. The next morning is when they snap out of it. Opening his eyes and seeing her standing at the foot of the bed dressed for work, one boy asked where Marcia was. "In the hospital," Marcia said. "Her appendix burst but she said not to wake you."

She still finds three boyfriends the optimum number. Three at a time. When she loses one, inevitably there is a stretch of one-night stands before the position is filled. That's right, "position."

She tests them, sets the timer, in a manner of speaking. A boy who can't get or keep an erection is out of the running. So are boys who want to marry her, want to have her all for themselves. Boys who are mean to her or start acting weird she doesn't give time to get dressed. When a farm boy slapped his belt on the palm of his hand and said he'd "sure like to thrash her little backside," she didn't care if he was joking, she shouted, "Danny!" up through the grate, and her Italian thug landlord bellowed, "Yeah?" and the boy was hopping across the floor into his cowboy boots.

If Danny thinks she's a hooker, he doesn't say so. If he's attracted to her, he doesn't show it. "Anybody give you any trouble . . . " is his sole hallway greeting, whether she's alone or not. She tells Pammy that he's her guardian angel. "The kind God sends when you stop believing in Him."

"What kind is that?" Pammy asks.

"Hairy."

Pammy looks up at the ceiling. "I couldn't sleep at night if I were you."

"If you were me, you'd have better things to do than sleep."

"Oh, don't talk like that!" says Pammy. Who was shocked enough to learn that Marcia wasn't a virgin. Who—and this is why Marcia stays friends with her—is just as shocked that she herself still is.

Pammy comes by Sunday mornings to vacuum the apartment and do the laundry, gasping at hardened balls of Kleenex between the sheets and at marijuana butts in the ashtray. These regular gasps give Marcia the impression that her place is being ventilated by uprightness, so who needs church? Meanwhile, at the kitchen table, Marcia rewrites Pammy's essays for her courses in twentieth-century American literature and the Romantic poets. Sunday afternoons she takes the subway to the Broadview station where her father picks her up in the car. He is the only man she knows who feasts on her mousy daytime appearance.

"You're looking well," he says enthusiastically.

"So are you," she says, but how he really looks is different. More different each week.

They all do, except for Joan. Joan, who is going to be fifteen, who of all of them should be changing, is frozen in a six-year-old's body. That isn't even it, though, not what Marcia is talking about when she says to Joan, "We haven't changed a bit." The Joan before her eyes is the Joan who has been in her mind all week . . . all Marcia's life, it seems. Like the kitchen clock, and the tin plates with the deep blue rim, Joan is a surprise because there she is—the same! Or maybe not even the same, just *recognizable*.

Her parents and Sonja mutate compared. Every Sunday they are taller, shorter, fatter, louder, smarter, dumber than the previous Sunday. What were they like before she left? She can't remember. Who are they, the elder inhabitants of this house, which itself is a foreign country she feels like a refugee from? She never noticed when she was living here that as soon as you walk through the front door there is a potato odour. It didn't used to bother her that no matter what they are having for supper her mother puts a plate of white sliced bread on the table. There are coat-hanger ducks on the kitchen wall. In the living room there's a footstool made out of old manuscripts. Get her out of here!

When her father drives her back to the subway she is anxious in case for some reason they don't make it—the car breaks down, or he does. The car reeks of turkey or ham from the mammoth doggy bag her mother pushed at her. Nothing is so primitive as that warm, smelly lump in her lap. As is the custom of these backward but kindly people, they have presented her with a goat's head. A pregnant sow's uterus. She will stuff it into a wastebin on the subway platform.

Months go by. A year, and another year. Joan turns seventeen and her school lessons with Doris and Gordon end. Doris says she has a feeling she never taught that kid a single thing she didn't already know. "Who's kidding who?" she asks Joan. She gets a part-time job at her friend Angela's lingerie shop on the Danforth, so now Joan spends whole days in the laundry room or "her office" as Gordon started calling it after he moved her books and magazines down there.

The whole family has given up wondering when she will finish her composition. Into everyone's subconscious a constant, irregular clicking has long since been absorbed to the extent that it is indistinguishable from dead silence. The clicking travels up the cold-air ducts. It is Joan starting and stopping tape and it is her echo of each click. If you are Sonja and sitting next to the duct directly above the editing bench, it is the sound of your knitting needles slowed down, paused over. It is no sound you register except on the level at which you know that the world is good and a click means "yes."

These days Sonja knits for a living. In 1970 when Schropps brought in automatic clippers she phoned a man who had once offered to sell some of her hats and scarves to department stores, and for what she can turn out in a week that man now pays her more than Marcia earns after tax, although Marcia has been promoted to manager and has her own secretary.

Sonja stashes her money away. Marcia spends hers. Not just on clothes but on books (her ambition being to read all the classics from Austin to Zola), china dishes, good sheets and towels, trinkets for her boyfriends. She eats out in restaurants that have linen napkins and wine lists and she has moved from living under Danny Vitalis to living above him in a two-bedroom apartment he renovated himself.

"Okay," he warned before showing her the place, "this is class." And she walked into a room that was wall-to-wall red shag carpet

("Hundred percent synthetic," Danny bragged), red velvet wall-paper and a chandelier you had to claw your way through.

The red shag is everywhere, including the bathroom, which has gold faucets, not real ("You kidding me?"), and a mirror on the ceiling above the bathtub. Along an entire wall in the master bedroom is a fake fireplace made of fake marble. You turn a knob and the plastic logs in the grate glow red. The opposite wall is a mirror.

"For you," Danny said, "I'll drop the rent to two ten." She was touched. "Girl like you," he said, "professional girl, needs a place that says, Hey, I don't need nobody."

Again, it was as if he knew her.

She didn't rent it just to spare his feelings or because she wanted to stay in his house. Or to pretend she was in Las Vegas. She *decided* to fall for it and then did (as she occasionally falls for a type of snake-hipped boy who dresses like a pimp, letting herself be persuaded by his version of who he is, since her version will get them nowhere). Her one-night stands say, "You live *here?*" and screech to a stop at the threshold, but after sex, lying naked in the blush of the plastic logs, they lounge like Hugh Hefner. There are sweet boys who see the place through Danny's eyes and are afraid to touch anything, and they are worth all the static-electric shocks the carpet can throw at her.

Her one-night stands fill the position of the third boyfriend. She always assumed that the position would be permanent short-term, but it didn't turn out that way and now she's glad. She runs into a gorgeous boy on the street, on the bus, and if he is game she brings him home. This happens five, six times a year. Mostly she is content with her two regular boyfriends, who come around on al-ternate nights and know about each other. Like her, they are con-stantly falling in love. The last thing they are is jealous. When she raves about the beauty of some other boy's body, they seem to take it as a personal compliment. They kiss her, softly. She thinks she knows how they feel. When they go on about another girl's heart-shaped ass or big brown nipples, she doesn't get mad. She is fascinated and often aroused, but the prevailing feeling is of being appreciated. If they love girls of all shapes and size, doesn't that include her?

Outwardly her two boyfriends have nothing in common with each other. One is tall, lean, dark-haired, doe-eyed, thoughtful. He is studying radio and television arts. The other is her height, muscular, witty, and has fuzzy blond hair, which is actually straight but when she met him he'd just got a permanent. He works at his father's shoe store. Both boys are always broke, so she picks up the tab when they go out. She is starting to know wines, and can advise them. "A white Bordeaux is nice with trout." She lends them books by authors she thinks they should like—Durrell and Greene, Kerouac. The dark one handles her books as he does her breasts—as breakable and priceless items he can't believe she just leaves lying around—and he returns them read. The blond one skims. Returns them, *if* he returns them, battered.

At midnight she goes to bed alone. Not long after moving to the third floor she discovered that she sleeps better in a room by herself. Midnight is closing time for her one-night stands, too, no matter how much fun she's having. Some boys she has to push out the door and they thrust a foot back in like travelling salesmen. She turns the lock, switches off the light and goes to the dining-room window, listening to them descend the stairs. If it's the dark boy, it could be a cat burglar. The blond boy, and the one-night stands who resent leaving, explode down, shaking the house. Only the dark boy never slams the front door. Then three to five seconds and they're on the sidewalk. From this window, if they're headed for the subway, she can watch them all the way to Bloor Street. She loves them so much! There they go. Away. "Don't look back," she thinks. They never do.

# TWENTY-ONE

A T AROUND eleven o'clock on the morning of Tuesday, July thirtieth, 1974, Joan turns off the two tape recorders. Half an hour later she removes her visor and goes upstairs and into her closet. It takes another half hour for Sonja to subconsciously register the silence, and when she does she feels dread. But dread is so unfamiliar to her that she mistakes it for hunger, and she pours peanuts straight from the jar into her mouth. That doesn't help. The sensation is hollow and electrical, chasing through her in little light-bulb bursts. Down her left side, down her left leg to her feet, up the other leg.

"What in the world?" she says and stops knitting. She feels like a movie marquee.

She stands. Falls back into the chair, heart banging. "Oh, I'm having a heart attack," she thinks, almost relieved. She pats her chest, absently, aware of something else now. Not inside *her*, inside the house, like a bad man. "Joanie," she thinks, and her whole body lights up, panicked. She stands again, knocking over the chair as she did when her water broke (the only other time she felt anything close to this). She hurries down to the landing. "Joanie!" she calls, and just like that other time her voice is a neigh and yelling won't help. Holding the railing with both hands she goes down the stairs. As she never did when she was in labour she takes deep breaths. "Joanie!" Not a sound from below. Not a click.

She is barrelling back up to the landing when the front door opens. It is Doris, home from the shop to make them lunch. "Joanie isn't in her office!" Sonja cries.

"So?" Doris says, but she hurries after her.

Joan is lying on her back, hands crossed over her chest. Remembering the episode in Grandma Gayler's casket, Sonja drops to her knees with a thud that slams a window. She pushes up Joan's sunglasses. Joan's eyes are open and focused but she didn't flinch at either the thud or the slam and she doesn't flinch when Sonja's relieved sigh wafts her hair.

"Go in," Doris says, giving Sonja a shove. They are both huffing like trains. Sonja crawls around to Joan's other side. Doris feels Joan's forehead. "She's cool," she says, although she can't really tell. It's hot in here and her own hand is burning. Joan squints, and Doris puts the sunglasses back over her eyes.

"Bunny, you took your visor off," Sonja says. She moves Joan's hands down to her sides. That's better.

"Were you having a nap?" Doris asks, disturbed to be putting this question to a person who never naps. She thinks of the ailments Joan has escaped—measles, chicken pox, mumps, the flu. This is a kid who doesn't even catch colds. Physically she's a late bloomer (you can say that again), so it's a long shot but maybe she is finally starting to come down with one of those childhood viruses. Except who would she have picked it up from?

"How about a cup of tomato soup?" Doris asks.

Tomato soup usually elicits a few gobbles. Not this time.

"What if I bring it in here?" Doris says. "Would you like that?" Nothing.

"Joanie?" She claps her hands.

"Mommy," Sonja whimpers. Never has Joan not imitated a clap.

Forget Dr. Ackerman, he'll say warm her fanny. Doris calls

instead the lesbian doctor Angela goes to and praises as being down to earth and humble. Dr. Amelia Shack. Who over the phone says that a few years ago she read an article about Joan in a medical journal. "She's never sick," Doris says, and Dr. Shack says yes, that was in the article.

She arrives within half an hour. Living up to her reputation, she doesn't object to crouching in the sweltering closet. When she has finished her examination Doris tells her about the pediatric endocrinologist saying that Joan might not live to see her twentieth birthday if she were some rare kind of dwarf. "An ateliotic dwarf," Dr. Shack clarifies, but shakes her head and says no, there aren't any signs of crisis along those lines. There aren't any signs of anything out of the ordinary. What about a cold coming on? Doris asks. Her first cold? Or maybe the flu? Dr. Shack shrugs. "Her temperature's on the low side," she says. All she can recommend is that if Joan is the same tomorrow, they should phone her. And to give her lots of fluids.

Doris reheats the soup that went untouched at noon. She props Joan up on pillows and nudges the spoon between her lips. It's like trying to feed a groggy baby, soup dribbling down her chin. "Oh, Sweetie, what's wrong?" she says, frightened. She places the palm of her hand on the top of Joan's head, over two pink-bow barrettes. Eighteen years too late she still feels as if this spot needs protecting. "What's wrong?" she whispers. Yes, she is the one who is always saying that telepathy is for the birds, but since her hand is there anyway she may as well see if she can pick up a message.

She can't. According to Marcia (who has been summoned from work by Sonja), that's because Joan has switched herself off. In her expensive grey linen pant suit Marcia lies in the closet alongside Joan and thinks, "What's the matter? Tell us. Please. Please." Last night she had a horrible dream about Joan shrinking to the size of a mouse and people almost stepping on her.

"What does she say?" Doris asks.

Marcia comes up on one elbow. Her mother's faith in her ability to read Joan's mind is scaring her as much as anything. "This has never happened before," she says. "I always hear her, even if it's not in words. But there's nothing. It's like she's not there."

Then Gordon comes home and tells them to calm down. As the only one who hasn't had a premonition, he isn't spooked to start with. "I have a feeling she's meditating," he says after taking a look at her. "A couple of days ago she was reading an article on Gandhi. She's probably fasting as well. Why don't we all just leave her alone for a few hours."

So they do. They eat Kraft Dinner in front of the TV and watch the six-o'clock news. The lead story is that it looks as though Nixon is going to be impeached.

"I hope he is," Doris says. "A liar that bad doesn't deserve to be president."

At eight o'clock, when Marcia goes to check on Joan, she has wet her pants. Still lying on her back, she has soaked the carpet. And she won't budge. Sonja lifts her, a dead weight, onto the bed, and then Gordon leaves the room while Sonja, Marcia and Doris clean her up.

"I can't believe this," Marcia says, tugging the soiled pink shorts down Joan's legs.

"She was toilet trained at eighteen months!" Doris says, near tears.

"Oh, she's like a baby!" Sonja whispers, because Marcia has just pulled down Joan's underpants, and Sonja is shocked to see that Joan still has no pubic hair.

Nobody gets much sleep. Marcia, staying overnight in Joan's bed, gets none. "What's the matter?" she starts out thinking, but that changes to "Why are we doing this?" Nothing is coming through to her other than the feeling that Joan could snap out of it if she wanted to. "Little brat!" Marcia finally says. She shakes her by the shoulders, then starts crying at how her head flops around. Near dawn she pries open her lips and pours the apple juice in. To hell with it spilling all over the sheets. Joan chokes, but when Marcia clamps a hand over her mouth and pushes her head back, she has no alternative except to swallow. "Just try dying of thirst," Marcia mutters, and one of them—she can't tell if it's her or Joan—is awed by how vicious she sounds. "Just try."

At eight-thirty in the morning Doris reaches Dr. Shack at her office. "Get her to Toronto General Emergency," Dr. Shack says. "I'll meet you there."

---

She tests normal. Blood, urine, x-rays, electrocardiogram. Dr. Shack admits her anyway, for observation. "You can say goodbye to her," she says, "then I'm afraid you'll all have to leave until visiting hours. We'll call you if anything changes."

What's she doing with her sunglasses on? And her barrettes back in her hair? Dr. Shack said that these were removed in Emergency. "No, nobody helped us," a nurse says in a childish singsong. "We must have done it all by ourself!"

"We happen to be almost eighteen years old," Marcia says coldly, unaware that she herself is using the plural. "So," she says to Joan. "We *can* move. We knew it."

"Do you think it *is* psychosomatic?" Gordon asks Dr. Shack.

"I can't tell you what it is. We'll have a clearer picture by the end of the week."

"The end of the week!" Doris cries. "I was thinking she'd only be in overnight!"

"Bye-bye, Bunny," Sonja says. She pulls the one flimsy blanket over Joan and tucks her in. She wants to go. She has just remembered Hen Bowden saying that white-haired people don't live very long, and she is feeling like a marquee again. What was the white-haired waitress's name? She has forgotten. "Joanie was Alice," she chants to herself. In case thinking about that waitress is a Sign. "Joanie was Alice"—all the way to the parking lot.

In the car she pulls her needles and a ball of moss green angora wool out of her purse and starts knitting Joan a warm blanket. Nobody takes her bet that she can finish it before tonight. Gordon drives Marcia to her office, then drops Sonja and Doris off at home before turning around and driving back downtown.

It's one-thirty. Too late for Doris to go to the shop. She slaps together three peanut butter and jam sandwiches for Sonja (she herself couldn't eat a thing) then does laundry. She decides that what she'll do with the soiled carpet in the closet is pull it up and hose it down outside, on the lawn.

The urine has dried but there's a stain. Where the books were, the nap has flattened hard as burlap. She's glad the books are gone, it makes her job a heck of a lot easier. Only the old transistor radio left . . . the pillows, the blanket, a hundred dust balls. And the pitch pipe! So that's where it got to. Oh, and here's a piece of chalk, a blue barrette. She tosses everything out into the bedroom and yanks up one end of the carpet.

What's this? Something tucked away. She unrolls it. A shirt, one of Gordon's it looks like. Writing on the back. Faded, the first and third letters all but gone. "HLL," she makes them out as. She thinks for a minute, reads the message out loud: "HLL WAS HERE."

HLL? Harmony La Londe? "What the Sam Hill?" she says.

Who wrote it? Not Joan, that's for sure. It must have been Marcia. Why, though? Well, Joan used to love to touch the embossed initials on Harmony's envelopes. So maybe Joan got Marcia to write out the letters. But why on a shirt? Now this doesn't make sense either: the "was here." Harmony was never here. And what's the shirt doing under the carpet in the first place?

A sob jumps into her throat. She shuts the door so that Sonja won't hear. "Please, God," she sobs, "I'm sorry I don't believe in

You. Don't take it out on Joanie. I'm sorry I stopped writing Harmony. If I broke her heart, I'm sorry. I'm sorry. I'm bad, I know. Kill *me*. Take *me*. Torture me first. Give me incurable cancer. But don't . . . don't . . . " She can't even think it.

She decides not to hose the carpet down after all. If there's no smell, why bother? She rolls the shirt up and puts it back where it was. She'll have to remember to ask Marcia about it.

But she forgets. Marcia arrives at the hospital an hour after the rest of them and starts crying to see Joan hooked up on intravenous. "It hurts," she says, holding out a bouquet of miniature pink carnations for Doris to take care of. "Oh, God!" she says, and stops crying. She swipes at her tears. "I got that from Joan!" She bends over Joan and raises the sunglasses. "What else?" she thinks. Joan closes her eyes. Her eyelids seem to have gone transparent, like a fly's wings. "What's the matter?" Marcia thinks.

Nothing. Only that it hurts.

Marcia looks at her father. "Does she have to have it?"

"She's still refusing liquids, honey." Out in the corridor a supper cart crashes by and he goes to the door and shuts it. One blessing of the day is that they were able to move Joan into a private room because of his company's insurance plan.

"I mean, is she trying to commit suicide?" Marcia cries.

"Marcia!" her mother says sharply from the bathroom.

"She hasn't pulled it out," Gordon says, referring to the i.v. "If she could, she hasn't."

"You know when she climbed in Grandma Gayler's coffin?" Marcia says. "Well, what if she has a death wish?"

"That's enough!" Doris cries.

Marcia rubs her eyes under her glasses. Sits on the edge of the bed and startles at the erotic softness of the angora against the back of her legs. As though somebody made a pass. She just now notices that it is still being knitted. It covers Joan, but Sonja is leaning forward in her chair at the foot of the bed and adding on more rows. Marcia sneaks a finger into Joan's hand. "Squeeze," she thinks, and remembers wishing for the same miracle from her dolls. "Is she any better?" she asks.

Gordon tugs his sideburns. "No worse. They did some more blood tests and they came back normal."

"Who would have thought she had normal blood?" Marcia says.

For three days that's how it goes. No better, no worse, no fight, no movement. Specialists are consulted and order yet more blood tests. Before Joan was admitted, she was already a well-known case in medical circles—the girl whose retarded physical development no syndrome could definitely account for. The pint-sized idiot savant. Now she seems to be attracting every white coat in the city, mostly useless curiosity-seekers or self-serving researchers, Gordon suspects, but how can he speak up when there's a chance that one of them might help her? Each leaves his mark on her inner arm. Arms scarcely wider than the i.v. tube, you'd think a needle would splinter them. Was she always this thin? Well, you can't tell Gordon she was always this white. It's not her regular bone pallor, it's like icing, like a glaze.

"She's trying to turn herself into a doll," Marcia says after an hour of staring at her and not getting through and then going outside to smoke a joint and coming back to stare at her for another hour.

"Is that what she says?" Doris asks. She is clipping Joan's toenails.

"She isn't saying anything. *I'm* saying. I shouldn't have thrown out my dolls."

"I agree with you there," Doris says. "But that has nothing to do with this."

"It does. I'm not sure what, it just does."

"For crying out loud!" (No flinch from Joan. They all glance at her to see.) Doris drops the nail clipper into her purse and whips the blanket over Joan's feet. She stands, rapidly tucks the blanket in, goes to the table and starts rearranging the mess there. "You sound like you've lost your marbles," she hisses at Marcia. With a sleight-of-hand speediness she moves around two drinking glasses and a "Get Well Soon" coffee mug.

"You still think she's doing this to herself?" Gordon asks Marcia. He pats her shoulder. He can see how Doris has hurt her feelings.

"I *know* she is," Marcia says.

A nurse comes into the room, but before she can speak, Doris says, "I don't want to hear that! I don't want to hear how she's doing this to herself! I feel like I'm in *The Exorcist,* for pete's sake! Everybody getting the heebie-jeebies and . . . and . . . peeing on the carpet!"

The nurse laughs. A nervous titter. (You can hardly blame her for supposing she is meant to, the way Doris, when she's this angry, sounds thrilled to death, but since that is out of the question the nurse's next guess would be that she is an overwrought mother trying hard to keep everybody's spirits up.)

That titter sticks with Marcia like a finger strumming the frets of her brain. The whole drive home in the car she is tortured by it. "This is awful," she says, clutching her head. No one asks, What is? Sonja, though, gives her the ball of wool to hold and that helps.

————

For the time being, Marcia has moved back home. In her own bed she thrashes and itches. In Joan's bed she falls into eight-hour comas. Wakes from them drugged, wondering where she is, where Joan is. Before she remembers, she can sense the bad news gathering outside the shattering crystal of her unconsciousness, and some salvation being extended, like a voice calling "Here!" or a rope dangling, but she is never quick enough.

Her boyfriends phone her at work and offer to distract her. She says, "I can't make love when I'm worried sick." Until now she didn't know this about herself. She didn't know that she still believed in God, but she must because she's praying. The whole family is, secretly, and coincidentally working the same angle—"Don't make Joan suffer for my sins, my unbelief. Punish *me*." They try to make deals. They say they will gladly give up their own lives, their love lives even.

Sonja, not having a love life, has already sacrificed half of her income. Until Joan is out of the hospital she is devoting afternoons and evenings to knitting receiving blankets for the maternity ward. Every night, as soon as she gets home from the hospital, she starts on another. Marcia lies on the chesterfield and holds the ball of white wool. The tug feels good, she says. "Like fishing."

"When did you go fishing?" Gordon asks.

"I didn't."

An exchange without looking at each other. They are concentrating on the TV, they have become TV addicts—her because every show is mind-blowingly incomprehensible, him because simple truths seem to be forthcoming by the minute and he feels that all these years he has been short-changing the medium. News bulletins about Watergate interrupt regular programming. "I am the only one in this room who really knows whether I am guilty or not guilty," says John Ehrlichman, and to Gordon he sounds like King Solomon.

Only Doris moves around, but that's Doris. She opens all the windows. She closes them all. Brings in glasses of beer and Coke, answers the phone. Sometimes she sits with a pile of magazines on her lap, tearing through them for coupons, but this lasts maybe a quarter of an hour. She tears through the photo albums. Except for baby pictures there are no pictures where Joan isn't covering her face or doesn't have her back turned. And yet Doris seems to remember a recent picture of her staring into the camera, and so she pores through the albums looking for it. Five minutes of that and she rushes outside to fill the bird feeder or trim the hedge. Rushes back in to make popcorn. You get the idea. Nobody says, "Relax." She is life carrying on, twitchy and off-kilter as you would expect life to be under the circumstances.

On Saturdays and Sundays they visit Joan twice, once in the afternoon and again in the early evening. Doris says that the prices in the hospital cafeteria are highway robbery, so after the first visit they return home for supper, and while the left-overs are heating up, Gordon goes downstairs to Joan's office. He doesn't intend to, he is suddenly there, opening the door.

Stooped over, just inside, he waits for his eyes to adjust to the dim light. He sees the reflecting silver strip along the bench, and the white-spined books on the shelves. He built these shelves. There are four on the west wall, five on the east, the lowest ones just off the ground and the highest a little taller than she is. He spent an entire Saturday afternoon arranging the books alphabetically and in subject order, but that same night Joan rearranged them in order of colour, a spectrum going from white to off-white to beige, brown, orange, red, purple and so on to black. White and black spines in opposite corners.

He limps to the stool and sits. Way down. He rubs the thigh of his bad leg. On each side of the bench, in two neat piles, are what he presumes must be the original tapes. Unlabelled, it goes without saying. How does she keep track of what's on them? he wonders. And why this tidiness, everything put away, as if she was finished here? Maybe Marcia is right, not necessarily about Joan willing herself into a coma-like state but about knowing it was going to happen. Jack once told him about an elderly parishioner of his, healthy as a horse, who matter-of-factly said, "I'm going to kick the bucket next week, better get another fellow to pass the plate," and the following Saturday night he died in his sleep.

"Jesus," Gordon says to have thought of that. And then he is crying in the dry-eyed, gasping way he has been doing all week. A sudden fit of panting followed by long exhalations, long sheets of breath as though he is blowing up a balloon.

When it's over, he feels nothing, not even drained. He looks around. The visor is on top of the tapes, and he picks it up and turns on the penlight to check the batteries. He sweeps the beam over the bench, over David Rayne's notes, over his own haggard, bewildered-looking face in the mirror, over a jar of pens and pencils, a bottle of rubber cement and, right in front of him, two more tapes still in their boxes.

Hold it right there. These tapes *are* labelled—"tape 1" and "tape 2" typed on a strip of white paper and glued to the boxes. At the bottom of the tape 1 box it says, "finished composition" and under that, "ready to play." He turns the boxes over, and on the tape 1 box a typed paragraph says, "On two different tape recorders (of course!) play the A sides of tape 1 and tape 2 at slow speeds and simultaneously, ensuring that the tape counters are in perfect synchronization with each other. At the end of the A sides, turn the tapes over and play the B sides likewise."

His heart starts hopping up and down. He shines the light on Rayne's notes, back to the tape 1 box, comparing the typefaces. He leafs through the notes, and there it is—where she cut out the words "tape 1" and "tape 2." He keeps turning pages and finds where the words "finished composition" came from. A few pages later is the hole that was the entire how-to-play-the-tapes paragraph.

It's not handwriting, it's not even *her* typing, but she selected the words from Rayne's notes and cut them out and glued them to the boxes, and that makes it written communication. Her first written communication. No matter what she has produced on the tapes themselves, *this* is a breakthrough.

He sits there for a minute waiting for his heart to stop jumping around. "Watch ye therefore: for ye know not when the master of the house cometh," he thinks. No. "We have seen strange things today." He is trying to come up with the right passage to fit the breakthrough, or at least his discovery of the breakthrough. There was a time he did this to impress Jack. Since Joan has been in the hospital he can feel himself doing it as penance for appealing to a God he doesn't even believe in. And, yes, to soften Him up. How many atheists have over a hundred New Testament verses under their belts?

"That they may see your good works . . . " No. He picks up the tapes. Switches off the penlight. "They were filled with madness . . . " No.

# TWENTY-TWO

THE TAPE RECORDERS are on the floor in front of the TV, their counters turning from one to two. It is four hours later. "We found the tapes," Marcia told Joan when they went to see her after supper. "We're going to play them as soon as we get back. We're going to have a concert." Marcia claims that Joan clicked her tongue at that. Nobody else heard, but they are all feeling encouraged.

Gordon has just taken his seat. Beside him, in her chair, Sonja knits. Marcia lies on the chesterfield with her legs across Doris's lap to pin her there, keep her still for this. Doris has already gotten up once because she thought that a cricket was the kitchen tap dripping.

"Now, no talking," Gordon says.

Out of the tape recorder nearest him a voice says what sounds like *tone, tone, tone.* But after several repetitions, it is obvious that it's *Joan. Joan, Joan, Joan* . . . Not sung and yet describing a familiar melody.

"Mister Sandman!" Marcia says.

"Shh," Gordon says.

Once more, at the same slow tempo, another string of *Joan*s instead of the *bum*s that "Mister Sandman" begins with.

"Who *is* that?" Doris says.

BARBARA GOWDY

"You," Marcia says, realizing.

"Shh!" Gordon again.

"I never said Joan like that."

"No!" Marcia says. "I know what she did! She taped you saying it once, then copied it, then she sped it up and slowed it down—"

"Quiet!" Gordon says.

Now the song itself starts, still that creeping tempo and not sung so much as spoken on key. Except that those aren't the right words. It is difficult to make out *what* the words are because of a muffling hum in the background and because, as Marcia said, half of them sound mechanically altered. No two words in a row seem to be from the same voice. "Is that me?" Marcia whispers, hearing a girl say *shrivel* at a normal pitch. "That's me!" she whispers, hearing *chuck. Heck* she hears and nudges Doris, who nods.

"We're all in it," Doris whispers, amazed. She has picked out Gordon saying *orange* and *peanuts*, Sonja saying *nostrils, father* and *jeepers*.

Gordon has heard *nostrils* and *jeepers. Peanuts,* to him, was *penis,* but he instantly decided it must be *Venus.* He is concentrating on the second tape, which is playing a short passage of murmured words whose rhythm is syncopated to the "Mister Sandman" rhythm. This voice is not different voices joined together, it is a single voice, female, either Doris's, Sonja's or Marcia's, it would have to be. He has figured out that much, that Joan was taping them, and he is already a bit apprehensive. What is the voice saying? He is about to get up and fiddle with the dials when the voice says distinctly and at such a high volume that it sounds shouted—"YOU CAN KEEP A SECRET, CAN'T YOU?"

Sonja stops knitting. "Was that me?"

"It sure sounded like it," Doris says.

"She taped us," Marcia says excitedly. "I wonder when she did."

"Well, those heaps of tapes she has," Doris says. "She might have been doing it for years."

"But I thought it would be her playing the piano," Sonja says.

"Shh," Gordon says gently.

On the first tape the "Mister Sandman" tune has begun again as before, with all of their voices speaking a word in turn. The words seem to have been chosen for no other reason than that they have the right number of syllables and the right pitch, although, as in the first verse, many words (and in some cases only parts of words) sound sped up or slowed down. Despite the hum these words are easier to make out than ones in the first verse were. *Tibby retard fly breast shebang carrot top Negro albino worms darn.* A nonsense jumble. And yet startling, some of them. *Tibby. Breast.*

Meanwhile, on tape 2, a voice (Gordon's) is murmuring another broken sentence of about seven or eight words. You can tell how long the sentence is because it is a rhythmic phrase being played over and over. Again the words are unintelligible until the end of the verse when suddenly they blare out, perfectly clear: "I THINK ABOUT HIM ALL THE TIME!"

Doris looks at Gordon. "*Who* do you think about all the time?"

He shakes his head. "My father," he says after a moment.

"Quiet," Marcia says.

A third verse of the same "Mister Sandman" melody has begun on tape 1. On tape 2 there's that incoherent voice—female and, even this early on, recognizably Marcia's. Marcia covers her mouth with her hands as she waits to find out what she's saying. She hopes it's not too personal. *Chinless neglected Bill Cullen tongue blood type . . .*

"Blood type?" Doris says.

"Bill Cullen," Sonja says with a smile. She has resumed knitting.

*. . . pediatric mango pop tongue erection . . .*

"Erection!" Doris says.

"Quiet!" Marcia says and glances at her father.

But Gordon is hardly listening. His heart is flopping around like a fish. He can't think. He can't remember. Did he ever mention Al Yothers to Joan? Did he say he loved him? My God, he has a feeling he might have. With a quaking hand he pulls his handkerchief out of his trouser pocket and dabs his forehead. *Okeydokey bean virgin* from tape 1. Is *bean* Jack Bean? *Virgin?* Who said *virgin?*

"I think maybe we should turn this off now," he says.

"What?" Doris says. "Why?"

"Listen!" Marcia shouts, and a second later her voice on tape 2 says, "WE WENT ALL THE WAY TONIGHT!"

She yelps, embarrassed.

Doris subtracts the number of years ago that Joan presumably stopped taping everybody (it would be when she began editing in the basement) from Marcia's age. "Hey, you weren't even seventeen!"

Marcia laughs. "So?"

"I don't know if this is the right time to be listening to this," Gordon says.

"If you don't want to listen, don't," Doris snaps. "Go for a walk. I'm staying right here."

"Can we just listen?" Marcia yells.

*. . . yours canary Ziggy cream cheese soft spot . . .*

The next voice on tape 2 is Sonja's. "THE TRUTH IS ONLY AVERSION!" it eventually hollers. Then on to the next verse and more of the same: from tape 1 a list of random words—*bosom baloney chinky crown lard*—spoken to the tune of "Mister Sandman," and from tape 2 an inaudible, repeated phrase providing a jazzy counterpoint.

What verse are they at now? The voice is Doris's. When it shouts, "WELL, IF THAT DOESN'T BEAT THE BAND!" she says, "Do I say that a lot?"

"You never stop," Gordon teases. His heart is settling down.

The next murmurer is female, and the last two declarations have been innocuous enough. Each verse is roughly two minutes long, so if the piece continues like this until the end, that works out to, what, twenty-five or twenty-four more verses, of which maybe six will feature him. And what percentage of everything he uttered at the threshold of that closet could possibly have been indiscreet? Less than one percent of one percent. "I suppose she wanted us to hear it," he concedes. "She wouldn't have left instructions—"

"Shh," says Marcia. The voice on tape 2 is hers. The clarification of the murmured phrase is all any of them are really listening for now, although they can't help hearing that oddly disturbing catalogue of words on tape 1—*padded ding-dong hammer pass*—as if a lunatic were raving in their ears while they were straining to catch an important announcement. "Boys," Marcia says. "I think it's something about boys."

"Oh, great," Doris says grimly.

It's about boys, all right. It's: "I HAVE SLEPT WITH SO MANY BOYS I HAVE LOST COUNT!"

"What?" Doris cries.

Marcia sits straight. "I never said that!" Did she? She may have thought it, but did she say it?

"Before you were seventeen?" Doris cries.

"I just said, I never said it!"

"We heard you!"

"Maybe you meant 'had a little snooze with,'" Sonja offers.

"I hope you're taking the pill!" Doris says.

"I'm taking it," Marcia says. "Not that it's anybody's business."

"Look," Gordon says, "let's keep in mind that these are edited tapes, and there are unnatural breaks between words. I think that what she did was extract a word from this conversation and a word from that conversation to manufacture her own sentence."

"Why would she do a thing like that?" Doris cries.

"I don't know," Gordon says. He doesn't even believe it. He is thinking of himself. Ahead of time, from a state of savage, efficient dread, he is constructing his excuse.

"Well, it's a big—" Marcia says and her breath snags. She can't say "lie." She can deny having said it but not having done it because that would be calling Joan a liar. Why did Joan tell everybody, though? She folds her legs into her chest and presses her forehead to her knees. *Robin queen quack bare Vaseline . . .* the song goes. The end of the verse is approaching.

It's Sonja's voice this time. "IN MY LAST LIFE I WAS THE LADY ON THE FLYING TRAPEZE!" it yells.

"Well, now you know," Sonja says with a chuckle. "But I'll bet you anything I was."

The next voice is Gordon's. He grips the arms of his chair. *Love,* he thinks he hears, and burning halos begin radiating from his skull. "WHEN YOU FALL IN LOVE, OTHER MIRACLES ARE INSPIRED TO SHOW THEMSELVES!" his voice finally proclaims.

He exhales. That wasn't so bad. He smiles at Doris, who stares at him. "I must have read it to her from some book," he says. Right! That's it! If anything risqué comes up, he'll say he must have read it aloud!

But for the next quarter of an hour, the declarations are harmless. Gordon's voice saying, "I FEEL LIKE BUCK ROGERS AT THIS POINT!" Doris's saying, "WHAT DO YOU THINK, SHOULD I LOSE TEN POUNDS?" "I ALMOST WENT THROUGH THE FLOOR!" from Sonja, and from Doris, "GIMME A PIGFOOT AND A BOTTLE OF BEER!" Marcia snorts at that one. "It's a song," Doris says stiffly. Marcia's voice says, "I SURE KNOW HOW TO PICK THEM, DON'T I?" and along the same lines, "WHY AM I ATTRACTED TO LEPER KEEPERS?" ("Leopard keepers?" Sonja says. "*Leper* keepers," Marcia says.) When Marcia's voice says, "I AM A WALL AND MY BREASTS LIKE TOWERS!" Doris glances at her.

"It's from the Bible," Marcia mutters.

"The Song of Solomon!" Gordon says heartily.

Doris sighs. Maybe what Gordon said about Joan manufacturing sentences is true. Who knows? The whole thing sounds crazy to her. She pulls Marcia's feet onto her lap and begins plucking lint balls from her socks and flicking them away. (As if, Marcia thinks, but is not offended, they are the countless boys she has slept with.)

In unison, the two tapes click off their reels. "That's the end of side one," Gordon says, slapping his knees and coming to his feet. He is feeling fine now. More than fine—fired up. As far as he is concerned, Joan's rhythmic variations are as sophisticated as anything he ever heard on a David Rayne recording. "This is extraordinary," he says as he turns the tapes over. "Disquieting in places, there's no question about that. But once you accept that her intention is to provoke, there are levels within levels—"

"I think it's weird," Marcia cuts him off. Her feelings are still hurt. Why did Joan pick on *her*? "And I think it's weirder that she was secretly taping us like a Russian spy."

"Those lyrics, or whatever you want to call them, are sure weird," Doris says. "When you think of all the thousands of words we must have said. And she goes and picks humdingers like *orgasm* and *bosom!* Who said *chinky*, by the way?" She twists around. "Oh, look, it's raining out."

"I suspect she chose them partly for their sound," Gordon says. "And to juxtapose a shocking word with a bland one. Okay." He flicks both switches. "Here we go."

"I hope we've heard the last of 'Mister Sandman,'" Marcia says.

"Well, I would think we *have*," Doris says, surprised.

"No, we haven't!" Sonja says as the first words come traipsing out—*blowing doughnut jerking kiddo* . . .

On this side, the tape 2 voices turn out to be spouting platitudes. "WELL, YOU CAN'T WIN 'EM ALL!" "LIKE I SAID, IT

TAKES ONE TO KNOW ONE!" "GIVE A GUY LIKE THAT
AN INCH AND HE'LL TAKE A MILE!" "SO I GUESS IT'S OUT OF
THE FRYING PAN AND INTO THE FIRE!" "I'M NOT GOING
TO COUNT MY BLESSINGS UNTIL THEY'RE HATCHED!"
(That one from Sonja.)

Gordon laughs, an attack of enormously relieving and slightly
out-of-control guffaws. "This is terrific," he says, wiping tears
from the corners of his eyes.

Another malapropism from Sonja ("A BIRD IN THE HAND
IS WORTH ITS WEIGHT IN GOLD!") has them all laughing,
Sonja as well, she isn't sure why. By now the tapes are almost run-
ning out. Only a few more verses to go.

"That sounds like me," Doris says, as the next murmured
phrase starts up. "Hold on to your hats," she says, grinning. And
from the tape recorder her voice shrills, "I LOVE TO HAVE SEX
WITH BARE-NAKED WOMEN!"

Sonja blurts out a laugh, imagining this to be another joke
(one she thinks she gets).

"Oh, my God," Marcia says.

"I never said that," Doris says quietly. A blush starts climbing
her throat.

"Of course, you didn't," Gordon says. He forces a laugh.

"I never said that," Doris says again.

"This is what I was talking about before!" Gordon says. "She
took a word from here, a word from there and spliced them together!"

Doris holds her hands in her lap. Her bearing is regal. "I would
never have said anything like that," she says in the same quiet and
startled voice.

"We know, Mommy," Sonja says. Of course they do! Why is
her mother so upset?

"I didn't . . . ," Doris says. And it's true, she didn't. She is certain she didn't. And yet it's as if her clothes have been ripped off

and she is protesting that these aren't her breasts, this is not her pubic hair. "A word from here, a word from there and spliced them together" is the perfect cover-up. Not even a lie. The lies that are tumbling into her throat she can swallow away and simply agree with what Gordon is saying. So why doesn't she? She opens her mouth. Breathes out nothing.

*. . . juicy twitch dead Cedric cleavage dumbbell climax . . .*

Meanwhile, Marcia has brought her knees back into her chest. She has never been on a bad acid trip but this is beginning to feel like one. Her mother's face is a colour of red you don't see anywhere in nature. In her mother's folded hands is a tiny naked woman. Her left hand, her wedding-ring hand, slipped under the waistband of Angela's bathing suit and went too far down. That happened. There is a shuffling in Marcia's head, an amassing, but from all directions her father's voice trombones and she can't concentrate. "Shut up," she says.

Gordon hears her, ignores her, goes on telling them about Brad Wagner. "You remember him, Doris! Great big guy, a football player before he became a writer. In *Poker Face* he had this character who was the spitting image of his own mother, he even used her real name, Thelma or Velma! I met her once. Sweet little old lady. But what does Brad have this Velma character do in his book? Chop up the milkman!"

"Holy moly," Sonja says.

"That's creative licence for you!" Gordon says. The pounding in his lungs seems to have locked into the rhythm of his voice on tape 2. Keep talking, he thinks. Drown it out. He can't. He is suddenly empty of words. And there go the words on tape 1—*mute squat Greenville flophouse*—marching right by him to the finish line. The rain outside he hears as Sonja (who is nearest the window) crinkling Saran Wrap. He looks at her, and her face is so untroubled that he experiences one sweet moment of safety before his voice on tape 2 shouts, "I HAVE ORGASMS WITH QUEER MEN!"

He stands. "What the hell?" Filtered through a sickly laugh.

"Oh, my God," Marcia whispers.

"Did you hear *orgasms*?" Gordon says at a strange tenor pitch. "That wasn't my voice! See, there you are right there! She spliced in one of you saying *orgasms*. Was that you, Marcia?" A blind careering in her direction. "What's she up to? Shock value, I guess. Bringing the piece to a climax." He yanks out his handkerchief and punches it at his wet face. "Here—" He strides over to the tape recorder. "I'll play that back. You'll see that it wasn't my voice."

"No!" Marcia cries. She leaps off the couch and grabs his arm. "Leave it!"

"I'm just going to demonstrate—"

"Leave it!"

They look at each other.

"That's me," she says about the next voice on tape 2.

He listens. Yes.

"I want to hear what terrible thing she has me saying."

"Well," he says, shaken.

They stand there in front of the second tape recorder listening to *blubber smokes Nazi candy bladder* and so on from tape 1. Behind them (neither of them can quite believe this) Sonja hums along with the melody. A moment before the murmurs clarify, Marcia realizes that the voice isn't hers after all, it's Sonja's.

"ALWAYS REMEMBER, BUNNY, I'M YOUR REAL MOTHER!"

"Uh-oh," Sonja says.

Neither Marcia nor Gordon budge.

"Me and my big mouth," Sonja says, and quickly rolls up her knitting.

Marcia turns to her. A trance-like rotation during the course of which Gordon swerves to otherworldly calm.

"*You're* Joanie's mother?" Marcia says faintly.

"Let's keep calm," Gordon says with a slow, pushing-down motion of his hands.

"Gulp," Sonja says. Her eyes squirrel around the room.

"*Are* you?"

"Yes, she's Joanie's mother," Doris says flatly. "She gave birth to her."

"Who's her father?"

The tapes flap from their reels. "We don't know," Gordon says. He switches the recorders off. "We never learned his real name."

"It was . . . I guess you'd call it a one-night stand," Sonja says. Now *she* is red and Doris isn't.

Marcia lowers herself to her father's chair. "Why didn't anybody tell me?"

"We should have," Doris says. "Ten years ago."

"So, you got pregnant and that's why you went to Vancouver," Marcia says, more to herself. She looks around at everyone. "So, Joanie's my niece," she says.

"I'm sorry, Sweetie," Doris says. Her eyes are tired and sad and affectionate. "Brother, this is some night, isn't it?"

"I just wish you'd told me. I don't understand why nobody told me." By "nobody" she means especially Joan. She means before now.

Gordon sits next to Doris. "I guess our thinking was, you'd tell Joanie, you know the way you two are, and that she had enough on her plate as it was."

"But *she* knew!"

"As it turns out," Doris says. She shifts on the chesterfield to study Sonja.

"Me and my big mouth," Sonja says again and covers her mouth with both hands.

"She's not my sister," Marcia says. Her eyes flood. "She's my niece."

"She's still Joanie," Sonja says, muffled through her fingers.

"That's right," Gordon says serenely. "Who she is has nothing to do with who you, or any of us for that matter, think she is."

He is so tranquil! Has he lost his mind? *I have orgasms with queer men!* roars in his skull but as if from behind glass. *I have orgasms with queer men!* It has the ring of an odd translation. He did not say it, of course. Under no circumstances would he have put it that way. So what *did* he say that she knew about him? And why did she want everyone else to know?

"I have orgasms with queer men," he says out loud. "I wonder how she came up with that one?" His tone of baffled innocence sounds just right to him.

Nobody seems to be listening. Doris is telling Marcia about the stigma of out-of-wedlock pregnancies back in the fifties. "Your life was over," she says. "Kaput." Gordon looks at Doris. Does *she* love having sex with bare-naked women? Given that his declaration told the truth, he supposes that hers did, too. He looks at Marcia. She has slept with more boys than she can count. How is it that he can conclude these things without feeling appalled? Well, he can. "Therefore whatsoever ye have spoken in darkness," he thinks, "shall be heard in the light. And what ye . . . " How does it go? "And that which ye have spoken in the ear in *closets* shall be proclaimed upon the housetops."

"Holy, Geez," he thinks. "Right on the money."

# TWENTY-THREE

H E DRIVES through the downpour like an escaped convict. Skidding away from intersections, passing cars on the inside and sending flares of water up over the sidewalks.

Beside him in the front seat Doris grips the armrest and her door handle. In the back seat Sonja and Marcia smash into each other whenever he rounds a corner. Nobody speaks, except for when Marcia says, "I wish you'd asked her why," and Doris says, "She hung up on me."

It was Carol, the friendly nurse. "You'd better get here right away," she said. That was maybe fifteen minutes after the tapes ended. Before she phoned, while everyone was saying that Joan was the same Joan, Marcia was aware of a fissure opening up between herself and Joan, a breathing space that hadn't been there before. Now, in the car, it's gone. Her bones rattle. There is a popping in her head. Her parents are homosexuals. She doesn't doubt that the tapes were spliced. She is certain that her parents would never have said anything like that in front of Joan. They are still homosexuals, though. Even if Marcia believed Joan capable of making up such tremendous lies, it's too late. Now she knows. She knows because she already knew, don't ask her how. Hearing it expressed was like hearing about sex for the first time. The details suspect, the fact unassailable and yet impossible to imagine. She looks at her father's hands squeezing the steering wheel. He is gay, she thinks and doesn't feel a thing. He is going to keep pretending he isn't, she thinks, and this penetrates, draws some blood.

They make it to the hospital in under twenty minutes. As they're going up the elevator the loudspeaker blares, "Code blue! Seven north! Room 259!"

Marcia says, "That's Joanie!"

"What's code blue?" Sonja says.

"We'll soon find out," Gordon says. When the elevator stops he shoulders through the doors before they're open.

Doctors and nurses are hurrying down the hall. "Oh, God," Doris says. She starts to run. They all do. Ahead of them two nurses turn into Joan's room. A nurse just inside the door says, "You can't come in here!" Doris shoves past her, and Gordon, Sonja and Marcia follow. Somebody shouts, "Make way!" It's a nurse dragging in a cart with monitors on it. They stand aside. The bed is creaking but there are so many nurses and doctors around it that they can't see Joan. One nurse is putting up another I.V. At the foot of the bed Carol is writing in a clipboard. She turns and says with light surprise, "Oh, Doris," as if she wasn't the one who phoned. She hands her clipboard to the nurse beside her, then motions the family to stay back, stepping aside herself, and now they see the doctor giving Joan mouth-to-mouth resuscitation. Doris grabs Carol's arm.

"She stopped breathing," Carol says in a low voice.

"When?" Gordon says.

"Three minutes ago. Four."

The doctor is now thumping Joan's chest with both his hands, one hand on top of the other. The bed creaks. A sound like people making love, Marcia thinks.

"Is there a pulse?" Gordon says.

Carol shakes her head. She says that she phoned because Joan was having trouble breathing.

"Is she dead?" Marcia whispers.

No answer. The doctor resumes thumping Joan's chest. Gordon's bad leg buckles. Sonja catches his elbow, but she has been feeling dizzy since the elevator ride and now she swoons, clutching his arm and dragging him down with her. When they hit the floor the whole room quakes, and Joan coughs.

"She's back!" the doctor says.

———

Six hours later, in Intensive Care, Joan is sitting up and taking sips of water from a glass. Wires are clamped to her chest and run from under her blue gown to a monitor on the wall, but this is regular procedure after cardiac arrest, it doesn't mean she's still in danger. Obviously she's not. She is making her animal sounds and looking alertly around the room. She has her sunglasses on. In only minutes after that cough she was imitating everybody's gasps and weeping. She breathed "Whoosh" when the toilet flushed. When the doctors and nurses left the room and Marcia lay down on the bed and thought, "What happened," she got a response—We were tuckered out.

"I mean, what happened *tonight?*" Marcia pursued.

We were beat.

"Why did we get sick in the first place?"

We were so exhausted. It was so exhausting.

"Why wouldn't we help ourself? Why wouldn't we eat?"

We were too pooped.

And so on, along those lines. But at least it was communication.

Dr. Shack, who showed up as Joan was drifting off to sleep, said, "Well, maybe it *was* fatigue." She didn't even raise her eyebrows at

Marcia's claim that Joan had spoken to her telepathically. "In all honesty," she said after taking Joan's blood pressure, "I have to tell you that she has me completely bamboozled."

"Join the club," Doris said.

In the car Marcia says that she asked Joan why she secretly taped them, and that Joan's answer was, "You are so interesting."

"I think, initially, she taped us for the fun of it," Gordon says. "For no reason except to have something to listen to when she was by herself. And then she read that article on David Rayne, and that gave her the idea of taking what we had said apart, taking—"

"A word from here and a word from there and splicing them together to make us say things we never said," Doris finishes for him. She doesn't mean anything by it. She is exhausted, that's all, and he has already told them this enough times.

"We were her instrument," Gordon says quietly. This he truly believes and is in awe of.

"We were her *audience*," Marcia says.

By the time they pull into the driveway the sun is up, a pewter light kicking out from between the houses. Straight overhead the rain is coming down hard, but who has the energy to dash from the car to the front door? Sonja, scarcely awake, shuffles behind Marcia with one hand on Marcia's shoulder. Inside, Sonja lumbers up the stairs and shuffles along to her room, where she falls on her bed without removing her wet dress or folding back her poodle-patterned coverlet.

Doris offers to scramble some eggs. Marcia declines, says, "See you in eight hours." She has a date with a hundred clues. In Joan's bed she lies naked on her back, crying and letting the clues spill over her. The front of Sonja's blouses being wet when she came back from Vancouver, and that sour-milk smell she had then. A man her father used to work with, an effeminate man named Elvis, coming up to her in a restaurant and saying too urgently, "Say hello to your father for me, will you? We were very, *very* close." And her recoiling, knowing that she would never say hello for him. Six or seven years ago at one of her father's book launches a man slid his hand around her father's waist and whispered in his ear something that the two of them laughed at, secretly—flirtatiously is how she remembers it now—and then the man saw her and his hand withdrew, smooth as a pickpocket's. That time when she burst into the kitchen, and Angela was standing behind her mother with her arms around her mother's waist . . .

At the kitchen table Gordon massages his eyes under his glasses and says, "A night for the record books."

"We should have told Marcia about Joanie," Doris says. She cracks eggs into a bowl, one after another in a ruthless delirium. "I can't figure out why we didn't. Why didn't we?"

"It was easier not to."

"Oh, *easier*," she says sarcastically. She pours milk into the bowl. "Oh, all right, then. Well aren't *we* swell parents."

"She'll be fine."

"Sure, why not? With her male harem to comfort her." She opens and slams drawers, searching for the wire whisk. "More boyfriends than she can count is how many? A hundred? Four hundred? Well, it's her business, that's what *she'd* say." She settles for a fork. "Anyways, *Joanie's* going to be fine, that's all I'm thinking about right now."

"It was a close call. Another minute—"

She winces. "Don't say it."

"Well, we were lucky."

"Luckier than we deserve. A pair of lucky so-and-so's. A pair of lucky homo—" She starts laughing. "Lucky homosexual—" She can't get it out but it's so funny. "Old-timers who love to . . . " The fork slips from her hand, clatters to the floor. She grips the counter as the hysteria retches from her belly.

Gordon gets up and stands behind her and holds her shoulders. Not too tight, even though she just blurted out what he has been doing somersaults for the past eight hours trying to disclaim, and as she settles down she wonders at his composure. Still shuddering and gulping laughs, she turns to look up at him and sees from his patient, instructive expression that he is going to give her that lecture again about Joan splicing the tapes.

She pulls away from him. "Stop it!" she says. "No more! Not with me." He glances worriedly toward the bedrooms and she lowers her voice. "Sweetie, I *know!*" She thumps her breast. "I've known for a long time! So let's both stop this song and dance!"

He blinks at her.

"The girls, fine," she says. "We can go on pretending to them, if you want to, I don't know. But between you and me, for the love of Mike . . . " She drops into a chair.

He stares at her but he is attending to himself. Everything knotted inside him has suddenly been yanked into straight lines. He hears his long breaths. He reaches up to prod the ceiling tiles. "How did you know?" he says. His heart beats loosely, unclenched.

"We could start with no sex."

"That had nothing to do with you," he says, balancing a tile on the tips of his fingers.

"Listen, I didn't really know anything until it was spelled out for me." A short laugh. "And, brother, did she spell it out or what? How *she* knew is the question. How she knew about *either* of us."

He sits across from her but does not look at her. "We must have been indiscreet," he says.

"I guess that's it. But who knew she had supersonic hearing?"

"Let me ask you this." He presses his fingers together at his lips. "Was it because we didn't have sex that you . . . that you . . . "

She helps him out. "Turned into a lesbian?"

The sparest of nods.

"I think I'd have kept it under wraps," she says, "you know, in fantasy land, and let me tell you there were a lot of dry years there before I took the plunge. But who knows what I'd have done if we'd had a normal sex life? I'm no saint, I found that out." She is remembering her seedy courtship of Cloris Carter, which eventually came to nothing.

Gordon nods.

"Can you believe we're even *having* this conversation?" *Mama may have* are the lyrics in her head. *And Papa may have* . . . "All civilized at the breakfast table. Oh, the eggs!"

"Not for me."

"How about coffee?"

"No."

"All right, let *me* ask *you* this. Because I've been wondering all these years. Do you find me disgusting?"

He is surprised. "No. Never." He looks straight at her. "Not disgusting."

"Just not sexually exciting."

He keeps his mouth shut.

"See, I never didn't find you sexy. So I must be what they call bisexual." She pats her hair. It's still damp. She is feeling more friendly toward him than she has felt in years. She'd like to sit in his lap, but as soon as this urge hits her so does a natural conclusion, and she straightens and says carelessly, "Do you want a divorce?"

She sees that she has jolted him, and says quickly, "I'm not saying *I* do. I thought you might, though, now that the cat's out of the bag."

"No."

"Well, good. Do you have a boyfriend?"

"There is a man I'm seeing, yes."

"Do you love him?"

"Yes. I do."

"Do you love me?"

"Yes."

"Is this guy married?"

"No."

"Doesn't *he* want you to leave me?"

"No."

"Anybody I know?"

Pause. "No."

"Well, guess what? I'm in exactly the same boat. I have a gal friend, I love her, she's not married, she doesn't want me to leave you, and you don't happen to know her." He lied about the last part, so she will, too. Back to the white lies. She can't say it's not a relief. "What are you staring at?"

"Your hair."

"My black roots." She rakes her fingers through the tangles. "I look like a two-bit hooker."

"That's not what I was thinking. I was thinking how . . . "

"What?"

"Exuberant your hair is."

"Exuberant! Ha!"

He reaches across the table and takes her left hand. "I don't want anything to change, Doris. I'm not unhappy. Are you?"

"Not unhappy? Well, this week was no picnic, but so long as Joan stays out of the woods. Sure, I'm happy enough."

"Let's go on as we have been, then. Why not?"

"What'll we tell the girls? I wouldn't bet my last dime that Marcia bought your splicing story."

"If she asks . . . Well, let's wait and see."

"Lie our heads off." A tired, reckless laugh.

"There's something to be said for that."

"Oh, my God!" she says suddenly. "She had no pulse!"

While she weeps, he squeezes her hand and gazes at her crumpled, red face, taking absolute responsibility for it, taking a curiously resigned comfort in it, as if it were a face made up in his mind.

———

When they visit Joan later that day she is under the blanket reading *Time* magazine. She is still in Intensive Care and hooked up to the cardiac monitor, but she is not panicking and this is amazing considering all the people and noise. Somebody combed her hair and put her barrettes back in. Maybe she dld. With moistened bits of Kleenex she has made herself earplugs. She points them out, tucking her hair behind her ears, and Marcia says, "I know what, I'll bring you your earphones. They'll work way better."

Joan gobbles.

A complete recovery it looks like, but Dr. Shack says they'll have to keep her in for observation another three or four days at least. So they stand around the bed for a half hour, looking at her motionless shape under the blanket, hearing the pages turn, then they leave.

In the car Marcia decides to go to her own place after supper. The reason is not her boyfriends, though they stretch out naked wherever there's a gap in her thinking. Let them wait. She wants to be alone. She wants to feel how she feels. Joan is her niece! Sonja isn't a virgin! Her mother and father are grandparents, homosexual grandparents! But . . . so? Should she talk to them about it? Should she talk to Sonja about it? She's pretty sure that Sonja didn't believe for a second that what their parents said on those tapes was true. She wonders if Sonja even knows what "queer" means. Here's what Marcia wants: to get to the last feeling, the one that comes after you're surprised, after you're upset, after you feel nothing, after the feeling after that.

But she doesn't get past *nothing*. Because once she is alone in her apartment, the fact that Joan was dead for five minutes takes over. She keeps thinking about it—"She was dead!"—and feeling vertiginous and then thinking it again as if she can't stop looking over a cliff she almost fell off. She wonders where Joan was during those five minutes, and how she brought herself back. You can haul back an entire dream by pulling on a wisp of it, but that's so precarious. When she asks Joan where she was, what she hears is, Gone.

"Where?"

Gone.

"To the cold and silver place?"

Gone.

This is on the Wednesday evening. On Thursday afternoon Dr. Shack gives the okay for Joan to be discharged, and Gordon and Doris go to pick her up. It is the eighth of August. You can't turn on a radio without hearing the news that President Nixon has resigned. In the car they hear Nixon say that he has never been a quitter, which annoys Doris, and she switches the radio off. "He might not be a quitter, but he sure as heck is a nincompoop," she says. "Anybody with half a brain would have burned the evidence the minute the break-in story leaked."

Joan is sitting on her bed. She is wearing her sunglasses and earphones and reading a hospital regulations manual. The green blanket is folded on her lap. Gordon says, "Do you want me to carry you?" She nods. In his arms she burrows her head under his armpit. In the car, even with her earphones on, there isn't a sound she doesn't echo—brakes squealing, Doris closing the glove compartment, an ambulance siren, the tires sizzling through a puddle.

When they get home, Gordon carries her from the car to the front door. Marcia opens it. She has just arrived from work. Joan stays put on the landing, arms at her sides, while Marcia and Sonja hug and kiss her and Sonja describes supper. Tomato soup, meat loaf, mashed potatoes, tapioca pudding—"All your favourites!" Joan clasps her hands, seemingly glad, then goes down to the basement.

"What are you doing?" Marcia calls.

They hear her opening the door to her office.

"Don't tell me she's going to make more tapes!" Doris says.

No, here she comes again, wearing her visor and with an armload of magazines. Up the stairs and along the hall to her bedroom. A minute later they hear the funeral march "Dum dum de dum . . . " on the piano.

"Is this a joke?" Marcia says. She goes to the bedroom and stands beside the piano. "This is a joke, right?"

If it is, Joan isn't smiling. (Not that she ever does.)

She plays honky-tonk piano until supper. After supper she sits in her closet and reads old *Life* magazines in the beam of the penlight. They leave her alone and watch television, President Nixon resigning on every station (Doris keeps jumping up to change the channel). It's Julie Nixon's virginal, out-of-style dress that annoys Marcia. She goes to the bedroom to say goodbye to Joan. She thinks she'll sleep at her own place tonight, but when she lies on the bed she drifts off. Joan stays in the closet reading.

It's after midnight when Marcia wakes up. She is alone. She climbs out of bed and goes down the hall to her parents' room and finds her mother standing at the window in (wow!) a baby-doll nightgown. "They're playing monkey in the middle," Doris says when Marcia is standing beside her.

At first, Marcia can see only Sonja, hopping and waving her arms like a crazy lady, and then she sees the striped beach-ball sail in an arc above Sonja's head like a fast-moving planet, and her father step out of a shadow to catch it. He throws it just above Sonja's reach again but not far enough, so that Joan has to race to retrieve it before Sonja does. Sonja pants and chuckles. She and Joan are both wearing white nightgowns.

"How long has *she* been playing with them?" Marcia asks. She doesn't even try not to sound petulant.

"I don't know. I just woke up."

"No, I mean, it was always just Dad and Joanie."

"This is the first time that *I've* seen Sonja out there. Mind you, I don't watch every night."

They are speaking softly, like interlopers. The crickets sound like tambourines.

"I'm going out, too," Marcia says.

"Oh, what the heck," Doris says, following her. "It's a big day."

Joan's echo of the screen door banging is so-so. As if she were expecting them she throws the ball their way, and Marcia catches it and tosses it to Gordon. Gordon tosses it to Doris, who tosses it to Sonja. They form a circle and keep tossing, industriously, carefully. Without a word. They could be people passing buckets of water to put out a fire. They could be a family spending a day at the beach together. If they were on a beach. If it was day.

A NOTE ON THE AUTHOR

BARBARA GOWDY is the author of two previous novels,
*Falling Angels* and *Through the Green Valley*, and the short
story collection, *We So Seldom Look on Love*. Her work has
received international critical acclaim and she has been published in thirteen countries. She lives in Toronto.

A NOTE ON THE BOOK

This book was composed using a digital version of Garamond, a typeface originally designed by Claude Garamond
in the early sixteenth century, and redrawn by Robert Slim-
bach and issued by Adobe in 1989. The book was printed on
acid free papers and bound by Quebecor Printing - Book
Press Inc. of North Brattleboro, Vermont.